PRAISE FOR VIV

"If you've never read a Vivian Arend book you are missing out on one of the best contemporary authors writing today."
~ Book Reading Gals

"A Rancher's Heart was a spectacular start to this new series and I am very excited to see what comes next for the rest of the Heart Falls crew."
~ Guilty Pleasures Book Review

"Brilliant, raw, imaginative, irresistible!!"
~ Avon Romance

"This story will keep you reading from the first page to the last one. There is never a dull moment..."
~ Landy Jimenez

"Arend became a favorite author of mine because not only does she write about sexy cowboys, she gives us families who love and take care of each other."
~ SmexyBooks

"This was my first Vivian Arend story, and I know I want more!"
~ Red Hot Plus Blue Reads

ALSO BY VIVIAN AREND

The Stones of Heart Falls
A Rancher's Heart
A Rancher's Song
A Rancher's Bride
A Rancher's Love
A Rancher's Vow

The Colemans of Heart Falls
The Cowgirl's Forever Love
The Cowgirl's Secret Love
The Cowgirl's Chosen Love

The Skyes of Heart Falls
A Cowboy's Bride
A Cowboy's Trust
A Cowboy's Claim

Other Heart Falls Series:
Holidays in Heart Falls
Heart Falls Vignette & Novella Collection

∼

A full list of Vivian's print titles is available on her website: www.vivianarend.com

A COWBOY'S BRIDE

THE SKYES OF HEART FALLS
BOOK 1

VIVIAN AREND

This is a work of fiction. Names, characters, places, and incidents either are the product of the author's imagination or are used fictitiously, and any resemblance to any persons, living or dead, business establishments, events, or locales is entirely coincidental.

NO AI TRAINING: Without in any way limiting the author's [and publisher's] exclusive rights under copyright, any use of this publication to "train" generative artificial intelligence (AI) technologies to generate text is expressly prohibited. The author reserves all rights to license uses of this work for generative AI training and development of machine learning language models.

A Cowboy's Bride
Copyright © 2024 by Arend Publishing Inc.
Digital ISBN: 978-1-998508-15-0
Print ISBN: 978-1-998508-21-1
Edited by Angie Ramey
Cover Design © Damonza
Proofed by Linda Levy

All rights reserved. No part of this book may be used or reproduced in any manner whatsoever without written permission except in the case of brief quotations.

1

Mid-September, Heart Falls

Despite the cool fall breeze swirling around him, a trickle of moisture slid between Aiden Skye's shoulder blades. His muscles hummed with a welcome ache after riding hard, and he savoured a deep breath of the fresh, crisp air as he leaned on the saddle horn.

A grin stretched his cheeks.

This place was perfect.

Three ranch dogs raced around his horse's legs, including Aiden's retriever, Dixie. All the beasts clearly approved of the land as well. Dust swirled as Aiden's two older brothers joined him on the ridge.

Thirty-nine-year-old Declan reached over his horse's neck to offer Aiden a firm handshake. "Other than the one time when you nearly came out of the saddle, you did damn good. As expected." Declan glanced at Jake, their middle brother. "You, on the other hand…"

Jake made an appropriately rude gesture then laughed.

"You're a mean son of a bitch, Declan. 'Come for a ride on our new property', you said. 'It'll be good to get back to your roots.' Five fucking hours later..."

"Not my fault your roots have spent more time planted in a cushy chair than on horseback lately." Declan leaned back and adjusted his hat, his smile nothing more than the faintest line as usual. "You'll get back into the swing of things soon enough. Aiden did well."

"Thanks." Aiden sat straighter, stretching his neck and shoulders. "Though I need a hot shower after that."

"Agreed. Plus food," Jake added, eyeing his brother. "I hope you have this part planned as thoroughly as the show and tell of the land and buildings."

The oldest of them tilted his head toward the barn. "Let's get the animals cleaned up. I figured we'd keep it simple this evening. Burgers, then time to meet some locals at the pub. I've only been a few times, but Rough Cut seems a decent place."

Good thing they'd all turned their horses toward the barn already, the dogs happily racing ahead. No way could Aiden have kept his expression blank enough to hide his amusement at returning to the pub.

Declan had done the final leg work in purchasing the animal rescue in Heart Falls, moving early to supervise renovations, but it had been Aiden's job to find the ranch in the first place.

His research trip three years earlier into the community had not only turned up the perfect location for their project, but he'd also enjoyed an amazing evening dancing and otherwise occupied with another visitor to town. The leggy brunette with pale-blue eyes had been a blast on the dance floor and a wildcat in bed.

Aiden spent the time grooming his horse and putting away tack wearing a wicked grin.

Around him, signs of change were everywhere. Through the nearest window, the building to the north was visible, where renovations were partially complete. Smaller but comfortable private rooms, each with their own bathroom, circled a second-floor kitchen and dining room that faced the Rocky mountains. Floor-to-ceiling windows let light pour into the open working area, and Aiden could already hear their future guests rave about how fabulous the space was for painting.

The artists' residences were the working cover that held their secret project together.

On the main floor below, half of the building had been divided into three living units for him and his brothers, each with a bedroom, bath, and private living space. The areas were complete in terms of plumbing and framed walls, but the rest of the work remained.

The other side of the main floor held five separate rooms as well as a joint bathhouse. The main reason for all the work. Not too many months from now, men who needed a safe spot to retreat for a while would find refuge here.

Aiden and his brothers finished their chores, put out food for the dogs, then strolled in a companionable silence back to the ranch house.

The place would've been bigger than necessary for the older couple they'd purchased the land and animal rescue from, but for their new project, it was just right. Once they were up and running, the extra rooms in the house would be for any women who needed a spot to hide.

On the north side was the primary bedroom and attached bath that would house a full-time live-in cook and housekeeper. To the east were the other three bedrooms, along with two more bathrooms, temporarily filled with Aiden's and his brothers' gear.

The rest of the house was equally simple. The tidy kitchen boasted a long trestle table that the previous couple had left because it had been built to fit. The living room held a wood-burning stove and room for two oversized battered and worn couches. The view beyond the windows was breathtaking, though, with the Rocky mountains in the distance and kilometers of open prairie all around them.

It was the perfect place to make a difference. Somewhere to feel utterly safe while a person built up their courage and found new ways to be strong.

They ate a quick supper then headed out. Aiden slid into the front passenger seat of Declan's truck seconds before Jake could claim it.

"Ass." Jake said without malice.

"Thank you." Aiden ducked instinctively away from the slap to his shoulder Jake offered, snorting in amusement. "It's been too long since we lived together, but it feels as if it was only yesterday."

"Agreed." Declan put the truck in gear and headed up the road, the faintest hint of a smile curling the corners of his lips. "I still have nightmares from those days. You're both so damn needy. Constantly yattering about."

The cab filled with soft laughter, considering the truth was the other way to the extreme. They might have been needy but getting that truth from any of them would have required torture and thumbscrews.

In the back seat, Jake sprawled easily, gazing out the window and studying the landscape. "It's good to be back together. It's definitely what Jeff would've wanted."

"Yup." Aiden and Declan said it at the same moment, the memory of their stepfather rising hard and fast.

They might have had shitty luck when it came to their biological donor, but the man who had been a father to them when it truly counted had more than made a difference. Aiden had been eight years old when Jeff had come on the scene. When their mother had suddenly passed away less than a year later, Jeff had moved a mountain's worth of paperwork and fought the bureaucracy to make sure *his* three boys didn't end up lost in the foster system.

Pay it forward.

The words were always there, hovering at the edge of Aiden's thoughts. Would he be able to make the same difference in other's lives that Jeff had made in his and his brothers?

A hand landed on his shoulder, soft this time, as Jake leaned in close. "We will," his brother promised.

Damn it. "Didn't mean to say it out loud."

"It's not as if we're not all thinking it," Declan said. "That's why we're here. That's why we're going to do everything we can, come hell or high water."

Jake hummed his agreement. "Make a difference. Do what's right. Pay it forward."

The three of them sat quietly while the phrases their stepfather had offered to three lost young boys echoed in Aiden's head. Jeff repeated the sentiments from the moment he'd stepped forward to say things had to change because Mama was gone. They were the last words he'd said before he passed.

Jeff had been gone for over fifteen years now, and they'd all had a boatload of life experiences.

Some good, some not so good, including relationship-wise.

Ten years earlier, Jake's marriage had lasted barely ten months before falling apart. Declan's beloved wife, Sadie, had died of breast cancer three years ago. Aiden had a few long-term girlfriends over the years, but no one who had been more than casually committed on both sides.

Heart Falls was a fresh start in many ways for them all. A place to set down roots and maybe do the next thing for themselves as well as providing a home base for others.

Aiden blinked as they pulled into a parking space behind the pub. He'd gotten caught up in the memories and hadn't noticed the distance vanishing.

Still, one thought rang through bright and clear. "Remember how we were trying to figure what to call the animal rescue and retreat house?"

"Because we can't keep calling it the Heart Falls Animal Rescue?" Declan slipped the truck into Park then glanced at his little brother with the faint smile that said he was highly amused.

"We can't keep calling it that because it's going to be *more* than that."

"Damn right." Jake lifted his chin. "What's your brainwave?"

"Not me," Aiden insisted. He let his grin break free when he realized this was the perfect way to trap the other two into going along with his plan. "It's Declan's idea. You said it, bro. Come hell or high water. The perfect place to not only rescue animals, but people."

Jake sat for a moment then nodded. "Leave it at High Water officially, so the delicate types don't flip out. But we'll know the truth."

"I like it," Declan said. "I am brilliant at times."

"You're definitely something," Jake taunted. "Fine. We have a name. Now I need a beer."

Aiden stood outside his door, waiting until his brothers joined him, a sense of satisfaction rising in his soul. A new home. A new goal. A new name. Maybe even the opportunity to find someone to spend time with—that would be new as well, although he'd take another dose of his wildcat.

A Cowboy's Bride

Looked as if their move to Heart Falls would be smooth sailing from here on in.

~

DECIDING what to wear for the evening wasn't the weightiest issue she had, Petra Sorenson decided. Nope, clothes were simple. She'd pulled on a pair of faded jeans paired with a black tank top and a checked button-down. She had pretty, but comfortable, well-worn boots planned for her feet. Her long brown hair had been gathered into a ponytail for ease while dancing. Most importantly, a couple of the girlfriends she knew from her many visits to the area were waiting for her to join them.

She just needed to get out the damn door before the evening was over.

Her problem was an overly enthusiastic big brother who didn't know how to turn off his excitement over having her move to Heart Falls. Their large family, with six siblings and Mom and Dad, had always been close, but tonight Zach's zeal buzzed at such a level it made Petra wonder if he was pulling her leg and *trying* to be annoying...

Well, hell. That's exactly what he was doing.

"Before you go, let me show you the office areas," Zach suggested. He pushed back from the supper table and bounced to his feet. "You can decide if you want to have your space there or—"

"I'm probably going to work remotely," Petra reminded him. "I'll check the offices tomorrow."

"There's a new colt in the barn. You have to see him." Zach blinked innocently, and his resemblance to a Ryan Reynolds wannabe was so unfair. "I can take a picture of you next to him to post to the family chat."

She usually had zero problems standing up for herself, but Zach, her sibling closest in age and childhood playmate, was her soft spot. Especially when he was being all sweet and seemingly focused on making her happy.

The jerk.

Petra met her sister-in-law's gaze, begging for an assist.

Thank goodness for female solidarity, because Julia laid a hand on Zach's arm and shook her head. "Hey, you aren't trying to get out of your promise, are you?"

Zach blinked, his smile fading slightly. "Um, no?"

Julia nodded decisively. "Good. Because for a minute there I thought you'd forgotten we're supposed to go over to my sister's tonight. Josiah and Lisa are expecting us."

His confusion wiped clean instantly as suspicion slipped in. "They are?"

"Yup." Julia kept a straight face, but when she twisted toward Petra, she winked. "We'll take care of the dishes. Go have fun with your friends. We'll catch up more later."

"Sounds great. Thanks for supper… and everything." Petra hurried to the door and shoved her feet into her boots, snatching her coat off the hooks. "Take me for a tour tomorrow, 'kay, Zach? Night."

She escaped into the warm fall evening, grinning as laughter erupted behind her in the cozy home Zach and Julia had built together.

So. Her brother *had* been acting like a turkey just to tease her.

Petra climbed into her truck and eased her way down the ranch drive, headed the short distance to town. If Zach wanted to play those games, she had zero problems handing out as good as she got. In fact, this was going to be fun. Tormenting her big brother was one of her favourite things.

She pulled behind Buns and Rose's café, happiness welling up when she spotted another favourite thing, friends.

Tansy Fields and Sydney Jeremiah stood framed by the backdoor of the café. One slightly under medium height and blonde, the other a petite redhead.

Petra shoved open the truck door and all but threw herself into their arms. "I missed you both so much."

Sydney squeezed her hard but escaped the embrace quickly. "Of course you did."

"We're extremely missable." Tansy snickered at herself. "Wait. That didn't come out the way I intended." She snuck in a hug before retreating far enough to examine Petra carefully then nodded with approval. "You look happy."

"I'm so glad to finally be here," Petra agreed.

"You *want* to be in a small town with one grocery store and two-and-a-half restaurants?" Sydney eyed her as if ready to pull on her doctor jacket and make a diagnosis before smiling. "I know exactly what you mean, since I did the same thing two years ago."

Since her brother had moved to Heart Falls four-and-a-half years ago, Petra had been on the receiving end of the wonderfully giving local female community. She'd been welcomed with open arms to any girls'-night-out events taking place during her visits. The mix of participants changed regularly based on who was free, and Sydney and Tansy were the two whom Petra had gotten to know the best, apart from her sister-in-law Julia, who the entire family loved to pieces.

Petra peeked into the shop. "I want to get caught up on everything you guys have been doing, but I want to get some dancing in as well."

"It's going to be much easier to stay in touch now that you're here full-time instead of flying in and out three or four times a year to visit your brother." Tansy pulled the door shut and locked it behind them. "Tonight it's a mini-girls' night out. Just the three of us."

"Wait. Forgot something." Petra raced back to the truck and snatched up her purse, sliding it over her shoulder before returning and linking her arms through both Sydney's and Tansy's.

They marched down the back alley toward Rough Cut.

"I'm opening the clinic at seven a.m., so I'm heading home at midnight," Sydney warned.

"That's my deadline, as well," Tansy said. "Baking tasks start at four a.m. for me."

Jeez. Petra didn't mind getting up early, but that was beyond her skills. "You're both going to hate me when I tell you I'm going to sleep in until noon."

Sydney snickered. "You can tell us that, but you'd be lying."

"Fine." Petra couldn't stop grinning. They knew her too well. "I hope to sleep until seven, but knowing my bratty brother, he'll probably stand outside my cabin window and crow like a rooster at five."

"Really?" Tansy hummed thoughtfully. "Let me know if I need to doctor his coffee the next time he comes in. Just a little retribution—that kind of thing."

"You're the best. I promise to let you know if it's necessary." Petra held up her pinkie, and Tansy laughingly linked their hands together.

Yup. Moving to Heart Falls was exactly what Petra had needed.

Jobwise, she was a skilled computer programmer. That, plus the other slightly less-legal vigilante adventures she'd been working on for the past year kept her busy. Yet both of those were tasks she could do anywhere.

What she needed the most right now were friends who liked her for herself.

Inside the pub, the dark wood and western style settings were welcoming yet intimate, with room to dance and room to chat. Tansy guided her and Petra to their favourite spot on the edge of the dance floor and settled in to examine the potential dance partners available that evening.

Tansy's running monologue of who was in attendance made Petra snicker. "Matt is a solid seven. Tony counts his steps, but he's a nine if you don't try to talk while on the floor. Joey is a seven, eight if he's had a few drinks—"

"And Jeb is a ten if you want to dance right now." A tall cowboy with a cheeky smile stood before Petra. "Hey, pretty lady. Long time no see. Want to take a spin?"

Petra leaned around him to grin at her friends. "Thanks for the play-by-play, but I think I'll go with this one first, no matter how he rates on the Tansy Dance Scale."

Both Tansy and Sydney offered a thumbs-up before going back to their calculating.

Petra stepped into the cowboy's arms and let him take the lead.

The quick pace of the current song didn't encourage chatting, which was fine. Petra needed this tonight. A chance to exercise her body without her mind whirling through possibilities and mistakes and goals for the future.

Because they were all there. The good and the bad and the impossible.

Right now was the time to establish a new attitude. Which meant shoving aside the sadness in her belly to keep it from dragging her down. The change in her relationship situation wasn't going to be an easy thing to simply ignore, though.

Not tonight. Not here and now. Do not dwell on it.

Maybe if she told herself that firmly enough she'd eventually follow her own excellent advice.

She was on the dance floor with only her second partner

when someone near the bar roared loud enough to grab the attention of everyone in the place. Mid-twirl in a rapid two-step, Petra didn't catch all the details, but it looked as if an argument had broken out.

Her dance partner jerked to the side, letting go of her in the process. Petra stumbled, struggling to keep her feet. The fighting cowboys surged onto the dance floor even as other men rushed forward to try to break them apart.

With curses flying and fists swinging nearby, Petra didn't know which way to turn. When one of the cowboys trying to break up the fight stepped suddenly to the right, Petra was slammed broadside with full force, her balance still too shaky to recover. She tumbled, bracing herself to hit the floor.

Instead, she found herself being swung upward, a firm grip around her back and under her thighs as she flew into the air away from the action.

Relief flooded in, and she curled herself tighter against her rescuer. She looped her arms around his shoulders and buried her face in the crook of his neck until he stopped moving. "Are we safe now?"

"Think so."

"Thank *God*."

She'd said it with conviction, but his answering chuckle seemed bigger than it should be. "No problem, Petra."

Her heart gave a kick as memories rushed in. That voice—

That touch.

Petra lifted her gaze and stared into the face of the man she'd enjoyed a one-night stand with on the night of Zach and Julia's wedding.

"Holy cow. Aiden?"

2

"Well now, wasn't this a nice surprise?

Aiden took a couple extra steps to the side, aiming for an opening in the crowd as the fight continued to rumble behind them. He was fully aware he was grinning at Petra with damn-near delight.

Petra squirmed slightly, her fingers on his shoulders pushing him back yet holding him close. As if she too wasn't quite sure what to think of this moment, but it wasn't a bad thing.

"This is a blast from the past. You saving me again." Amusement danced in her tone. "Plan to put me down anytime soon?"

He met her gaze, examining her features and the long brown strands that had escaped her ponytail. She looked nearly as good as she had after he'd tumbled her into bed the first time. "Sure you *want* me to put you down here? Because I can find us somewhere more private."

"Very funny." Her eyes rolled slightly before she tapped his chest. "Okay, now that I'm not shocked out of my mind, let's start with you helping me to my feet."

Fine by him. That's where they'd start, but not where they'd finish. Not if he had anything to say about it.

He lowered her but kept the hand around her back snug enough that she landed torso to torso. The heat of their bodies meshed.

Petra shook her head but smiled as she examined his face. "You're a cocky bastard."

"How cocky, you know intimately," he reminded her, delighted at the flush of red that brushed her cheeks.

Another woman arrived, the human equivalent of a pry bar. Impossibly, within seconds the petite redhead had managed to wedge herself between him and Petra as if it were the most natural thing in the world and not a defensive move. "You okay, honey?"

Aiden couldn't resist. "I'm just fine, sugar."

The redhead lost her charm and offered him an evil glare, silvery eyes flashing menace.

She opened her mouth, probably to lambaste him, but Petra moved first, spinning slightly to position herself next to her friend. "We're both okay. Aiden saved me from falling on my ass."

His gaze dropped involuntarily. It was one fine ass, but that was probably not a comment he should make at this moment. Not with the redhead and another woman joining their gathering.

"Ranch hands are such idiots," the newcomer commented before thrusting her hand toward him. "I'm Tansy Fields. Nice catch there, hotshot."

He took the offering. "Aiden Skye. I aim to please."

Petra laughed. It was a soft sound, her head down as if she

were trying to hide her response, but he heard it, and something warmed inside.

The night he'd picked her up had been memorable. Pleasurable without strings. Seeing her again brought to mind all sorts of wonderful distractions. Just because he had a job to do here in Heart Falls didn't mean he couldn't also have some fun.

He ignored Petra's posse as much as possible, focusing solely on her. "You steady enough on your feet to try the dance floor again?"

Petra glanced at her friends. "Sydney. Stop growling like an attack dog. Aiden and I have met before. He's got my seal of approval."

Disappointment danced over Sydney's face. "Well, drat. I just got a new scalpel I wanted to try."

Scalpel? Dear God.

Tansy smacked the back of her hand into Sydney's arm. "Stop being mean to the nice cowboy."

"But it's so hard to tell the nice ones from the not so nice ones," Sydney complained, gesturing toward the dance floor. "I mean, one minute everything's flowing smoothly, and the next, testosterone is rumbling all over the place."

A very inelegant snort escaped Tansy. "Please. You rarely complain about rumbling testosterone." She danced her attention between Petra and Aiden then made shooing motions with her fingers. "Go on. Dance."

Aiden tucked his arm around Petra again, ready to guide her to the floor. Amusement was still there though, so he tilted his head toward where his brothers stood at a nearby high top, drinking their beers now that the crowd and the fight had settled. "Those two cowboys are nice. I mean, nice enough, in a not very nice way," he corrected.

As expected, Tansy's gaze darted over to land on Jake and

Declan. Her expression turned to admiration then flicked back to Aiden. "If you're lying, we will get revenge."

"They're my brothers," he admitted. "The grumpy one is Declan. The one who looks as if butter wouldn't melt in his mouth is Jake, but they both know their right feet from their left."

Then he ignored the mischief he'd arranged and guided Petra onto the dance floor and back into his arms. The music shifted to something slower, and he tucked her tight against him.

"Neatly done," Petra watched her friends for a moment before focusing back on him.

"I was highly motivated to get your friends otherwise occupied." He turned her smoothly, welcoming the pressure of her curves against him. "You're looking good."

"Thanks. You're looking like you're here, in Heart Falls."

He paused. "Is this a trick question?"

"No. But I could've sworn that night we spent together you said you didn't live here."

Aiden leaned her over his arm, staring into her eyes as he dipped her with the utmost control. "You said you didn't live here either."

"Touché."

He pulled her upright, and they danced in silence for a moment, deep appreciation for the way she moved in his arms rising again.

"After I danced with you last time, I knew I wanted you in my bed," he admitted. "You're so responsive. Makes it easy to guide you, which means both of us get to enjoy the *dance* as much as possible."

Petra smiled, the hand on his shoulder rising until a gentle caress drifted over the back of his neck. "My sisters always told me that if a couple couldn't dance well vertically, they couldn't dance horizontally, either."

"Makes sense." His body was heating up from all the contact points between them. She knew it, the minx. Her hips swayed the slightest bit more than necessary so that the thickening ridge of his cock was brushed more intensely. "We going to do more dancing tonight than right here? Right now?"

Heat rose in her eyes, but her head shifted slightly from side to side. "I'm interested, but that's not something that can happen tonight. I've just moved to Heart Falls, and I'm still settling in. This isn't a great time for me to sneak away, no matter how much you tempt me."

"Well, that's the saddest thing I've heard in a good long time." And yet, to be truthful, he was a little relieved. Figuring out the logistics of taking her home, with all of them settling in would be awkward, to say the least.

It also made him question what had appeared to be a perfectly reasonable living arrangement. Temporarily sharing a house with his brothers was one thing. Agreeing to remain celibate for months was another. Aiden was sure he wasn't the only one.

First thing on the agenda at tomorrow morning's meeting was a check-in of the building situation at the new High Water ranch.

He spun Petra because it brought her in close and let him torment himself with thoughts of what he'd have to wait a little longer to enjoy.

"Here's the good news," Petra told him, her eyes flashing with mischief, aware of what he was doing and fully on board. "Since I am living here now, when you're traveling through the area you'll know where to find me. Maybe this time we could exchange phone numbers. Keep in touch."

She was brilliant, beautiful, and one of the high points of moving to Heart Falls. "I'd like that very much."

The song was coming to an end, so he guided her back toward the side of the room. A quick glance told him that both his brothers were still on the floor with Sydney and Tansy.

He grabbed his phone and opened his contacts. "Type yours in."

She eyed him for a second then tapped in her name and number. "Please do not end up being weird this time around. My phone is set to Do Not Disturb from midnight till eight a.m., so if I wake up to find a long message of increasingly fucked-up messages, or a single dick pic, I will forward Sydney your number. And your address if necessary."

Aiden laughed. He took the phone from her and quickly typed in his information, hitting Send on the message. "There. My address for you to send to Sydney in case I get weird. But I promise the only ulterior motives I have regarding you are crystal clear."

She glanced down as her phone pinged with his incoming message. Petra blinked, and her head snapped up. "What's this?"

"My address," he said again. "Since I now live here in Heart Falls as well, we won't have to wait for me to travel through the area to give you a shout to let you know that I'd like to get together. Got any plans for Friday night?"

∼

PETRA'S FRIENDS were never going to let her live this down. Especially Tansy's sister, Rose, who they'd all been wildly teasing because Rose's one-night stand was now her fiancé.

It seemed Petra had managed the same damn thing—

At least in the messing up the *we're doing this one time and* it's only for fun because I'm never going to see you again *kind of way. Not in the* this is a full-on relationship and we're going to be together forever *business.*

Not that she had anything against marriage. She had a ton of shining examples of how to do it right in her parents and her siblings. But she wasn't ready to take the plunge yet.

Her last boyfriend had left a nasty taste in her mouth.

Her brain was still in scramble mode when Aiden tucked his fingers under her chin and lifted, smiling into her eyes. "Did I throw you for a loop, darlin'?"

Petra shrugged. "You know you did, but it's okay. Just taking a moment to wrap my brain around it, that's all."

Aiden nodded. "We'll go at your speed, but we had a lot of fun last time." He paused. "Or at least I had a lot of fun, and I tried to make sure you did as well."

"Oh, it's not that at all," Petra reassured him. "That night lives on as fodder for my battery-operated pleasure-fests."

He blinked, then his grin grew even wider. "Good to know. And damn if you didn't just give me a visual that's going to entertain me for a hell of a long time."

A quick glance at the dance floor showed that her friends were heading her direction. "Your brothers? You've all moved here?"

"We've taken over the animal shelter," Aiden informed her.

Oh, *really*? Petra had been in town for less than twenty-four hours, but she'd been kept up to speed over the past months, between Tansy's texts and Rose's emails, regarding everything going on in their extended family. AKA, Petra knew that their Grandma Sonora, who used to own said animal shelter, was moving, but not who had bought the place.

Small towns were small. There wasn't much that happened without it affecting someone you knew.

Tansy arrived at that moment, swinging into Petra's space. "You're not going to believe what Declan just told me."

"That the Skye brothers are the ones who bought your grandma's place?" Petra laughed as Tansy planted her fists on her hips and pouted. "Look, I don't get to pull a fast one on you very often, so *ta-da*."

Sydney dipped her chin at Jake then took off back onto the dance floor with another partner.

Jake shrugged then gestured toward a table of ladies in the corner. "Declan. You coming?"

"Thanks for the dance, Tansy." Declan shifted a little uncomfortably.

Tansy went full-on Tansy. She grabbed him by the collar and tugged him down to plant a kiss on his cheek. "I had a great time dancing with you, but we have zero chemistry. So go—there's some lady out there you'll light up the night with, but it's not going to be me."

Declan's rarely present smile slipped fully into place. "I had a great time dancing with you, too. Plus, you are about the most blunt-spoken woman I've ever met. You let me know if you need me to act as big brother. Anytime."

The next moment both Declan and Tansy took off in different directions leaving Petra and Aiden standing there.

Amusement rose hard and fast. "So much for triple dating," Petra offered.

"Thank God," Aiden said. "I meant it. They're not assholes, but I like dating to be a two-person event, not something run by committee. Jake tends toward liking things very much by the book. Very straight and narrow. Declan is a lot more likely to go with the flow and make last minute changes."

Which made things even funnier. Petra tugged Aiden toward the exit. "Maybe they have too much in common.

Sydney makes lists of lists. I swear she organizes her day with three backup calendars and a host of alerts. By comparison, Tansy flies by the seat of her pants the entire time. She's a fantastic cook, yet she somehow does it without ever setting a timer. It's as if she's got this internal stopwatch that tells her exactly when things need to happen."

They were outside now in the cooling fall night. Petra had already forwarded Aiden's contact information to Tansy, but considering everybody in town would know who the Skye brothers were before the day was out, she felt safe enough alone with him. Again.

She linked her fingers in his and tugged him down the boardwalk until they were outside of the pub's bright lights. "You okay with this?" she asked.

"Don't know. Do you plan to take advantage of me, Ms. Sorenson?" Aiden leaned against the wall of the mercantile and pulled her between his legs. "What will I do when I'm at your mercy?"

"Hopefully you haven't forgotten all your moves," Petra teased back.

She pressed her hands to his chest and slowly slid them upward. The soft fabric of his brushed-cotton shirt contrasted nicely with the powerful muscles under the material, and she hummed happily.

Easing closer, she tilted her head and lifted up on her tiptoes to offer her lips.

He needed no second invitation. Aiden cupped the back of her head, cradling her as he gently brought their lips together. A single brush, pleading and tender. The breath rushing past her warm compared to the cool night air. He pressed his other hand against the small of her back, and everything lined up so perfectly that Petra sighed again.

Another kiss, this one with lingering pressure. Another, his fingers guiding her head slightly to the side to take it deeper, slipping his tongue over her lips before easing away. And again, making contact and sending a thrill through her that made goosebumps rise and an ache start deep in her core.

His breathing kicked up a step, and the kiss turned into a taking. He owned her, controlled her. Ravished her lips in a way that made her head spin and her heart pound and everything in her ask for more.

Her memories had not failed her. Not one bit.

Petra wanted to climb him right there. To hell with being smart and waiting until the time was more appropriate. This man knew how to make every one of her *yes* buttons chime loudly. Consistently.

It was Aiden who tightened his grip on the back of her neck and, with a groan, separated his mouth from hers. He tipped his head so their foreheads met, and the two of them damn near gasped in each other's faces, trying to catch their breath.

"Holy shit."

Petra whispered it, but Aiden heard, and he chuckled. A barely there sound more noticeable because his entire body rocked against hers. Which also was not easy to take because there was so much more she wanted to do.

He smiled, eyes bright with amusement and lingering passion. "I agree. Holy shit."

She put her hands back on his chest, rearranging herself until the room between their upper bodies had vanished. She leaned on him, his hands resting easily on the swells of her buttocks.

"We are going to do…each other…again," Petra promised. "But no matter how much I wish I could change my mind, I'm still going to go with door number two this time. Not tonight."

"Agreed, again." Aiden's gaze roamed over her face. "You just moved to town. I just moved to town. I've got a long list of things that need to be accomplished and can't be put off, but I want to see you when it works."

The way he worded it sounded like more than wanting to get together for a booty call, and Petra hesitated. "Just so you know, I'm not looking for a boyfriend right now."

His shoulders lifted in an easy shrug. "Finding a girlfriend wasn't on my to-do list. But we've got some amazing chemistry between us. Seems a shame to not at least enjoy that. If that's something you're looking for."

The moment of panic passed. "We do have chemistry."

His lips twitched. "Did you want to go back on the dance floor and torment ourselves for a little longer?"

"Definitely," Petra agreed. He went to straighten but she pressed her palms to his cheeks and shook her head. "But first, we stay here. I'd like about three or four more kisses like that first one, please."

"Please and thank you. Very polite, just like a good girl." Aiden sank back against the wall, teasing his fingers along the crease where her butt and legs met. "Good girls get all sorts of things they like."

Oh. My. God. The zap that went through her at his words could've powered a small space station for a full day. "You talking that way shouldn't make me this hot."

"Don't try to analyze it." Amusement danced in his eyes. "If it works, it works."

Petra couldn't agree more as his mouth crashed down on hers. She thoroughly enjoyed having her brain scrambled with kisses that left her aching and needy and happier than she'd been in a long time.

New beginnings. A place to start over and get her feet under her. Sometimes that was exactly what a person needed.

3

*A*iden hovered over the coffee pot until it boiled. Amusement rose as Jake and Declan also filled mugs as if their lives depended on it.

They settled at the trestle table and drank in silence.

Aiden wasn't sure why his brothers looked like the walking dead. Him? He'd slept like crap. Far too many dirty images had raced through his head to allow for sweet dreams. Plus something more...

It was the oddest thing. Naturally he'd dreamed about Petra and sweaty hot sex, but there'd also been other images. Like the two of them walking hand and hand, and one of being curled up together in front of a fire. Sweet and homey mental pictures that were as distracting as the sex thoughts.

Petra was going to be trouble, he knew it to his core.

It wasn't until they were on their second cups that Aiden felt human again.

"It's a good day to get started on what comes next." Jake opened his notebook and tapped the page. "Can I simply hand over your lists of what needs to be done, or are we going to sit and argue about them first?"

Declan shrugged. "I've got my own shit to accomplish. I can get to whatever's on your list at some point, I suppose."

"We all have a ton to do," Aiden pointed out. "But let's lean into our strengths, remember? From this point forward, Jake organizes the overall schedule, and we dictate in our areas of expertise."

Their older brother eased back in his chair and folded his arms over his chest, coffee mug resting on the table in front of him. "I've got no argument with that, and you know it. Hell, the renovations would have stalled a dozen times if I hadn't had the checklists and contracts, in triplicate" —he glared momentarily at Jake— "to shove in the contractors faces to light their asses on fire. But there are animals I promised to go pick up over the next couple of days. Make sure that's worked into the schedule."

Jake nodded. "I've got that in there. We need to finish prepping the dorm rooms, the retreat space, and the room for our on-site therapist. I've broken down the remaining tasks into what we can take over now that we're all here and what we still might like to hire out. We've got at least a couple of months of work before the big spaces are livable. Oh—and we need to keep looking for a housekeeper."

"The living quarters for us, as well," Aiden tossed out. "I know it's lower on the priority list, but let's make sure we keep that moving as well."

Declan raised a brow. "The pretty brunette from last night?"

"Shut up. That conversation is over, move on."

His brothers exchanged knowing looks.

Jake leaned forward on his elbows. "No, this is interesting. And alarming— Remember. No making waves in Heart Falls.

We need to get High Water firmly established so everyone local knows they can trust us."

"Or better yet, forgets we're here," Declan added.

Christ. "I'm not about to haul the woman off against her will so she's crying bloody murder or anything. I just said let's not forget we'd all like privacy sooner than later." Aiden sipped his coffee, pleased that he'd managed to say it without any indication that his interest might be more than casual.

After the dreams he'd had last night? He knew when to follow his hunches, and something was telling him Petra was potentially more than a one-night-stand repeat.

"Privacy would be good," Declan agreed. He snagged one of the papers from under Jake's hand and tapped on the blueprint drawings for the barn. "Another thing. Now that I've thought about it more, I want to suggest a couple of changes to this. We need a bigger place for the guys to hang out together that isn't the barn."

Aiden gestured around at the fire and the giant table where they currently sat. "We'll have this space for meals and family gatherings."

"Which is great, but I agree with Declan," Jake said. "It's important to use this space as much as possible, but they'll need somewhere else where they don't have to mind their manners as much, since the ladies will be in here."

Jake tugged more design blueprints from the pile, and for the next half-hour they made suggestions and altered plans. The sharing felt right and was a big reason why Aiden knew this was going to work.

They might be very different, but all three of them had the same vision and the work ethic to make it happen.

The rest of the morning was taken up with a million different tasks. Everything from dealing with furniture deliveries to setting up a small office space so Aiden could go online and put in more orders.

Dixie greeted him eagerly every time he headed outside to touch base with his brothers. "Good girl. You like it here?" he asked her, ruffling the top of her head.

She sat on her rump, tail wagging furiously, a wide doggie grin on her face that clearly stated her approval.

He took off just before twelve to run into town and grab lunch.

Walking in the door of the Buns and Roses café was like walking into heaven. The sweet scent of cinnamon buns and rich chocolate hung on the air, and the size of the meals on the tables he passed walking up to the counter gave him a pleasant buzz of anticipation.

When he hit the counter and looked into the big brown eyes of Petra's friend Tansy, Aiden grinned widely. "We meet again."

Tansy blinked then flashed him a smile. "Hey, cowboy. So you're not just a good dancer and a good kisser, you're also very smart because you know exactly where to go for the best food in town."

The dark-skinned woman with long black hair pulled into a neat braid working the coffee machine glanced over her shoulder and examined him closely. "Tansy. How would you know he's a good kisser, and why haven't I heard more about this?"

Aiden kept his position instead of checking to see if everyone else in the shop was staring at them, although he imagined they were. Small town and all.

Tansy waved a hand. "Aiden, this is my twin sister Rose. Rose, this is the gentleman Petra told us all about. In detail."

Well, damn. Aiden kept his grin in place, but he was fairly certain he was also blushing. "Hello, Rose."

"Hello, Aiden. Welcome to Heart Falls." Rose stepped forward, wiping her hands on her apron before offering him a handshake. "Sorry. Lunchtime rush. We'll find a way to grill you later."

So be it. "I look forward to it. In the meantime, I need food to go."

Tansy took his order then gestured him to the side. "Wait there. I need to keep the line moving, but I'm not done with you yet."

"Yes, ma'am."

He laughed at the expressive eye roll she offered. Then he stepped to the side as commanded, standing against the wall and out of the way while he took the time to examine the people and the café.

The shop had done a good job of making the place cozy and a touch on the eclectic side. It did not look like a typical small-town diner. The walls between the coffee shop and the next-door flower and knickknack store had been mostly taken down, and there were tables available throughout the floor space. Bright bouquets and interesting local handicrafts were displayed everywhere.

The constant low buzz of voices said it all. People were comfortable here. Aiden approved.

With a couple of other people working behind the counter, it didn't take long for his order to be up. Tansy brought it to him, snagging him by the arm and hauling him toward the front door. "You're with me."

Aiden went willingly, amused that the Heart Falls ladies seemed comfortable dragging him around. Not that he was displeased with the concept, but it did make him wonder.

Just outside the door, Tansy whirled on him and pressed the bag into his hands. "You didn't order enough food for the three of you, since I assume this is for your brothers as well. I tossed in some extra roast beef sandwiches and a half-dozen muffins."

"Thank you."

She nodded decisively then narrowed her gaze. "What are you doing with Petra?"

"Well according to what you told your twin sister—and you will have to explain how that's possible sometime—what I'm doing with Petra is kissing her. And doing a good job of it."

Tansy's gaze remained intimidating but her lips twitched as she fought a smile. "You're a sly one."

"I'm private," he corrected. "I'm all for Petra sharing whatever she wants to share with her girls, but if you want details, you need to ask her."

He got a kick out of it when Tansy's glare morphed into a pout. "Dammit, I hoped you'd say that, and I wish you hadn't. Petra didn't spill the beans last night other than mentioning she was happy you were here and that's all she wanted to say about it for now."

"I'm certain that if you put your mind to it you'll be able to encourage her to share more. You strike me as the resourceful type."

Tansy took a deep breath then grinned. "Dammit, I *like* you. Why do you have to be all charming and stuff?"

Aiden shrugged. "Just lucky, I guess."

She patted him on the chest then tilted her head toward the door. "I need to go before my sister puts out an APB. But rest assured I will work on Petra and learn everything I need to know. But so far, I don't plan to warn her away from you."

"I always enjoy having a good wingman at my side," Aiden said. He lifted the bag in the air. "Thanks for this. Next time I'll pay it forward and buy the guy behind me in line his lunch."

Tansy waved goodbye and pushed through the door, but she had a thoughtful expression on her face.

He meant every word about Petra deciding what she shared with her friends. Everyone needed someone to talk to, and he was thankful he once again had his brothers. Not everyone was so lucky.

Aiden demolished his portion of the food en route home, stopping just long enough to stick the lunch bag in the fridge. Then he took off with the list Jake had given him which included a massive stock up grocery run in the nearest big community.

Hours later, once the trip was done and he'd found storage places for everything, he got started on steaks and fries with a salad for dinner. All of them could cook to some extent, but it wasn't his favourite thing.

Still, he liked to eat, which meant cooking was required.

He had the barbecue fired up and the fries in the oven when a message came through on his phone.

> Petra: Hey. You asked me out for next Friday and I never responded. Up for a picnic supper? I know a great place we can ride to. Or if you want to drive, we can do that.

> Aiden: Hey, darling. A ride to a picnic spot sounds amazing. Need me to bring over my horse? Five o'clock? Six?

> Petra: Nope to bringing your horse. My brother co-owns a dude ranch, so we have horses. If you can make it for five, that gives us more time before we lose the light. I'll pack the meal if you bring the drinks.

> Aiden: Five is perfect. I'll bring dessert as well. I make a mean Jell-O.

> Petra: I don't know if I should be terrified or not.

> Aiden: Lol. Looking forward to seeing you. Sweet dreams until then. Or not so sweet…

> Petra: I'm not ready to start sexting with you, sir. Not that it wouldn't be fun, but I'm sitting in the living room with my family and getting squirmy and bothered right now is not in the plan.

> Aiden: Okay. Getting you squirmy and bothered is on hold until a better time. Have a great evening. We'll chat soon.

She responded with a thumbs-up to his final message, but it was enough.

Aiden whistled as he returned to his cooking, and thoughts of exactly how he'd get Petra to the point she was squirming under him were a happy distraction.

~

PETRA SPENT a wonderful day with her brother and sister-in-law. They wandered all over Red Boot ranch, checked all the animals and the venues for both weddings and the dude ranch.

She hung her arms over the railing and stared at the teeny white colt standing under foot with his mama. She took a quick picture and posted it to the Sorenson family chat group their father had set up years ago.

> Petra: Photo proof that I'm here at Red Boot ranch. This place is amazing, and spending time with Julia is so much fun. Oh, and Zach. He's okay too. I guess.

"It really is beautiful here," she said to Zach as she tucked her phone away. She glanced over as he leaned lazily on the fence beside her. She smiled to discover his gaze was fixed on Julia where she stood across the yard chatting with some of the hands. "I'm very happy for you, big brother. Not only about your new home, but the people and your wife. Julia is perfect for you."

Her brother grinned, gaze remaining on Julia. "She is pretty perfect, and I'm very happy." He turned his attention to Petra. "I'd be happier if you'd let me go beat the shit out of your ex, but since I know you're far too good of a person to allow that, let's focus on making you at home here in Heart Falls."

Ugh. "Are we going to have that conversation already?"

Zach shrugged. "I don't like that he made you cry."

Petra twisted and leaned her elbows on the rail behind her, staring toward the Rocky Mountains in the distance. Patches were bright yellow where larch trees were reacting to the dropping fall temperatures. Snow would be coming soon, but right now everything was on the cusp between warm and cold.

It was a good place and a good time to make a fresh start, she decided.

She met her brother's gaze. "Curtis wasn't who I thought he was. Which is mostly on him for being a jerk but partly on me for not seeing it sooner. It's up to me to move on, and that's going to be far easier to do here in Heart Falls than back in Manitoba, where everywhere I go, someone will want to know the details of why we broke up."

"Some people here in Heart Falls knew you were seeing someone," Zach pointed out, cringing a little. "Maybe more than a few? I'm sorry, but I like to talk about good things."

"And for a while it was a good thing," Petra assured him. "I get it. It'll still be easier to say we broke up when they don't know him."

Anger flashed in Zach's eyes again. "I know you don't want his knees broken or anything, but I'm more than willing to find a way to hit him in the pocketbook. I have the resources," her brother assured her.

Petra kept her expression blank. What Zach didn't know was she had some skills in that area as well. The temptation to use her recently honed hacking skills to hijack her ex's finances was a hard battle, but so far she had won.

Telling Zach about her illegal side gig was out of the question. Instead, she offered him her full attention. "With your contacts, you could probably go in and mess with his investments from now to eternity. If I ever feel particularly vindictive, I'll let you know."

Zach extended his hand. "Deal."

She used his hand to pull him into a tight hug. "Thanks for finding me a job."

He ruffled her hair, pointing a hand toward their office building. "As if you needed my help. You could walk into any place in any town and get a job dealing with their tech, but I'm glad you're going to do it for us. My partner is glad you're going to do it for us."

Zach's partner, Finn Marlette, hated computers, which always struck Petra as funny in this day and age.

She briefly wondered what Aiden's job was and where he sat on the technology scale.

Like every other time her thoughts had drifted toward Aiden that day, she found herself smiling. They had an evening picnic date planned for two nights from now. She still wasn't sure if she was comfortable bringing him back afterwards to the small cottage she'd been loaned at Red Boot ranch. It seemed too soon, even though everything in her was craving the mindless physical release of some truly spectacular sex.

If she were being honest, it was probably too soon for her

big brother to deal with. The last thing she needed was Zach going overprotective, both for her and Aiden's sakes.

The question was still on her mind when she got together with Tansy and Sydney the following night.

Tansy had hot wings in the air fryer, Sydney had made a salad, and Petra's contribution had been to stop at the grocery store and buy three liters of ice cream plus chocolate and marshmallow sauce.

She didn't tell her friends that she was so distracted she'd gone back to her truck twice to grab her shopping bags.

Sydney took the treats from her with an appreciative nod. "All four food groups are represented. We're set."

Tansy considered. "Vegetables, protein, dairy…?"

"Oh please, nothing so proper as that." Sydney gestured around them. "Wings. Salad, a.k.a. the illusion of something healthy. Plus ice cream, and of course this."

She pulled out a bottle of tequila.

Hell, no. Petra raised her hands in protest. "The last time we drank tequila, I felt it for a full week."

"Just a welcome-to-town shot," Sydney promised. She cracked the bottle and poured them small glasses, handing them around. She lifted hers in the air. "To Petra, who can take names and kick ass but also knows when it's time to run."

Petra considered then realized it was probably the wisest toast she'd heard in her life. "You should've said that when I was a little tipsy, because I would've offered homage to you from now till eternity."

Sydney raised her glass in the air and they clinked them together. "To Petra."

"To Petra," Tansy repeated.

"To friends," Petra insisted.

The burn of the liquid down her throat was a reminder of

what it felt like to be alive. A little bit of pain mixed with the sweet.

Her happiness was up to her. Her choices, her decisions. While the last six months had been tough, and she wouldn't have wished it on anyone else, she was here now, stronger because of it.

Ready to make a difference.

"Before we do anything else, we have gifts." Tansy pulled a bag from beside the couch and passed it to Petra. "Welcome-to-town gifts. Small ones from me and Sydney."

"To prove we planned ahead," Sydney added with a glare at Tansy.

Tansy snickered.

Petra discovered a hard object wrapped in tissue. "Candles? I love candles."

"We know this," Tansy fluttered her fingers to hurry up. "Unwrap. This century."

Tempting as it was to tease her friend and remove the paper slowly, Petra didn't have the patience. She tore it off and held candle one aloft and read out loud. *"I'd Shank A Bitch For You."* She snickered even as she peered at the much smaller writing underneath. *"Right In The Kidneys.* Thanks, Sydney. It's a sweet sentiment, and totally you."

"You're welcome." The petite woman grinned. "Anytime, anywhere."

"Read mine," Tansy demanded.

This one also made Petra grin. *"BESTIE: the one who will tell you that you are full of shit but support any and all stupid choices you make when called upon to do so."* She hugged Tansy. "You guys are the best."

"We're glad you're here," Tansy said, a hint of seriousness in her expression. "And now, let's eat."

They dove in hard on the wings and treats, conversation

flowing rather than liquor. It had been over a year since they'd truly gotten to catch up, and all of them had big news to share.

"I could have the door of the clinic open from five in the morning to past midnight, and there'd always be somebody in the waiting room," Sydney told them. "Of course, I'm not doing that," she said quickly when Petra began to ask a question. "I run the clinic four days a week, based on my priorities. Then I make a lot of house calls."

Tansy jerked her thumb at Sydney as she explained to Petra. "She's visiting all the seniors who either can't get out or refuse to get checked. They call her Captain Jeremiah because when she shows up, nobody dares countermand her orders."

"Oh, please," Sydney said dryly. "It's *General* Jeremiah, thank you very much."

"Good for you," Petra said. "You're probably still working more hours than a regular nine to five."

"I don't think there's a doctor alive who works a regular nine to five," Sydney offered. "Trust me, I'm getting enough sleep, especially compared to my interning days. This is why I wanted to be in Heart Falls. If I'd wanted tons of billable hours, I'd have gone to the big city."

"You'd think sometimes we were in the big city the way people moan about a lack of access," Tansy complained. "Buns and Roses is also what we want it to be. Coffee, breakfast, lunch. I'm not staying open for dinner where people book tables then don't show up."

It was a different business than Petra had ever worked in. "They really think they're in charge?"

"The customer is always right." Tansy said perkily before sticking out her tongue. "Bah, humbug. I believe in customer service, and I believe in serving a good product, but if it's not on the menu, don't ask for it. I get that people have allergies, and I absolutely make sure I have menu choices available for them, but I'm not listening to somebody who sneakily tells me how to make their omelet, including how many shakes of salt, and the pan temperature, and which spatula to flip it with."

"They don't," Petra goggled at the idea.

"Oh, they do. Or at least attempt to. Then I seem to mysteriously run out of ingredients." Tansy's grin was pure evil.

"Chefs are supposed to be temperamental and a little diva-ish," Sydney leaned back in her chair and rested her hands on her stomach. "Oh my God, that was delish. If you did decide to open a place that served dinner, you could cook whatever the hell you wanted and people would buy it up in a minute."

"No set menu," Petra added. "Cook what you want and they will come."

Tansy was uncharacteristically silent for a moment. She leaned forward and spoke quietly. "I've been giving some thought to what I could do. I mean, for different work."

Both Sydney and Petra sat up like a shot. "Close down Buns and Roses?" Petra asked.

Tansy made a rude noise. "No, not that. We've got it running well with enough staff that it's pretty routine. But sometimes I do get a wild idea of wanting to cook something different. Plus, truthfully, living here over the shop is boring since Rose moved out."

"You want a new roommate?" Petra asked. "Because I don't have to live at the ranch. I could come stay with you."

Tansy smiled. "I would adore you as a roommate, but I think it's more than that. This was where Rose and I found our independence. Now that she's engaged and living with her sexy Irishman, I feel as if I'm supposed to do the next thing as well. Which might involve not being in the apartment. Move on, move forward."

A sentiment which Petra could absolutely agree with. She

nodded slowly and laid her hand over Tansy's. "Well, if you change your mind, let me know. I'm the last person to say you're wrong. I moved provinces at thirty-three to get a fresh start."

The two of them nodded back, solemn expressions on their faces.

Sydney wrinkled her nose. "I know you don't want to spend a lot of time rehashing what happened with your ex, but if you ever need a sounding board, we're here for you."

Because while Petra had told them she'd broken things off with Curtis, she was still too embarrassed to share the details. "I know, and I love you for it. But for now, what we all need to relish is that *we* are in charge. Of where we work, and how much we work, and who we work with. That's a good thing," Petra insisted.

"Amen," Tansy said as she lifted her ice cream spoon in the air.

Sydney nodded. "We're also in charge of something else. Specifically, where we play, how much we play, and who we play with." Her gaze fixed on Petra. "So. Aiden?"

A laugh burst free, because these two had, over the past years, subtly snuck into her very soul. They were trustworthy and they were honest and they were women Petra connected with to the tips of her toes. Which made it easy to share the truth. "Aiden is a delicious distraction I'm looking forward to. But there's no rush. Sometimes anticipation makes everything that much sweeter."

Conversation turned, swirled into laughter and teasing and good solid female friendship. When Petra made her way home later that night, it was with a heart full of happiness and the lingering memory of Aiden's smile and looking forward to being in his arms in a couple nights.

Anticipation *was* a wonderful thing.

4

Mid-morning Friday, the High Water ranch house already looked a lot more like a home. By some weird magic, the shipment of mattresses and bedroom furniture Jake had ordered weeks ago arrived only a few minutes before the towels and linens.

Aiden and Jake took a pause from drywall work in the artists' retreat space and spent a couple of hours assembling beds and arranging furniture. They'd gone with simple choices, and everything in the bedrooms was mix and match. By the time Declan stopped in for his third cup of coffee, he gave a slow nod of approval as he marched through the rooms to see what they'd accomplished.

"Not bad." Declan stepped toward the window in the room where Aiden's gear was shoved in the closet to get it out of the way of the new twin bed. He peered outside and made a noise. "I'll adjust that yard light so it doesn't shine in this room all night."

"Good idea," Jake guided them toward the kitchen. "Did

you finish the idea list of outdoor furniture? Or find a place for a firepit?"

"Got a start on the list. I'm still not sure I've hit the right amount between too sparse and too busy. But the spot I picked is dead on. One of you should come and check after lunch so you can tell me I'm a genius." Declan glanced around hopefully before his expression fell. "Do we have plans for lunch? Jake, you set the schedule."

"I phoned over to Buns and Roses," Jake admitted. "I know we've got stuff in the fridge, but once the furniture all arrived, we've been going full tilt ever since. I'll cook supper."

Aiden checked his watch. Thirty minutes to go until lunch still, but they may as well plan this now. "Does one of us need to swing over there to grab food at noon?"

Jake shook his head. "Tansy said she had somebody who could run it over for us, but not to get in the habit because they didn't offer a full-time delivery service."

"Sounds fair," Declan said with a nod. "I like her."

"You like anyone who kisses you on the cheek," Jake teased. "Big brother to how many women now?"

Declan shrugged. "A lot of the reason why High Water will work is because we'll be able to scare the crap out of the people who need it, but the innocent know they can trust us."

Which was a sobering pull back to reality about exactly who would be coming to live in the rooms they were setting up.

The sound of a car in front of the house brought Aiden's attention to the window where a familiar car had pulled to a stop. He swore softly. "Don't kill me. I forgot to mention I got a text this morning from my contact with Alberta foster care, Danielle. She said she planned to stop by today. No other details."

They all turned to the window. Jake sighed heavily. "We're nowhere near ready, but we've made a good start. She probably wants to reassure herself we actually bought a place."

Declan put his coffee cup down on the island and headed toward the front door. "No use in standing here wondering."

Aiden met Danielle as she stepped from her car, glancing around at the house and barn. In her late fifties, she was neatly dressed in a smart outfit that would fit equally in a family setting or a boardroom. He'd met her while volunteering with troubled teens at his previous job in the Crowsnest Pass area, and he knew she had a passion for doing what was right, even if it meant colouring outside the lines.

"Danielle. Good to see you again."

"And you." She gave him a quick hug. "I know this is sooner than you expected, but I was passing through after a meeting in Calgary. I thought I'd take a chance and see how things were going."

"We'll let you take a look around," Aiden suggested. "If you've got any suggestions, you let us know. There's been a lot happening and some things to catch you up on, but first off is making sure you're okay with our plans."

Danielle greeted both Jake and Declan then opened the trunk of her car to display a pair of boots. "I know it's probably the least ready, but I'll admit that the animal rescue holds a great deal of charm for me. You got any cats or dogs around for me to say hello to? My husband is allergic, so this is the only chance I get for some creature cuddle time."

Declan tilted his head toward the barn. "Come on. I'll give you a tour and show you what we're planning for the men's dorms."

"When you're done, come back inside. You can check the house then join us for lunch," Jake offered. "I ordered more than enough, and she'll be bringing it by just before noon."

"Wonderful." Danielle took another quick glance around

before holding up her boots. "Let me change, then I'll be ready for my tour."

Wasn't much they could do in the living room to make it cozier. They had chairs at the kitchen table and not much else yet, so Aiden didn't bother trying. Danielle understood how this worked. How you could only do so much at a time.

Jake put plates and cutlery on the table, though. "We should at least try to make a good impression," he mumbled when Aiden laughed. Then they both worked on their own tasks until Danielle and Declan were back.

Aiden took her for a quick walk-through. He was very thankful they'd tucked away all their stuff because with the new beds all made up with comforters in a soft blue, everything looked, well, pretty. Welcoming.

Danielle stopped and looked at the primary bedroom for the longest time then joined them at the kitchen table. "Okay, in case you're worried, I'm impressed. I can tell you're serious about making this a place of refuge and a stepping stone to better lives. Thanks for keeping my trust."

"Making High Water a safe spot for those who need it is our priority," Declan assured her.

"Whatever checks and balances you need in place, we'll go along with," Jake repeated. "We want that, so that everyone feels safe."

She met Jake's gaze. "Thank you. I know, and I wouldn't have started this in the first place if I didn't trust you all at a gut level. So here's where I admit I came over with an ulterior motive. I know you absolutely are not ready—there's no way you could be." Danielle paused and seemed to go off in a different angle as she directed her next question at Aiden. "When does the housekeeper move in?"

Some sixth sense made him hesitate. He didn't want to admit they'd had zero luck in finding someone. "Not for a bit."

Danielle sighed, settling back in her chair as if exhausted. "It was a long shot, but I had hoped that by some miracle you already had someone in place." She met each of their gazes in turn. "There's a young woman I heard about who's in a bad situation. She's sixteen, and I'd like to get her out in the next twenty-four hours, but I can't bring her here unless you have a woman on-site."

The front doorbell rang followed by the door slowly swinging open and Petra walked in, arms wrapped around an enormous box. "Hey, guys. Sorry about that. I leaned on the door, and it opened. I brought lunch." Petra spotted Danielle and blinked. "Hello. I'm sorry. Didn't mean to interrupt."

Beside Aiden, Declan had bolted upright and now shot to his feet. He hurried forward and took the box from Petra. "Perfect timing. Thanks so much." He spun and dropped the food on the nearest counter then to Aiden's surprise, his brother wrapped an arm around Petra's shoulders and marched her to the table right beside Aiden's chair. "Petra, this is Danielle."

"Nice to meet you," Petra said. She smiled, but her confusion was clearly rising.

A hand landed on the back of Aiden's collar as Declan all but hauled him to his feet. Not knowing what was going on, Aiden went willingly enough and ended up standing beside Petra.

His brother stepped back and gestured to the side. "Danielle, I'd like you to meet Petra. Aiden's fiancée."

∽

IT WAS PARTLY her fault for not paying attention. Petra had been more interested in sneaking a peek at Aiden than giving the other woman at the table her full attention. But—*what?*

"Um—"

"Like Aiden said, there's been a lot happening, and this is part of it." Declan twisted to face her and Aiden, winking with the eye that was away from the older woman. "Isn't that right?"

Petra still wasn't totally sure what she had heard. It sounded an awful lot like the word *fiancée*, but that made no sense.

The next moment, though, Aiden slipped a hand around her waist and tugged her against him. "I'm thrilled that Petra said yes."

He turned and pretended to nuzzle her neck even while whispering frantically. "Please go along with this. I'll explain everything as soon as I can, but it's important."

Well then. Petra glanced between Danielle, Declan, and Jake, noting with some amusement that each of them had a vastly different expression on their face.

Declan continued to stare in his somewhat stone-faced matter but with an earnestness that made Petra pause. Jake looked horrified. He'd pasted a smile on his lips that made him look slightly ill.

But it was Danielle who turned the tide for Petra. The older woman was genuinely relieved and happy. "Oh, I am so pleased for you, Aiden. And for you, Petra. Aiden's a wonderful man."

"I think so too," Petra offered sweetly. Only she slipped an arm behind Aiden so she could pinch his butt.

What. The. Hell?

Danielle leaned forward and spoke softer. "I assume this means she knows everything that's going on with the shelter and all the requirements we discussed."

"We're still working through the final details," Aiden said quickly. "But the bottom line is if you have someone who needs a safe place to hide, we're ready to have her come to the ranch. Petra will be here."

The urge to curse the entire group soundly and walk away without another word vanished after hearing *needs a safe place to hide*. "Aiden will fill me in on everything I need to know," Petra assured Danielle.

The older woman nodded firmly and pushed to her feet. "Thank you for the offer of lunch, but with this good news, I'm going to carry on to make sure I get everything done as quickly and quietly as possible. I'll text the details as soon as I can, Aiden. As always, if you need anything, let me know, and my husband and I will see what we can do."

Getting Danielle out of the house became a symphony of movement. Aiden tugged Petra farther back into the house, allowing Jake and Declan to escort Danielle to her car.

The instant the front door closed, Petra jerked free from Aiden's grasp and raced for the living room window.

Aiden ended up right beside her, the two of them staring as if making sure the woman had truly left.

"I'm pretty certain I need to kick somebody's ass right now," Petra said as calmly as possible.

"That makes two of us." The anger in Aiden's voice was clear. "I'm very thankful you didn't call *bullshit* and stop that in its tracks, but trust me, Declan blindsided me as well."

Petra met his gaze. "Really?"

"He was the only one of us to think fast enough on his feet. I just about messed it up before I realized what he was doing."

"What the actual fuck?" Jake nearly roared as he re-entered the house hard on Declan's heels. "They're engaged? What's going to happen when Danielle discovers that's a damn lie?"

"That's a problem for down the road. We'll figure it out." Declan marched up to Petra. "Sorry for dropping that on you. Thanks for not mucking it up. Come have lunch, and we'll explain what's going on."

"I'd appreciate that," Petra offered. "And for the record, the only reason I'm not hightailing it is that comment about getting somebody to safety. You bought an animal rescue."

"It still will be, partly." Aiden gestured toward the table. He waited until she sat before taking a chair opposite her. "But we're also quietly building a safe house. Somewhere for people who slip through the cracks for whatever reason. We plan to give them a home here for as long as they need."

"A safe house?" Petra thought through what she knew of the social system. "That doesn't seem the kind of thing you do within a few months of buying a place without a lot of red tape involved."

"Which is why we're avoiding the red tape," Jake confessed with a grumble before meeting her gaze. His dark grey eyes focused sharply. "Look, I worked in criminal services for over fifteen years, and far too often I saw people who just needed a bit of a break to be able to turn their lives around. But the system isn't set up to make that happen, either because of a lack of resources or a lack of give a damn."

"I've done a lot of volunteer work with problem teens," Aiden offered. "It's nearly impossible for someone who's willing to put in the work to find a new path when they're stuck in a bad family or a bad situation that's not of their choice."

Declan cleared his throat. "Since we're spilling all the beans, we'll let you know that we've got the resources to commit to this, and a willingness to make it work, even if it means saying *fuck it* to red tape. If that's not something you're comfortable with, I get it. But we would ask if you could stretch your morals for a short period of time. One of the parameters we agreed to was always having ladies working the ranch so that any women who needed to retreat had peer support. We're in the process of hiring a live-in housekeeper and cook, but until they're in place, it sounds as if we need you."

"But as Aiden's fiancée?" Petra glared at Declan. "What the hell?"

This time, it was Jake who sighed. "No, that was a brilliant move. Danielle's still in the system, secretly working on our behalf. She's not going to agree to a random woman we temporarily drop into place at a moment's notice. We've helped her help others in short-term situations over the past few years. While she trusts us, she's also rightly put in checks and balances. We promised she could vet the housekeeper before we brought them on, but a fiancée is different. None of us would get involved with a person who wasn't able to join our venture one hundred percent."

Petra sat back in her chair, mind whirling. Of course a fiancée made sense—if she truly was one. "What a tangled mess."

Aiden leaned forward, hands pressed to the table. "I'll do anything I can to make this work for you for as long as it's necessary. Declan's right. I hope you don't walk away for the sake of whoever it is that Danielle thinks needs our help in the next twenty-four hours."

Damn the man. Petra met Declan's gaze. "First, fuck you. You're quick on your feet but also a complete jackass. I'm torn between admiring you and wanting to kick you off a bridge."

"Join the club," Aiden and Jake said with near-perfect synchronization.

Petra snickered then pointed toward the box on the counter. "You'd better feed me. I think the adrenaline rush is wearing off, and I'm going to balk fast if I don't get some food into me."

Jake opened the box and put food on plates while Declan grabbed drinks from the fridge.

Aiden shifted position closer to Petra's side. "You okay?" he asked softly.

"Oh, I will be. I guess, somehow." She met his gaze. "This is one hell of a situation, but I'll do it. You're all so clearly telling the truth, and I have a soft spot for people who step across lines to do things the system can't fix."

Relief shone on his face. "Sorry we got you into this."

"Yeah, and you're going to be even more sorry. But we'll talk about those details when it's just the two of us. We're going to need a little bit bigger plan than Declan realizes."

Aiden nodded. "Food first? That'll give us time to talk about what our overall plans are here for Hell or High Water. High Water to the community."

Oh, she liked that. "That's a very evocative name."

Aiden took a couple of sandwiches then passed her the platter. "It's meant to be. The three of us have had experiences that mean we know what it's like to face an ultimatum and be willing to do anything to come out the other side whole."

"Okay." Petra waited until everybody had filled their plates. "Tell me the plan so I know what I've signed up for. At least temporarily," she said quickly to Declan. "Because you need to keep looking for that Danielle-approved housekeeper, got it?"

"Of course." Declan said firmly.

As far she could tell, it was a rock-solid promise.

She sat back and enjoyed Tansy's excellent lunch while the three brothers painted a picture of what High Water would look like, and she listened as closely as possible.

The animal rescue would be the connection to the community. The artists' retreat house, with small group workshops scattered throughout the year, would bring in money to help fund the ranch. Running both of those plus the rest of the ranch chores would create jobs for the temporary guests to do while they prepared for their next step.

All the while, though, a part of Petra's brain was trying to decide what on earth she was going to tell her family and friends who knew the engagement was a lie. *A small deception. A temporary situation for the greater good.*

God, that sounded pathetic even in her brain.

Nope, she wasn't doing this on her own. Aiden was going to have to help her. But the more the brothers shared, the more she came to realize she couldn't walk away.

Not now.

5

*A*iden wasn't sure who he should hit first. Declan for getting him into this situation or himself because the image of Petra in his bed again was vivid and demanding, and he absolutely needed to not go there.

This was about High Water, period.

Maybe after the deception was done they could retest some mattress springs, but for now, Aiden was determined to be an utter gentleman and offer her nothing but respect for the help she'd been hijacked into offering.

Fuck his life. He was definitely punching the daylights out of Declan, first chance he got.

The meal was over, and Petra, who had spent most of her time nodding, grabbed Aiden by the arm. "You and me. We need to talk, stat."

"No prob." He tilted his chin at Declan. "Okay with me adjusting rooms and the rest of it?"

"Have at 'er. Less than twenty-four hours. Knock yourself out." Declan met Petra's gaze again. "Thank you. We'll find a way to make it up to you."

"I don't need a reward." Petra lifted her chin. "Not for doing the right thing."

"Good." Declan nodded sharply before he and Jake carried off the remainders of the lunch, stuffed them into the fridge, then left the room.

The big open space suddenly seemed awfully small. Aiden folded his arms over his chest and leaned back in his chair. "So. Logistics."

"How good of a liar are you?" Petra asked. Her eyes snapped, her expression serious.

"As good as I need to be," he offered.

An enormous sigh lifted her shoulders. "Damn good," she warned. "Also, I understand the need for secrecy, but this is nonnegotiable. My brother and sister-in-law need to know the truth. Because otherwise, this deception will not fly."

Tangled, but he got it. "You trust them?"

"More than I trust you," Petra offered dryly.

Aiden snorted. "Valid. Anyone else? I mean, we won't be shouting that we're engaged from the rafters, but it's a small town. I get how things work."

She made a face. "You had no choice in the matter, what with Declan running off at the mouth like that, but here's the twist. I was seeing someone, but broke it off recently."

Shit. He eyed her carefully. "Really? Damn, I'm sorry."

"No need to be sorry, but this is why my brother needs to know the truth. And my two best friends, who are rock solid. When others in town hear you're my fiancée, they won't blink. That part might work to your advantage. Some people will assume you're the guy my brother mentioned in passing. My ex isn't local, but from Manitoba where I used to live."

Which was good news for High Water, but still. "You're okay with this, though? After being that close to someone, pretending to be with me might suck."

"Only if you turn out to be a jackass." Petra lifted a brow. "I called things off when I discovered *he* was a jackass, and that's all you need to know about that. But it means I'm a free agent. I wouldn't have kissed you the other day if I wasn't. Don't waste energy feeling sorry for me."

"Deal." His mind still flew through the possibilities of what the guy did to screw up that badly and how good it would feel to clock the bastard. "Which means I'm pulling us back to logistics because we have a deadline ticking. First priorities. You need to move in, and we need to make sure the new ranch hand—which is what we're calling our guests—has a comfortable room to claim as her own."

Petra offered a wry smile. "I was just talking to Tansy about my living options. I guess this makes that decision easier." She stood, pulling out her phone. "Instead of our picnic, does supper with my brother work for you?"

God. "Sure."

Her grin turned downright evil. "Did I mention I'm the youngest in my family?"

"Great. With a protective older brother?" Aiden winked. "It's fine. I can handle him."

"Oh, I'm sure you can talk your way around Zach. It's my four older sisters you need to worry—"

"*Four?*" Aiden's gut fell. "Maybe I should start running now, just to be safe."

She snickered then patted him on the cheek. "Zach is the only one who lives here in Heart Falls. The others we can ignore for a while because we will not be shouting to the universe about the engagement. I need to get my stuff together, but that won't take long as I haven't unpacked. So first, let me help you get the new hand's room set up. Plus, you can give me a tour so I know where stuff is. If I'm going to help, and I plan to, I need to know the lay of the land. I'm not signing on to be chief housekeeper and cook, but I'll do my share. Just as if I were a roomie."

"Deal. And I promise to keep this as simple as possible for you."

"I promise to make sure my brother and sister-in-law listen while you explain the situation, although I can't promise they won't toss threats your direction."

"I get it. I have brothers too," Aiden tilted his head toward the window where Jake and Declan were visible unloading boards from a truck. "Threats of death and dismemberment are like love taps."

They worked together smoothly for the next hour, Petra's sharp wit making Aiden grin multiple times before she called it quits.

"I'm going to run interference ahead of time so that supper goes smoother." Petra made a face. "I hope you don't have too many skeletons in your closet, dude."

Aiden frowned. "I thought you'd want me there to explain things to your family?"

"Oh, you'll do your share of explaining. But giving Zach a couple of hours to dig into your history will make him far more reasonable to deal with. Unless said skeletons cause issues."

One area where Aiden had zero worries. "He won't find anything."

Her gaze narrowed. "That's interesting wording."

Aiden tossed her a grin but didn't mention that Jake's contact from his police force days had made certain all their records were clean as a whistle and very, *very* nondescript. "Have fun, and I'll be there a few minutes early. If it's safer to escape the country, text me."

Petra laughed as she walked away.

He still wore a smile when he tracked down his brothers in the barn.

They weren't as cool and collected as they paused and gave Aiden their full attention.

Scratch that. Declan was calm as usual, but Jake blustered as he tucked his notebook under his arm. "She still going to do it?"

"Said she would," Aiden offered dryly. "I didn't scare her off in the past hour."

"Told you everything was fine, Jake. You need to relax and trust my instincts more." Declan tilted his chin at Aiden. "We've figured out living quarters for now. You're still in the house—security for the ladies. Take the room I was going to use."

"Makes sense." Although it was close enough that the temptation of Petra down the hall was going to be a thorn in his side. "I'm going to Red Boot ranch tonight to meet her brother. She insists that he know the real situation, and I agree."

"He's solid." Declan nodded slowly. "Jake, stop scowling. You did a background search and cleared everyone at Red Boot ranch when we first checked out Heart Falls."

"The more people who know what we're up to, the more loose ends," Jake growled. "That's my complaint."

"Then the sooner you get in touch with some of your military and RCMP contacts who want to spend time here, the better. Plus, contact the therapist and see if Kevin can move up his arrival. Layers of people we trust in place will help calm you down if nothing else." Aiden pulled the notebook from under his brother's arm and glanced at the detailed checklist for the day still to be completed. "I can deal with items seven and eight before I head out. As soon as I get a feel for Petra's brother, I'll text confirmation so we make sure Danielle keeps rolling on that new ranch hand."

"Deal." Declan raised a brow at Jake. "You got that stick worked out yet?"

"Fuck you." Jake sighed. "Fine. Use your gut, Aiden. We'll back whatever play you make."

Aiden wanted to show up early, but in the end, it was past five when he rolled up the drive into Red Boot ranch. Straight-as-an-arrow fence lines ran from the nearby buildings into the distant west. Neat rustic rental cabins were strategically placed in a jagged line so each faced in a slightly different direction toward the gorgeous scenery of the Rocky Mountains to the west, the rolling foothills painted with fall sunshine.

Petra had informed him the last in the row was Zach and Julia's place. As Aiden hurried from his truck, with Petra's purse that he'd found on the bench by the front door tucked under his arm, a solidly built man stepped to the front of the porch and folded his arms across his chest. His expression and body language screamed disapproval.

To hell with it. Aiden went for passive aggressive and waved cheerily as he took the stairs two at a time. "You must be Zach. Great to finally meet you. Petra's told me so much about you."

The man's lips twitched. "Really."

Aiden thrust out his free hand. "Of course. Also, your charitable work with Sorenson Enterprises is noteworthy. You didn't also inherit your father's inventor's gene as well, did you?"

Zach raised a brow. "You've done your homework."

"I figured you'd be researching me and mine within minutes of hearing the mess we sucked Petra into." Aiden lifted his shoulders in an easy shrug. "We get it."

"I want to hate you, but between Petra warning me off and my curiosity, you get to live a little longer."

Aiden let his grin shine out. "Always my favourite option.

If you need to try to hit me or something, we can do that later. I'm hungry."

"*Try* to hit you?" Zach shook his head disapprovingly. "Please."

"Youngest of three boys," Aiden informed him. "I'm fast."

"So you'll run away?"

"Duck, if nothing else. Yup," Aiden agreed.

Even as Zach grinned in response, a heavy sigh sounded from behind him where Petra had stepped into the doorway.

Pushing past her was a second woman with deep-red hair, a wide smile, and curiosity in her bright eyes. She motioned them forward. "If you've finished the obligatory *threat exchange* portion of the evening, get inside. Dinner is ready."

~

It should have been awkward, or at least uncomfortable, but from the minute they hit the table, it was as if Aiden had been a family friend for years instead of a newcomer.

"I can't share all the details," he said at the start, meeting their eyes in turn. "In some ways, the less you know, the better it is, but Petra says you're trustworthy. Which means you'll understand that when I don't answer a question, it's for your safety and the safety of others."

"I only want to know two things." Julia eyed them both. "How long does this deception need to last? And what happens when it's over?"

Good questions. Petra faced Aiden. "Don't know the first part, but I figure it's possible to have a friendly breakup. Neither of us will have to leave town or anything drastic like that."

"Absolutely. Mutual decision to go back to being friends. It would be best for both of us to have no villain in calling it off. High Water plans to be here for years."

"Red Boot ranch isn't going anywhere, and as long as Petra wants to be in town, this is her home." Zach offered him the potatoes.

Aiden accepted the dish and scooped a healthy portion on his plate. "How long is going to depend on how quickly we get our housekeeper-slash-cook in place and how many ranch hands we get in the meantime. How attached people become to our situation. If the woman who shows up tomorrow needs you to stick around for a few months while she finds her feet, I hope that's okay."

Petra waved a hand. "I didn't imagine the engagement would be called off instantly. But you do know I'm not a therapist or anything."

"That's not your role. We have a trained expert who'll be joining us sooner than later. I expect you will get a lot of the kids—sorry, ranch hands—bending your ear, both because you'll be in the house and because you're a woman. We're all going to get quick lessons from Kevin when he arrives so we know how to guide those conversations to his court." Aiden's smile softened, growing a little sad. "It's hard to wrap our heads and hearts around, but some ranch hands will come into High Water and leave a few days later. Those are the ones who have a better spot to live while they make a change, and we're just a safe place on the journey. The ones who will need a home could be there for a while. We won't know much about them until they arrive, not even their names, because until they walk in the door, it's their right to change their minds and say no, and the less we know about them, the safer they'll be."

Zach asked a few questions, and Petra did as well. Then Aiden turned the tables and got Zach and Julia talking about Red Boot ranch.

They were passing around plates of pie before Petra got an elbow in the side from her sister-in-law.

Julia leaned closer. "He's smooth."

Petra looked Aiden over again, admiring the muscular lines of the man as he spoke with Zach. Aiden had been a lot of fun on the night they'd fooled around years ago and again on the recent night when they'd kissed.

Smooth only began to describe him.

"You're drooling," Julia said softly.

Petra wiped her hand over her mouth then stiffened as Julia snickered. "You're such an ass."

"Maybe, but you were one step away from eating him up with your eyes. You sure you know what you're doing?" Concern clouded Julia's tone.

Which was rich, coming from her. Petra raised a brow. "What? You have an issue with fake engagements? Really?"

Julia's cheeks flushed. "Zach and I weren't a fake engagement."

"Oh, excuse me. Fake dating and accidentally married." Petra stared at the ceiling and considered. "Yeah, I can see how this is totally different."

Julia laughed softly. "I was just thinking about how tempting it's going to be for you to get more involved. He seems like a good guy with strong morals and a smokin' body."

Petra nearly snorted her water out her nose, glaring at Julia. "Comments on his body are not appreciated."

"Just saying. He's temptation, and you are sort of on a rebound right now." Julia winced. "I wasn't going to say that, but..."

"You're showing amazing restraint and not asking what actually happened that first time Aiden and I met that made both of us willing to throw ourselves onto a limb like this."

Julia rolled her eyes. "Please. As if it's not obvious."

Nope. Not falling for it. Petra leaned closer and whispered her response. "That's my brother's favourite ploy. Pretend you know more than you do and hope the beans get spilled. Not a chance, sis."

A pout curled Julia's mouth. "Not fair. You know all my best cards."

"I do trust Aiden." The words popped out so easily Petra blinked.

Julia leaned into her side. "You also have a heart of gold, and helping others pushes your *yes* buttons. I'm just saying we're here for you, even as you dive into the deep end."

"High Water begs for a dive or two."

"Cannonballs are my favourite," Julia volleyed back.

Petra snickered.

Across the table, Zach waved his hands in the air enthusiastically as he shared some story. Aiden nodded, but his gaze was on Petra, and for a moment, it was as if there were only the two of them in the room.

His sweet mischievous grin teased the butterflies in her stomach into motion. The great unknown was right there, and she needed to walk forward to find out what might happen next.

Aiden was going to walk with her.

It felt far too simple. Far too right. But after a lot of *not simple* and *not right*, Petra welcomed it.

Aiden insisted on helping with cleanup and dishes after the meal. His arms loaded with plates, he winked at Julia. "We'll let your husband get in some time with his sister so she can work a little harder to convince him I'm not worth shooting."

Julia rolled her eyes. "He's not the one to worry about if you need shooting."

He blinked then flashed his sweet grin at Petra. "I like her."

"That's good. She's a dead shot at fifty paces," Petra warned.

"She's also a medic. If she shoots you, she'll patch you up after," Zach offered.

"Now this sounds intriguing. Tell me more." Aiden carried the plates to the counter as Julia responded.

Zach held out his hand to Petra. "Come sit on the deck and tell me everything is okay."

She tucked her fingers into his elbow and tugged him down the stairs toward the arena instead. "Walk. I need to gather my things and toss them into the truck. I guess I'm moving tonight."

Zach strolled beside her quietly for a moment. "You sure you're good with this, sis?"

"More than good. I think I need this." Petra rested her head on his shoulder briefly then straightened and sped up their pace.

"To lie to the entire community?"

"To make a difference." Petra glanced around at the gorgeous mountains. Heart Falls was a place to make a new start, but just having pretty things around her wasn't going to be enough. "Curtis did a number on my confidence," she admitted.

Zach cursed softly then offered her a very fake smile. "Please tell me when you decide he'd look better without his arms."

"You know that's never going to happen, so let the idea of vengeance go." Petra stopped them beside the arena, stooping to pet the soft nose of the colt that came to greet them.

Zach leaned on the railing, disgruntled expression turning to acceptance. "So living at High Water will let you make a difference?"

"To one woman who needs a safe place to land—yes. More than that, I don't know. And in a way, I don't care. If I can help

A Cowboy's Bride

one person, I want to do it." Damn it. Tears were rising, unbidden and unwanted. Petra brushed them away with her fingers, turning her head to the side.

"Hey, kiddo. None of that, now." Zach tugged her in close and pressed her face to his chest. A big brother hug that was perfect and exactly what was needed. "You always did find the best ways to experience new things. Okay, fine. I'll back you in this. We'll make the engagement fly and keep it quiet from the rest of the family. You'll have to post pictures carefully. Stick to the usual *ooh* and *aah* over the nieces and nephews as expected."

He squeezed her one more time then let her go.

Petra took a deep breath. "Good. I'll still get the work done for Red Boot that I promised, but can you give me a couple days before I start? Just until I get my feet under me at High Water."

"Not a problem. Take the time you need."

They wandered toward the house, chatting quietly. By the time they made it back, Julia and Aiden were waiting on the front porch. Julia held a cup of tea in her hands, and the two of them were laughing.

Zach grumbled. "Your *fiancé* is far too charming."

"Same could be said of you." Petra ducked from Zach's mock swing. "How often did you actually get in trouble, big bro? And how often did you sweet-talk your way out of punishment?"

"I'm a saint," Zach started, only to set Julia off into laughter.

He moved in on her, finger pressed to his lips.

Aiden slipped down to Petra's side. "You have things to move?" he asked.

She nodded. "Not tons, but you can help me load up." Petra glanced up at the house and shook her head. "You two are too adorable for words. Thanks for dinner."

"Thanks for trusting me," Aiden added.

"Make sure you keep that trust." Julia said quietly.

Zach eyed Aiden for a moment longer then nodded once. "Good luck. I hope your new ranch hand settles in quickly."

"We'll stay in touch," Petra promised before heading to the cabin where her things were stashed. In a relatively short time, she was already leaving her fresh start for something entirely different.

Funny how quickly life could change.

6

Sydney lifted the box Petra pointed to obediently, but her expression matched the tone in her voice. Kind of a mix between disbelief and amusement. "You're moving into Tansy's grandma's old house."

"You're holding my bathroom stuff, so yes. Follow me. Tansy said she'd be here in five, so please hold your questions so I only need to explain once."

"Fine," Sydney offered smoothly. "Do I need to grab the bottle of tequila I have in the truck for this conversation?"

"You have truck liquor? Is this something I should be worried about?" Petra stopped in her tracks and eyed her friend. "I'm not even kidding. Not one bit."

Sydney waved off the concern, pushing Petra into the house with the box in her arms. "I have it in case I get to some old-timer's place and they're being a pain in the ass about accepting treatment. Plus, it's cheaper than whiskey, so I don't feel bad making them do a shot or two then pouring the extra over a site I need to sterilize quickly."

Petra could only imagine a small-town doctor getting away

with that kind of medical treatment. Unorthodox, but what needed to happen to help.

Like the concept behind High Water.

At least her conscience had no problem fully jumping into the deception. Now to make sure the other most important people in her life were in the know and on board.

They were back at the truck, grabbing the third and final load, when Tansy pulled up in her extremely beat up minivan. She scooted over and grabbed a suitcase, shaking her head even as she did so. "I am so looking forward to you explaining what's going on. Because that text message you sent saying to get our asses over to the animal rescue and be prepared to zip our lips and swallow the key was cryptic, even for you."

"It will all make sense," Petra promised.

Sydney's head swung to the side as she eyed the three trucks parked on the far side of the gravel beside the newly renovated second building. "The guys aren't helping you move?"

"They would have, but Aiden suggested I give you two a call." Which was a brainwave Petra appreciated immensely the more she thought about it.

He'd also muttered something about staying out of range of Sydney's knife skills until the coast was clear, which was extra smart on his part.

"I don't mind being grunt labour, but please satisfy my curiosity, ASAP," Tansy ordered. "Also, I have a pie in the van if we need it."

Sydney's laugh was quick and sharp. "Be careful. Petra's going to be worried that you have van pie. That's a dangerous habit. It could become addictive, you know."

Tansy lowered her voice to a hush. "It started innocently enough. It was just a few apple turnovers, and the next thing I knew I was hauling out the pecan and pumpkin every night."

Which meant the three of them were all laughing as they stacked the boxes labeled *coats* and *shoes* beside the door then carried the final suitcases into the primary bedroom.

Petra patted the bed. "Sit."

Sydney lifted a brow then spoke to Tansy. "This must be big. She's making sure we're stable so we don't fall over."

Another snort escaped. The tension that had slowly built as Petra considered how to tell her friends was dissipating quickly because of who Sydney and Tansy were.

Still, Petra made sure they were solid before she sat on her suitcase and faced them. "I'm moving in to help the Skye brothers with a small deception for a good reason. We're all trusting you with a big secret, but I know that you'll be one hundred percent behind what I'm about to tell you."

It didn't take long to share the outline of what was going on, mostly because both Tansy and Sydney kept their mouths shut, although Tansy wiggled a whole bunch, pinning her lips together to keep from blurting out questions.

But when Petra stopped and looked at her friends expectantly, there it was. The exact response she'd hoped for.

Sydney dipped her chin firmly, although she still looked a little worried. "I've got your back. Plus, you tell the boys that if they need medical assistance for any of their ranch hands, especially the ones who are too skittish to hit the hospital, they should let me know right away."

Which was something Petra hadn't thought about, but she was sure the guys would be grateful for. "I'll pass that on."

Tansy lifted her chin. "You have my full support, which means the guys do as well. We can keep our mouths shut. This sounds like something that could make a big difference in people's lives. That's worth a little lying, I think." She glanced around the room and out the window before meeting Petra's eyes again. "Two questions, though. How does this work with the thing brewing between you and Aiden?"

Petra considered the question seriously. She did like the man, and the very hot and needy thing between them was real, but neither of them were adolescents without any control. "The pretend engagement and me living here is a temporary situation to help somebody who needs it. If there's going to be anything between Aiden and I, it can wait until a more appropriate time."

Tansy muttered something soft and low, too quiet for Petra to catch, but Sydney heard because she snickered. "True."

"Share with the whole class," Petra warned.

Her friend's grin widened before Tansy admitted, "I said *good luck with that*. I mean, did you see the heat waves coming off the two of you? The sexy pheromones were nearly overwhelming."

Of course, she hadn't seen them, but Petra had felt them and knew exactly what Tansy was talking about. Still—

Petra sat up straighter and bullshitted her way ahead. "What's your second question?"

Clearly an attempt to avoid the discussion, but thankfully Tansy went along with it. "I'll give some thought to suggestions of who they might hire for a housekeeper and cook. Can you tell Declan to get in touch with me? I need to know a few more specifics about salary and the rest of it."

Another brilliant idea. "Of course, but I think it'll be Jake giving you a shout. He seems to be the one dealing with those details."

Tansy shrugged. "That's fine. Now, let's get some unpacking done so we can move on to the apple-pie-eating portion of the evening."

It was just that simple.

Shortly after ten, Tansy's red taillights disappeared in the distance as she turned onto the main highway and headed back into Heart Falls.

Sydney watched her leave before examining Petra one last time. "It seems you've got your heart set on this, but I hope you know we'll be looking out for you."

"I wouldn't want it any other way," Petra told her friend earnestly.

She stood on the porch for a while once they were gone, staring at the mountains to the west. The sky was fully dark with stars sparkling here and there, poking through the clouds. Off in the distance, coyotes howled, and a few remaining crickets and frogs serenaded the night. She hadn't seen hide nor hair of any of the Skye brothers, but a scent of smoke carried on the air, which she suspected came from a fire pit.

She could go track them down but decided against it, turning back into the house and taking a slow stroll through the entire place.

She peeked into the nearly empty kitchen drawers and cupboards. The place was bare bones to the extreme, but it wouldn't take long to make it cozy, especially if another woman was around to help.

Petra peeked into the room they'd set up for the new ranch hand, standing for a moment and sending all the positive energy possible into the space. Hopefully the young woman would find peace and courage and even laughter during her time at High Water.

Walking a little farther, Petra cast a glance into the room where Aiden's things were neatly organized. He didn't have a ton of stuff, but then, she only had what fit into her truck. Not a lot to show for over thirty years of life.

Yet far more than some of the ranch hands would show up with.

The thought put her world into a whole new perspective.

She pulled the door closed on her own room and set about unpacking, followed by a quick shower then crawling under the brand-new sheets on the queen-size bed.

It might have been minutes later, or hours, but she was warm and snug and mostly asleep when footsteps sounded in the hall and the door to Aiden's room closed.

She fell asleep wondering if the sense of being in the right place was so crystal clear because it was real or because she wanted so badly for it to be true.

∼

AIDEN WOKE the same way he'd fallen asleep—far too aware of the woman in the room next to his. Whatever Petra wore for cream or used as a shampoo was enough to make his whole damn body sit up and take notice.

He dressed quickly and headed to the kitchen. Maybe if he made the coffee, it would push the scent of her from his head.

Once the regular coffee pot was up and running, he checked the meal schedule on the fridge that Jake had made and started hauling ingredients onto the counter.

He had ham frying in the electric skillet and pancake batter ready to go when the first of the family showed up.

"Everything ready?" Jake asked as he sniffed appreciatively.

"I've got the pancakes under control. You can pour the orange juice. Did you see Declan yet this morning?"

"He gave me a wave and said he'd be in soon. Petra awake?"

Aiden checked the heat on the griddle then turned it down a little. "I didn't hear anything yet. How 'bout you text her and tell her breakfast will be ready in fifteen minutes?"

"Will do."

They went about their tasks quietly. Jake finished then filled his coffee mug and dropped into a chair at the table.

Aiden glanced at him. "You're brooding."

Jake glared back then released an enormous sigh. "God, I hope this works."

"You need to trust karma a little," Aiden offered with as much positivity as possible. "One person at a time. One day at a time."

"I know, and I believe in what we're doing." Jake made a face before meeting Aiden's gaze. "I thought we'd have more time before things got rolling. I mean, we won't have the artists' retreat rooms ready for months. I'm guilty of using that as my target to get my head wrapped around...everything else."

"I hear you." Aiden flipped the pancakes on the grill and considered. With Jake's need to get everything lined up properly, and all his checklists done, the huge change in plans had to be making his brain whirl. "If I can offer a suggestion?"

Jake snorted. "I recognize that tone. Don't try to counsel me, counselor."

Amusement rose. Maybe in some other life Aiden would have taken official training. For now, all he did was run on gut instinct. Still, people seemed to listen when he followed through on his hunches. Part of the reason they were here in the first place, setting up High Water.

"Advice as your kid brother then. We have all the time in the world to get everything in place for the paying guests. The ranch hand who's about to arrive? She'll need things to do to distract her." Aiden watched as Jake's eyes widened with understanding. Jake was great at lists. Not so great at remembering the human element that went with them. "Danielle will give us the details we need to know to keep the woman safe and help her to find her independence, but too much time to wallow in memories of what went wrong is not what we want."

"Solid thinking. I'll make a list of current chores that even a newbie can handle on their own. Good idea?"

"It's a great place to start," Aiden said.

Jake's gaze darted to the side, then he rose to his feet as Petra entered the room. "Morning."

Petra pulled to a stop. Her smile took in Jake before her gaze bounced to Aiden, who'd just transferred the first batch of pancakes to a plate. "Morning. Anything I can do to help?"

"I've got it under control. I'm first cook today," Aiden informed her. "Grab a coffee then go ahead and relax. Declan will be here soon."

"Okay." She stepped past him, opened the right cupboard, and grabbed a mug.

Nice. She was already figuring the place out. "I take it you got settled in fine? How did it go with your friends last night? Other than the thumbs-up you sent—thank you for that."

"Really good." She filled her cup then turned back to the table and paused. "Jake, I hope you don't plan on standing every time I get up from the table."

"Just when it's the polite thing to do," Jake assured her with a grin.

"You'll get used to it." Aiden poured the next batch of batter and flipped the ham as he spoke. He glanced over his shoulder in time to see Petra's amusement as she found a seat and Jake settled back in place. "Our dad was a stickler for manners. If Jake kept his ass in a chair when there's a woman standing in the room, Jeff would reach out from beyond the grave and whack him one upside the head."

"A love tap I learned to avoid quickly while he was raising us to not be hellions," Jake informed her.

"If I'm supposed to be family, you don't need to be formal around me," Petra reminded him.

"Not being polite to family is worse than not being polite to a stranger." Declan spoke firmly as he closed the door behind him and stepped across the room in his stocking feet. "Morning, Petra. Were you comfortable last night?"

"The room is great. And I love that you have chickens and roosters. My parents had them on the farm, and I've missed waking up to the sound."

Ha. Aiden loaded the ham onto a plate and set it on the table then paused to smirk at Jake. "See?"

"You're an ass," Jake told him mildly.

"I'm an ass who's right," Aiden retorted before nudging the ham plate toward a confused Petra. "Jake thought we should avoid having roosters around because people don't like them."

"No," Declan corrected. "I'm pretty sure he said he didn't want them around because *he* doesn't like them. Which is why I made sure we had a nice big flock with a rooster in his prime."

Petra snickered even as she stabbed a piece of ham then passed the plate around the table. "Oh, family."

The remainder of the meal flew past, a small mountain of pancakes consumed along with all the ham slices Aiden had cooked. Petra shared the offer from Sydney for her silent doctor services and Tansy's offer to help find a housekeeper.

"You've got good friends," Jake said quietly.

"The best," Petra agreed. She patted her stomach. "That was delicious, Aiden, but don't expect me to eat that much every morning. I'm not a hard-working cowboy."

"No, but you are part of the household now." Declan looked thoughtful. "You need to tell Jake your favourite meals so they get added to the rotation."

"Jake's our planner of plans," Aiden explained.

She smiled. "You'd all better hope my favourites aren't your least favourites."

"It's food." Declan shrugged. "There's not much you could put on the table that we won't demolish."

"Speaking of which..." Petra turned to Jake. "While you're adjusting the menu plan, you can add me as a cook. Same number of meals as you're each doing."

Declan shook his head. "We don't expect you to—"

"If I live here, I expect to do my part," Petra cut in. "Also, which of you is the master planner for how much I'll owe for room and board?"

"Fuck that." Aiden couldn't stop himself. A sharp kick in the shins just made him swear again as he glared at Jake. "Petra's heard swearing before, and it was called for."

"No swearing at the table. No swearing in front of the ladies." Jake turned an angelic smile on Petra. "But I agree with Aiden. You're helping us a lot. We don't expect you to pay for the privilege of living with us."

"I'd be paying for rent and food no matter where I lived," Petra pointed out.

"Not here," Declan added his voice to the chorus. "If you want to help cook and clean up until we hire a full-time person, it'd be appreciated, but not expected."

She lifted her chin firmly. "Fine. I won't fight you on the rent issue, but I want on the schedule. It only makes sense, you know. The young woman who's showing up will expect me to do *some* work around the place."

True. Aiden started stacking the plates. "You got time to do a revamp, Jake?"

"Yup, along with that chore list we talked about." Jake shoved back from the table and nodded politely at Petra. "We'll work you being head chef for a few meals into the next rotation since we've already done groceries for the next week.

In the meantime, feel free to cook treats. We'll all do that at times."

"No problem," she assured him.

"I'll be back later to hang up extra hooks at the entrance. Probably shouldn't overwhelm the woman." Jake slid out the door.

Petra raised a brow. "Is he talking about me, or the new ranch hand?"

Declan made a soft noise of amusement. "Both?"

Aiden outright laughed.

"I'm headed out as well. Let me know if you need anything." Declan slipped from the room as silently as he'd entered it.

Aiden grabbed the plates in front of him and headed for the sink, speaking over his shoulder to Petra. "You're welcome to help me clean up, or do you have things to do this morning?"

"I have no other tasks for the next week except settling in here. What time do we expect Danielle to show up?" Petra stepped in front of the sink and got the hot water going.

"Should be around ten from her text this morning."

She nodded. "I'll wash, you dry and put away until I figure out where everything fits."

Aiden grabbed a dry cloth and stood ready, leaning back on the counter as she squirted soap into the water and got started on the glasses. "We're running on the most basic items right now. Declan suggested we wait for the cook to decide what else she, or he, needs. So cleaning up should be simple. We have an industrial size washer on order, but it won't be here for a while."

"Breakfast plates for four is not a lot to hand wash," Petra said as she dove into the task.

"Dishes for five starting tonight. If we end up with a full house at some point in the future, we could have up to twelve at the table." He grinned as she whistled. "Yeah. That's why the dishwasher's on the way."

Petra washed quietly for a bit then met his gaze firmly. "I'm glad to be a part of this. I'm glad to be here at the start of High Water."

The sincerity in her eyes was pure.

A sudden spark of something hot and soft flared in his chest. Nothing sexual, even though she still pushed all of his buttons with her soft grey T-shirt and faded jeans over gentle curves. The sensation of being part of something bigger than he'd ever expected was there, and the sense of rightness.

It wasn't *just* about the sexual tension between them, and that was good. "I'm glad too."

The doorbell rang, shattering the peaceful connection.

An instant later, the front door cracked open, and Danielle called a greeting. "Hello. Anyone here? We're early."

7

"We're in here," Aiden answered.

Snatching her hands from the water, Petra snagged the towel from Aiden's fingers and hurriedly dried off. She walked behind him slightly, stopping a second too late when he froze a step earlier than expected. Their bodies made contact, so when he inhaled, huge and sharp, she felt it.

It wasn't Danielle walking into the room that had caused his reaction, but the slight figure behind her. The girl slipped through the doorframe and tucked herself as close to the wall as her backpack would allow. As if she were a chameleon, and if she stood still enough, she'd vanish from sight.

She was thin—too thin, Petra thought. The girl's light frame would always look delicate, but her white skin was crepe-paper pale, as if she'd never been in the sun. She looked as if a strong wind could blow her away. The contrast of full breasts on such a small frame looked wrong, and Petra already guessed one of the problems she'd faced in the past. This girl who was young enough her face still held a hint of baby fat was built with curves that belonged on a much older woman.

Dark brown hair hung in mats, and ratty clumps tangled around her face. She held her head tilted toward the floor, but her eyes were up and wary as if watching so she could duck if necessary.

Still, Petra saw hidden strength in those eyes. Stone grey, but bright, like the eyes of a cat analyzing and judging. Sharp and alert. She hadn't lost all hope yet.

Danielle continued, her voice a gentle breeze dancing over eggshells. "We met up a little early and the traffic was incredibly light. I knew you wouldn't mind, so we came straight here. Jennifer, come meet Aiden and Petra. They'll be your hosts for the next while."

Aiden spoke softly. "Hey, Jennifer."

No one in the room missed the way the girl flinched when he spoke, but she took a couple of shuffling steps off the wall to stand partly hidden behind Danielle. "Hi."

Petra's heart pounded at the base of her throat. She had no idea what the girl had gone through, but this moment was beyond uncomfortable. This wasn't what stepping into the sanctuary of High Water should feel like, and the longer silence hung in the air, the more she knew to her core that this was her moment.

She acted on instinct, stepping from behind Aiden and folding her arms over her chest. Petra deliberately eyed the girl from top to bottom then nodded before speaking as bluntly as she would have to her friends. "Hi, Jennifer. This is your home for as long as you need it."

Jennifer nodded but didn't directly meet Petra's eyes.

"So, to start, what do you want us to call you?" Petra asked.

The girl finally lifted her head, confusion on her face. "Like a made-up name?"

"You can pick something completely different if you want, but I was more thinking that Jennifers are rarely called by their full name. I know some Jens and some Jennies." Petra shrugged. "Give it some thought." She turned to Danielle, mentally apologizing to Aiden for taking control of the situation. "Anything else you need to grab from the car?"

"No. Jennifer's got all her things with her," Danielle answered. "I have contact info for Aiden, though."

Petra waved a hand as if it were inconsequential, although it had to be the more detailed information regarding Jennifer's story. While that was important, this was even more essential. "We'll leave you to it then. Jennifer, we'll get you settled in your room in a minute. Aiden and I were doing the dishes, and I hate to leave a job half done. Put down your backpack and come help."

Then without waiting to see if the girl would follow, she headed back to the sink.

Low voices drifted on the air behind her, but nothing but silence from the young woman. Petra worked on putting things away—probably screwing the job up royally, but it kept her attention off Jennifer for a few brief moments.

Partly to see what she did without an audience.

Petra twisted back to grab a set of glasses and stifled a gasp when she discovered Jennifer had made it to the sink without so much as a single floorboard creak, despite wearing a pair of thick soled shoes. The girl moved like a ghost.

"You mind washing?" Petra asked.

"No."

Petra pointed to the sink. "There are gloves under there if you want. One of my older sisters uses them all the time to save her manicure. My hands are in terrible shape most of the time, and I rarely get manicures, so I never bother with them."

Jennifer dipped her hands into the water and took a deep breath, letting it out slowly before reaching for the first plate.

"Aiden says the new dishwasher is on its way, but until

then, we'll have to hand wash stuff. You like washing or drying better, usually?" Petra asked.

Jennifer shrugged.

"Me too. I don't mind either of them, except the Thanksgiving my sister Rachelle hauled out her wedding dishes and set the table formal-like, which means four or five plates and bowls per person. Then at the last minute she decided the fancy stuff couldn't possibly go in the dishwasher." Petra left the clean mixing bowl from Aiden's pancakes on the counter for later, then leaned in closer in the hopes of catching Jennifer's gaze. "There were twenty-four people at the table that meal."

The girl's eyes darted her direction for a second. "*Twenty-four?*"

"I have a big family," Petra offered dryly. "And some of them brought friends. It was a hand washing nightmare. We outlawed fancy dishes at family events after that."

Jennifer kept washing, but she eyed Petra a little more closely.

Yeah, her huge extended family was usually a great *break the ice* topic.

She shared her favourite dishwashing disasters including the time Zach and the brothers-in-law decided to create a washing assist using levers and pulleys. The resulting disaster ended up with a flood that poured down the stairs when one of them took out the tap controls and they'd somehow blocked the access to under the sink and couldn't turn off the water supply.

By the time the dishes were clean and put away, Danielle and Aiden had vanished onto the porch. Petra less heard the door clicking closed than noticed the subtle relaxing of Jennifer's shoulders.

If the girl was going to be that skittish every time a guy came around, with three brothers in the house at regular intervals, this was going to be problematic. Not knowing what Jennifer had gone through, it wasn't a judgment on her reaction. Just more like a fervent hope they could get through this stage quickly for all their sakes.

It had to suck to be constantly jumping at shadows.

They both dried their hands, then Petra tilted her head toward the living quarters section of the house. "Now for the grand tour. You'll have a room to yourself and a shared bathroom. You can lock the bathroom door on the second bedroom side for now if you want since there's no one in there. And there's a lock on your door to the hallway as well," Petra said, leading the way and trusting that Jennifer would follow.

The steady step of boot heels across the wooden floor reminded Petra. She stopped by the bedroom and motioned the girl to go ahead of her. "I don't think your bag is big enough for you to have a spare pair of runners or slippers, do you?"

Jennifer stared around the room, her head swaying from side to side as her eyes grew big as saucers. She ignored the question completely. "This is for me?"

"Yup. You're in charge of keeping it clean, although if it's clean enough there's no fire hazard or rotting food, I'm not fussy. There will be some tasks you'll help with around the house, but we'll wait and see what else gets added to that list after Aiden and Danielle have talked, all right?"

The girl blinked hard, lifting her head far enough to peer through the mess of her hair and take in Petra from top to bottom. "Is this a good place to live?"

It was the kind of question that should be either whispered or demanded, but the sheer hopefulness in the girl's voice just about broke Petra in two.

She lifted her own chin. "I'm not the type to stay somewhere that sucks. Trust me on that one." She snorted. As evidenced by rooting up her whole life to get away from the inconvenience of meeting her ex or his friends. Or his fiancée. "I expect there will be some learning curves between all of us as we set up this place." Petra waved a hand around her. "If you haven't noticed, you're the first to arrive. Which means you get to help us figure out what we're doing right and what we're doing wrong."

"If you're not hurting me or trying to get into my pants, I figure it's a pretty good improvement already." It came out with the most snap and fire Jennifer had offered since walking in the door.

A flash of anger rolled up one side of Petra and down the other. Not at this poor child, but at the assholes who had made a young girl utter such a phrase. "If somebody tries to do the first, I have a friend who will poison him, and I'll bury the body six feet under." Petra stepped closer, planted her hands on her hips, and gave Jennifer the absolute truth. "And if anyone tries the second, I have a friend who knows how to remove vital parts of their anatomy, so they'll never try again. Not with anyone."

One of the first true smiles she'd seen flickered across the girl's face.

So, bloodthirsty threats were the way to go. Good to know.

Dwelling on the idea wouldn't make Petra's blood pressure go back to normal. "Next part of the tour, Jennifer. This way to the bathroom. There's nothing too—"

"Wait." The girl stepped closer. "I want to be called Jinx."

Petra considered, her face had to be some twist between amusement and an adult exasperation. "Really?"

The girl lifted her chin. "You said I could pick a name."

Petra raised a brow. "That I did. Okay, Jinx, I'll show you the rest of the house, and then we'll see if Aiden's done so we can take a tour of the barns."

Jinx. Petra wasn't sure if the name meant what the girl felt like or what she wished on the people around her. But for now, it was a solid decision she'd made for herself, so Petra would deal with anybody who didn't follow along.

~

It wasn't until the door closed behind him that Aiden realized exactly how much fury he'd been holding inside.

Danielle laid a gentle hand on his shoulder, guiding him off the porch and toward the barn.. "What was it that got to you the most? The look in her eyes or the fact she's so young?"

"All of it." Underfoot, Dixie whined softly, sensing Aiden's anger. He gave her a brief pat then stepped away, inhaling deeply to try and wash some of the rage from his system. "I don't think it would be a good thing if I was to ever meet the people who put that expression on her face."

"Trust me," Danielle offered. "I've been fantasizing rather vividly about what things I would do to them if it were possible. But right now, the biggest thing is that Jennifer's out of that situation and in a place where her life can improve."

Which was what he needed to focus on rather than using his resources to discover who needed to be buried in a shallow grave. "It's not going to fly," he warned. "Having her on as a ranch hand. She's far too young for that to work."

"Agreed. I didn't realize it until I picked her up today. Sometimes girls at this age can get away with pretending to be older, but she looks young. Younger than she is." Danielle all but snarled the words.

Looking for a solution helped control Aiden's temper. "I might have an idea." They'd made it to the barn, and from across the open walkway, Jake and Declan put down their tools and paced quickly toward them. "She's welcome here, but I don't think it's going to be for a short time." He shook the envelope Danielle had given him. "Unless there's something in here that says she's got a safe retreat spot elsewhere."

Danielle shook her head then lifted her chin to his brothers, sharing with all of them. "Her parents died when she was five, so she's been in foster care for a while. The paperwork outlines more details, but to summarize, she's had two stable placements. A year and a half ago, the older couple she'd been with for eight years had to withdraw from fostering because of health issues. Her new family has a long history of fostering and a good track record. They have a birth son about Jennifer's age and a slightly older daughter, and it should have been a perfect match. Instead, it's been a disaster. They've persuaded the other authorities that she's been acting up and causing problems, which is why they're being firm. I'm convinced something bigger is happening. She's run away at least three times I know about. I couldn't get anyone to agree to look closer, so I stepped in and quietly asked if she wanted out."

"Is that how you're playing this one?" Jake asked. "That this time she's been successful in running away?"

Danielle nodded. "She left hints indicating she was headed to Toronto. That's a big enough place for a girl like her to get lost, and it's far enough away from Red Deer that I don't think anyone will bother trying to track her down."

"Red Deer isn't that far away from Heart Falls. You think it's safe for her here?" Aiden asked quietly.

"Safer than where she was," Danielle snapped before taking a deep breath. "She insisted she didn't need to see a doctor, that she hadn't been raped, but she has all the signs of dealing with sexual abuse."

Another rush of fury flashed through Aiden at the thought.

Danielle offered an apologetic smile. "You are her best shot right now," she said.

"Then here she'll stay," Declan offered with no hesitation.

"She's damn skittish." Aiden made eye contact with his brothers. "Petra's going to have to call the shots a lot on this one."

They both nodded.

"She's too young to be a ranch hand. But she could be family. Declan."

His brother met his eyes.

Aiden hated to go there, but it was necessary. It had only been three years since Declan's wife Sadie had died. Shortly after she'd passed was when the Skye brothers had seriously began planning for the setup of High Water. It didn't make her loss any less painful for his brother.

"Sadie's folks fostered kids. They live remote enough now that they won't know, and there's no high schools in their new area. That way Jennifer can still share the parts of her past that she wants to without the need to pretend her birth parents are still in the picture. You okay with that idea?"

Declan never hesitated. "Of course. Jennifer coming here would make sense. We can play it up that she plans to go to school in Calgary after she graduates."

"I'll get in touch with my contact," Jake offered. "Get her ID, get her set up in the school system. It shouldn't take long."

"I'm going to pretend I didn't hear that," Danielle said quietly. "Contact me if you need to, but from here on in, I'm going to keep out of the details as much as possible. Jennifer has my number in case of emergencies, and I'll stop by at times to check in, but the less interaction between us once people know she's missing, the better."

Jake shook her hand. "If you need us, call. That's why we're here. That's why we're building High Water."

Declan tilted his head toward the house. "If there's nothing else you need to tell the three of us, I'll walk you back to the house. You can say goodbye to Jennifer, and I'll let her know about her role in the family."

"Thank you for being men I can trust. I wouldn't be doing this if I didn't believe you were rock solid." Danielle met each of their eyes in turn before resting her hand briefly on Aiden's arm. "And thank goodness for Petra. You've found yourself a wonderful woman."

The praise only sent another wave of frustration over Aiden as Danielle joined Declan and they headed toward the house.

Petra *was* a good woman. Thank God she'd stepped in to help.

But it was also maddening since Aiden had thought her a good woman before all this, and now the chances of him doing anything about the connection between them had temporarily vanished.

Nothing mattered right now except making sure Jennifer's world improved from the hell it had been.

He pushed past Jake to the barn, fury rushing through him. He smashed his fist into a feed sack resting on a nearby haybale. The jolt of pain radiating up his arm barely disturbed the fire flaring inside.

Dixie whined softly, dancing away slightly but refusing to leave.

"That bad?" Jake asked quietly, slipping up behind him.

"She's a fucking baby," Aiden snarled. "I walked across the room, and she looked at me as if—" He closed his eyes and tightened his throbbing fist, trying to breathe away the anger. "If I ever find the son of a bitch who put that look into her eyes, he'll have breathed his last."

Which probably wasn't a thing he should confess to his brother who spent fifteen years as part of the police force.

But when Jake spoke, it was without censure. "I hear you.

And I mostly agree with you, but we need to let that shit go. She's out of a dangerous situation, and we need to help her step forward. We need to make this a place where she can bloom. If we have to put up with a few cringes and being stared at as if we're the bogeyman until she learns she can trust us, I can deal. So can you."

"Counselling the counsellor, are you?" Aiden growled in an attempt at normality.

"You usually give good advice," Jake admitted. "She needs time to get over her past trauma, and like you suggested, some good old-fashioned chores and safe family space might be the best way to do it."

Which was true, but one other thing needed to change. "I don't think me sleeping in the house is going to fly," Aiden said. "Not even with the suggestion that I'm there for their safety."

"Crash out here with us but put Dixie in the house with the girls," Jake suggested. "Problem solved."

Unexpectedly, a chuckle escaped. "Dixie?" He knelt and ruffled her ears, accepting the enthusiastic tongue bath she instantly offered to make him all better. Aiden nodded slowly at his brother. "That'll work."

The thought of the three females together in the house settled some of Aiden's agitation. Especially since one of them was a well-trained guard dog with very sharp teeth.

Jake tilted his head toward the house. "Want me to help grab your stuff so you can move out? Maybe if we go now, Petra can make us look less scary."

Maybe, but Aiden thought he knew an even better way. "Let's have Jennifer come meet Dixie outside. The girls can explore the animal rescue then come to the fire pit. Animals are the best kind of distraction," Aiden suggested.

"Good idea." His brother shuffled toward the nearest pen, patting the nose of the horse that came forward and shoved his head over the rail. Jake sighed. "It's not like making a checklist, is it? This is going to involve a whole lot of playing it by ear."

"Yup."

Jake sighed again. "I hate playing it by ear."

Aiden stroked Dixie's head again and breathed deep a few times, working hard to find a peaceful center. No, it wasn't going to be one step forward after another without some hiccups in the path, but it would be worth it in the end. That was the truth he had to cling to.

Come hell or high water, they'd make it work.

8

*P*etra had just finished giving Jinx a brief peek into the other rooms, including her own, when a knock rang against the front door.

Jinx instantly hid herself behind Petra's body even though the sound was followed immediately by Danielle's cheerful call. "Hello again, ladies. I'm getting ready to leave but wanted to say goodbye first."

"Did you need anything else from Danielle?" Petra asked the girl quietly.

Jennifer, or Jinx, as Petra needed to start thinking of her, shook her head.

"Declan needs to talk to you two, but I don't need to be part of that conversation." Danielle paced across the room, closing the distance until she stood a few feet shy of Petra and Jinx. "You're safe here. But I hope you'll also find a way to be happy."

Jinx nodded then wiggled forward far enough to thrust out her hand. "Thank you for believing me. I know you took a big chance to help me, and I appreciate it. I won't forget."

Danielle gently shook Jinx's extended fingers then gave Petra a smile. She mouthed the words *thank you* then turned to leave.

Just outside the open door, Declan offered Danielle a handshake of his own, waiting until she was to her car before stepping inside. He took slow steps into the room, his stocking feet sliding over the floor with a soft *whoosh, whoosh*. He tried to make himself as small and unintimidating as possible, which was ludicrous considering the breadth of his shoulders and the sheer bulk of him.

Once more into the breach. Petra offered introductions. "Jinx, this is Declan, Aiden's big brother. Consider him your own Stay Puft Marshmallow Man."

Declan snorted. "Thanks for that image."

Jinx tucked herself up against Petra's back again. "Can we talk outside?"

"Let's use the table," Petra suggested.

They intended the house to be the gathering place for the family and ranch hands. It would be hard to make that happen if Jinx couldn't even sit at the table without being frightened.

So, once again, Petra took charge. Pointing at chairs, she put the entire massive rough-hewn surface between their current trouble. "Declan, you sit there. Jinx, you get this chair and I'll sit beside you. Sound okay?"

Jinx nodded silently.

Petra sat, Jinx sat, then Declan settled where she'd put him, directly opposite Jinx.

Petra met his eyes. "I asked what she wanted to be called, and she's decided on the name *Jinx*."

Declan raised a brow, but his expression was thoughtful rather than dismissive. "I like it. And that goes with what I needed to talk to you about. We've been thinking about what you should use for a last name. We didn't know you were so young, Jinx. Which means you can't be a ranch hand. You have to be family."

The girl's entire body stiffened, and the fingers in her lap clenched so tightly her knuckles turned white. "What kind of family?"

"I was married to a wonderful woman who died three years ago." Across the table, the huge man softened, his expression so sad Petra wanted to give him a hug. "You could be Sadie's adopted foster sister, which makes you my sister-in-law. That would put thirteen years between the two of you, but that's not outrageous in a foster situation. Her parents recently moved to a remote part of Saskatchewan, so nobody would think anything of it for you to come finish your high school here. You could head off to Calgary for University in a few years. It means you don't have to remember lies about your entire life history. Just the past few years."

Petra kept her expression as blank as possible, but she had jumped in on the deep end. This wasn't an appropriate time to say something like *I didn't know that you'd been married* or *I'm so sorry for your loss*. Because Declan had obviously loved his wife very deeply.

Jinx's hands loosened, and her chin dipped slowly. "That makes sense. And less lies is good." She lifted her head far enough to look Declan in the eye. "I'm sorry. About your wife."

Declan didn't smile, but his lips softened. "Me too."

Petra's phone buzzed with an incoming message. She slipped it from her pocket and glanced at the screen.

> Aiden: When you guys are done talking with D, can you bring Jennifer outside to the barn? We want her to meet the dogs.

> Aiden: Oh shit. I hope she's not afraid of dogs.

> Aiden: Can you find out, gentle like, and let me know?

She glanced up to discover both Jinx and Declan watching her. Petra laid her phone face down on the table. "Sorry. That was rude. Aiden wants to know if you're afraid of dogs."

"No." Jinx blinked. "Should I be?"

Across the table, Declan chuckled softly. "We have some well-trained guard dogs. I bet Aiden thinks maybe one of them could be yours. If you'd like, they could live in the house with you."

"A dog?" Jinx nodded slowly before breathing out steadily. "I'd like that." A frown furled her forehead. "What's my last name going to be?"

"My wife's maiden name was Tremont. You'd be Jinx Tremont. Well, you'd still be Jennifer Tremont for the authorities, but that's a simple change we can do easily. I think that sounds pretty good, don't you?"

Jinx nodded then eyed the table between them and offered a rueful half smile. "Sorry for being so scared—"

Declan held up a hand to stop her. "You do not need to apologize. Not now, not ever. I don't think you'll always feel this way, but until you learn that you can trust us, we'll have some awkward moments. That's fine. I swear my brothers and I will *never* do anything to hurt you, and we will do everything we can to keep those around you from hurting you. No matter what it takes. Maybe that's hard to believe right now, but that's okay. You go on being scared. We won't take offense. Just let us know if we need to back off and give you more room." He glanced around at the open dining and family room. "This is where a lot of food happens, so I don't think you'll be able to convince us to not show up here at least three times a day."

Jinx ducked her chin then deliberately lifted it. "That makes sense. I kind of like food, too."

"Good. I'm planning on hooking you into being my assistant during my turns to cook around here." Petra leaned toward Jinx. "I'm not a very good cook, so you might be very happy to help me. It means more edible offerings on my night."

This time Jinx outright snickered. "Okay." She tentatively met Declan's eyes. "Can we go meet the dogs now?"

"Wonderful idea. Let me give Aiden a head's up that we're on our way." Petra grabbed her phone and messaged back.

> Petra: The girl who shall henceforth be known as Jinx has informed us that she is not afraid of dogs, and I've already called dibs on her being my chef's assistant. We're headed your direction. Don't worry about trying not to look scary. Jinx knows to let you know if you're misbehaving.

A moment later Aiden messaged back.

> Jinx? I can handle that. Come to the animal rescue building first. She may as well get to know the lay of the land.

Petra nodded as she turned to Jinx. "We're all set. On to the barn."

It was clear Jinx didn't have a lot of experience with animals from the way she kept looking around the barn with wide eyes—but wide eyes full of curiosity and not fear.

She let Petra guide her in petting the nose of a horse. She scooped up a couple of the kittens one after the other and gave them cuddles.

But it was when they met the beautiful golden retriever by the fire pit that something bloomed on the girl's face.

Aiden held the dog's lead, but it was clear that was more for show than anything else. The dog stopped perfectly when he did, slipping forward silently when he adjusted his stance a few feet to the right.

"Jinx, I'd like you to meet Dixie. Dixie," Aiden spoke down toward the animal. The dog looked up at him instantly, her full attention fixed intently. "This is Jinx. Guard."

The dog's rear wiggled as her tail wagged, but she didn't move from the spot, tilting her head toward Jinx and panting lightly, the edge of her tongue hanging out.

"Put your hand out," Aiden directed. "Then say, *Come, Dixie*, and she'll come to you. If your hand is out, she might give you a lick or two, but then she'll sit down and wait. You take your time getting used to her. You can scratch her along the muzzle or between the eyes if you'd like, but as long as you let her take a sniff and say hello, that's all you have to do."

"Sound okay?" Petra asked.

Jinx nodded, pushing her hand forward far quicker than Petra expected, though she did swallow big before following Aiden's instructions. "Come, Dixie."

Dixie crossed the distance, bumping her nose into the centre of Jinx's palm. Then her butt was back on the ground, her tail thumping again as she sat and offered a wide doggie smile.

Jinx tentatively lifted her hand to stroke the dog's head, but Petra's gaze drifted to the brothers. Watching three grown men try and make themselves smaller was amusing, or it would be if the reason it was necessary wasn't so sad.

Still, the introduction was going well, and when Jinx looked up at Declan and offered a real smile, hope bloomed in Petra's chest.

"She's nice. What else do I need to know?"

Declan tipped his head toward his brother. "Aiden will have to teach you. Dixie is his girl more than the rest of ours."

"But don't worry about that," Aiden hurried to add as Jinx's expression clouded. "We have other dogs, and we're going to have more, so it's okay to share one with you. Dixie is a special girl, and the rule is whoever needs her the most gets her."

"She's a cuddler." Declan shook his head as if somewhat disgusted. "Dogs aren't supposed to be cuddlers."

Jinx dropped her gaze, but Petra heard a snort, and when the girl glanced up at Declan, a bit of amusement lingered in her eyes.

They made their way back to the house. Jinx stuck close to Petra, but with Dixie pacing close enough to brush her legs and nudge her nose against the hand Jinx held at her side, it was a more positive trip than Petra had hoped for.

Aiden and Declan settled onto the bench on the porch to take off their boots when Jinx's calm seemed to vanish between one breath and the next. Petra glanced around to see what might have caused the change.

"What are you doing?" Jinx asked.

Aiden tucked his cowboy boots under the bench then glanced at her, confusion on his face. "We don't wear work boots into the house."

"That's the surest way to get a towel snapped at your butt," Jake agreed, using the boot jack to remove his own footwear.

It was the same rule Petra had grown up with, so it was only natural to lean down to prepare to loosen her own laces. She paused though, as Jinx eased her way to the edge of the porch, no longer sticking to Petra's side like glue.

It was sheer instinct that made Petra straighten at the exact second Jinx twirled and fled down the stairs and onto the gravel, headed for the main road at an all-out sprint.

~

"J*INX*." Petra's shout echoed even as she threw herself off the porch after the girl.

"What the hell?" Jake snapped, trying to jam his feet back into his boots so he could chase them.

Didn't see that one coming, Aiden thought. He too was shoving his feet back in his boots when Declan laid a hand on his shoulder. "Petra's got her."

The three of them stood there on the porch feeling rather useless as the two women talked about halfway down the drive. Jinx stood in one spot, staring at the ground while Petra waved her arms vigorously. No shouting, but obviously some very intense communication, at least on Petra's part.

"Wonder what that's all about," Declan said softly as Petra offered her hand to Jinx. The younger woman reluctantly accepted the grasp and let Petra guide her back to the porch.

Dixie wove in and out of them, worried because something was wrong that she couldn't see.

When they were within speaking distance, Petra met Aiden's gaze. "Just a slight misunderstanding. Everything's okay, but I need Jake and Declan to get in the house and chill for a bit if that's okay."

Aiden had never seen his brothers vanish so quickly.

"Aiden is sticking around because I need his help," Petra said firmly, grabbing him by the hand and pulling him onto the bench beside her. "You can sit there, Jinx."

She pointed to the bench on the other side of the door. Jinx moved meekly into position.

It felt like a juggling act, Aiden realized. He didn't want to move too quickly for fear he'd spook the girl, but something wasn't right. "What can I do?" he asked Petra quietly.

"In the bedroom. There's a pair of runners on the floor in my closet. If you grab them and a pair of socks, that should be good." Petra took off her own shoes, speaking calmly to Jinx even as Aiden slipped into the house. "Remember what we said about how it's okay to get scared? We're not always going to get it right, but you've got to trust us enough to tell us when something frightens you and not just take off."

Aiden missed what Jinx said in response because he was in the house, waving off his brothers' questions as he hurried into Petra's room to find the requested shoes.

It hadn't seemed as if it was going to be this hard, he realized, rushing back to the porch. This whole trying to help people. Somehow he'd assumed that because they needed help, it would make things roll easier, and maybe in a way he'd be right for *some* people.

But as he stepped onto the porch and found Petra kneeling in front of Jinx, the girl's foot in her hand, that's when it finally sank in that they were starting with someone who might be their biggest challenge ever.

Jinx sat stiffly, staring at Petra.

Petra's mouth was tight as she accepted the shoes and socks. "You want to tell us both what happened here? Because Aiden and I are a package deal, and I don't want to have to be the go-between all the time. I know you've got things you want to keep secret, and that's fine for now. But there are some things you need to let the guys know, got it?"

Aiden moved until he was behind Petra, sitting on the edge of the porch at her back. Which was when he noticed that the soles of Jinx's feet were scarred. Not just faint lines, but worn calluses and ridges, as if they'd been hurt so badly the skin had been damaged.

Fingers curled around his wrist, and he realized he'd been squeezing Petra's hip. "Who did that to you?" he asked Jinx.

"Me. By running away." Jinx swallowed hard. "I didn't feel safe, so I ran. They didn't like that, so they took away my shoes. The next time I ran, I climbed out my window. I didn't know someone had broken a whole bunch of beer bottles under it." She looked up and met Aiden's eyes. Her gaze slipped to Petra and back. "I still ran because I figured even having my feet all sliced up was better than sticking around."

Jesus Christ. "We're not taking away your shoes," he assured her. "It's a custom, that's all. No outdoor shoes in the house. But if you want to have shoes on all the time, you go right ahead. None of us will say a word."

"You got that?" Petra asked.

The girl dipped her chin.

"We need you to let us know if we're stepping into something that's scary for you. We're not demanding all your story," Petra said quickly, "but we can't fix what we don't know is broken. Give us a chance."

"Can you do that? Can you try?" Aiden asked.

"I'll try." Jinx accepted the socks and slipped them on quickly, all her focus on the footwear until they were tied on tight. She nodded rapidly then looked up at Petra. "I don't like being so scared. I don't want to be, but sometimes—" She took a quavering breath. "You aren't going to send me away, are you?"

"Absolutely not," Petra assured her. "But we should go claim our lunch before Jake and Declan eat it all."

"My brothers are a horde of wild boars when it comes to cleaning out the contents of the refrigerator," Aiden offered with as much levity as he could possibly muster. "Petra's right. Hesitate too long, and we'll be scrounging for leftovers."

They'd barely walked in the room when Petra motioned for Jinx to wait. "Hang on. I too have fancy inside designer wear. I just need a moment to find them." She sighed then grimaced, making a face at Jinx who hovered near the door. "I have the memory of a sieve at times. Fortunately, I also have technology."

Petra grabbed her phone and opened an app, then paced

forward as if following a compass. The boxes she'd left beside the coat rack were quickly re-sorted as the bottom box was brought to the top and restacked against the wall.

A bright hum of approval rang out as she pulled a backpack free then grinned at Jinx. "I knew they were close. Thank goodness for AirTags." Petra shook the backpack upside down, and a pair of slippers fell to the floor.

She slipped them on then casually gestured toward the kitchen table. "Ready if you are."

It was impossible not to gape. Aiden stood for a moment and simply admired the shining dragons adorning Petra's feet. They were more glorified socks than slippers, with rainbow colours and sets of shimmering wings that extended upward from the surface, as if two dragons were gliding in for a landing.

Jinx stared as well, her mouth hanging open slightly.

"In case you're wondering, Petra's one of a kind," Aiden informed the girl.

Petra pursed her lips and blew him a kiss. "Right back 'atcha."

She slipped her arm around Jinx's shoulders and guided her to the table.

Aiden hurried forward to offer his brothers a reassuring nod. "We accidentally hit one of Jinx's hot buttons, but it's dealt with. Also, Jinx has already made a positive addition to our rules. House shoes are now an option here at High Water."

"We can handle that," Jake said easily before tilting his head toward the left. "Sandwich fixings are on the counter. Make what you want to eat then join us at the table."

By the time they all settled, Aiden sat at the head of the table. Petra sat to his right across from Jake with Jinx beside her, directly across from Declan. Dixie rested on her haunches between Jinx and Petra, a look in her doggie eyes as she peered between them as if she couldn't believe her good luck.

None of them said anything when Jinx secretly snuck the dog bits of her sandwich throughout the meal.

Jake opened one of his unending to-do lists and began reading through it.

Declan listened and nodded, but he shrugged when Jake asked if there was anything he wanted added. "I've got enough to do dealing with the animals since we don't have community volunteers right now." He eyed Jinx. "Since you don't seem to have a problem around the animals, I'd appreciate it if you helped me with some of the chores."

She nodded slowly then glanced to the left when Aiden spoke.

"Chores, yes, but we need to get you registered for school. Which means you need to make your own list, maybe with Petra's help. What kind of things you'll need, like clothes and the rest of it."

Jinx's eyes went wide. "Is it safe for me to go to school?"

Aiden nodded. "We have to deal with the paperwork, but it shouldn't take too long. So you have time to make your shopping list."

"I know somebody we can ask for help," Petra offered. "It's been a long time since I was in school, so while I have no problem taking you shopping, I won't be much help deciding on styles."

Their newest family member took a small bite then chewed it very thoroughly as if she was thinking hard. "I don't need anything."

A snort escaped before Aiden could help it. "Well, that's a bunch of—" he paused.

"Bullshit?" Petra offered.

This time Jake laughed.

Petra leaned in toward Jinx conspiratorially. "They have an

aversion to swear words. I'm pretty sure you've heard *bullshit* before."

"Both the word and the meaning," Aiden said. "But our Daddy said we weren't supposed to say those things around ladies. Which Petra knows and thinks is hysterical."

"Because it is," Petra said with amusement. "But back to the point, I agree with Aiden. Jinx, you need stuff. A phone and shoes and all the regular school supplies, and that's part of what living here means. You get to have the things you need. Maybe that feels weird, but that's okay. You don't owe us anything except to try and keep finding the best new life that you can."

Moisture was gathering in Jinx's eyes. And while Aiden was one hundred percent on board with positive emotion, it seem like a good opportunity to keep things rolling.

He pushed to his feet, picking up his plate. "If everyone else knows what they're doing for the rest of the day, I have drywall to deal with." He came back to the table and laid a hand on Petra's shoulder, leaning down to speak softly in her ear. "Message if you need me."

She twisted her head slightly, and their cheeks brushed, and he was far too aware of how close her lips were to his. "Two steps forward and one step back is still forward motion," she offered softly.

Amen to that.

Declan was beside him as Aiden headed out the door. "That poor kid."

"She's got a lot of spunk. I mean, she's scared shitless right now, but once she gets her feet under her, I think she'll be okay."

"I'm glad we don't have anybody else coming in right now, though," Declan said. "Except we need to get in touch with Kevin."

"Jake said he'd be on that this afternoon." Because having a trained counsellor on the property as soon as possible was a necessary thing.

The afternoon vanished between installing the final drywall and beginning to mud the rooms that would be used for the artists' retreat. Aiden slipped into the house, intending to grab a quick shower then move his things to the barn when Petra caught him. She motioned for him to join her in the corner of the living room.

He had to ask. "You had AirTags in your *slippers?*"

She blinked then offered an eye roll. "No, in my backpack. I have a bad habit of leaving things behind. I got tired of losing stuff, so I've gone proactive and sewn them into all my main bags."

"Makes sense."

Across the room, Declan was cooking supper. Jinx stood a few feet away at the counter to the side of him, cutting up vegetables for a salad.

"That's a whole lot more hopeful than I had imagined," Aiden said quietly to Petra before examining her face. "I didn't get any messages from you. I assume the afternoon went smoothly?"

She raised her brows. "We had no more panic attacks. Jinx was great helping with the animal chores. When we came back in here to check online for school information, it went better than I expected." She took a deep breath, her gaze darting to the kitchen as she lowered her voice. "We do have one problem."

"Spit it out. Nothing worse than my imagination getting fired up."

Petra glanced at her hands as if examining them closely. "Jinx is happy she gets to have Dixie in her room. Said she's never had a dog, and it was considerate that my fiancé was willing to share his."

"Of course." He caught her fingers in his to stop her from fidgeting. "Petra. What is *wrong*?"

She sighed. "Jinx said that between Dixie in her room and you and me in the primary bedroom, she feels safe enough to sleep tonight."

"But I'm not sleeping—"

Petra raised a brow.

Okay, he wasn't always this slow. "Oh."

"Yeah, *oh*." This time she said it with amusement.

His brain whirled through everything that meant. "She wants a guy in the house, but she probably won't like it if I'm not in the room with you where you can keep an eye on me, right?"

"If we're thinking through worst case scenarios, yeah. That's where my puzzle solving went as well." Petra looked him in the eye. "So, roomie. I guess you may as well move your stuff in with me. But I'm warning you now, I get the right side of the bed."

9

The entire day had been one adrenaline rush after another. By the time dinner cleanup was complete and they all gathered in the living room on the side where the TV was, Petra's nerves had an unfamiliar jittering sensation to them.

She was smart enough to understand why it was happening —empathy for Jinx and how she must feel if nothing else—but it left Petra a little unsteady.

So full of conflicting emotions. Anger and frustration and hope and fear of doing the wrong thing or saying something that would crack Jinx's fragile courage.

It was also perfectly natural to feel the attraction that was there between her and Aiden. Every time their eyes met, a shiver ran up Petra's spine and the memories would flood back in. The delicious night they'd spent together was something Petra had been fantasizing about getting an instant replay on.

And now they had to share a room?

Jinx had been given the oversized recliner, which was barely big enough for her and Dixie. The dog had taken full advantage of house privileges with great enthusiasm, crawling into Jinx's lap and pouring over the arm rest.

Petra stood awkwardly, considering her options, until Jake stepped to the front of the room and took control.

He gestured her to the couch. "We haven't been here at High Water for long enough to have many set routines. Since I'm the one with the good head for timing and organization—"

"And a bigger head for being bossy," Declan muttered.

Aiden outright laughed as he settled on the couch beside Petra and Jake scowled. "Don't make that face. Trying to round us up and corral us is one of your favourite things, brother."

Instead of glowering, Jake dramatically rolled his eyes. "If you two are done being comedians?"

"Pretty sure I've got a few more lines in me," Aiden offered instantly.

Declan didn't say anything this time. Just smirked into the coffee cup he'd refilled after the meal was over.

Jake shook his head, but he wasn't the one Petra watched with fascination. Jinx had her arms around Dixie's neck, her eyes wide as if their comedy routine had her mesmerized.

Petra didn't think the light-hearted badgering was fake—too much true affection came through in the way the brothers spoke to each other. But Jinx was eating it up, and the longer the guys teased as Jake sat to the side of Declan and began updating the progress list, the more her mouth hung open in shock.

It was a nice normal family situation as far as Petra could tell. Not that much different from what she and her own family were like on a regular basis.

Which meant this kind of light banter was probably nothing Jinx had experienced for a long time, if ever.

Petra had snuck a quick read through the papers Aiden had tucked into her pocket, which gave the bare bones of what

Danielle had been told of Jinx's living situation. Jinx would tell more about her past in the days to come once she was ready, but for now, it was all about building trust one hour at a time.

Which meant Petra had this first evening to get through as well.

Followed by a night sharing a bed with Aiden.

What did she want?

It was one thing to have upturned her entire life to help—and the longer the day went on, the more grateful Petra was that she'd been in the right place at the right time for that. But did it mean she had to put her own desires on hold when it came to her and Aiden?

Fooling around would offer the perfect endorphin rush to deal with the current situation.

An elbow nudged gently into her side. "Teacher wants to know why you're not participating," Aiden teased.

Petra blinked and discovered all eyes on her. She'd been so caught up in her own head she'd lost track of what was going on. "Sorry, you have to say that again."

"Keep your girl awake over there," Jake grumbled before turning back to his papers.

Aiden curled his arm around the back of the couch which snuggled Petra in closer. He grinned down and waggled his brows. "Can't have the boss unhappy."

Only Jinx's eyes were on them, and her body language was stiffer than before. Petra twisted on the spot, curling her legs under her. Aiden's arm fell away even though they remained side by side. She poked him in the chest with amusement. "You don't need any encouragement to get distracted. What was the question, Jake?"

"Eventually, we'll have different evening activities lined up. Things like schoolwork, or prep for the artists' studio. But for the most part, we'll take the evening to relax. I asked if you'd share what goes on *your* list for evening relaxation activities."

Heat rumbled through her as Aiden laid a hand on her thigh. His hands, all over her... That was one relaxing evening activity that was *not* going to be named now, no matter that it leapt to mind.

Petra considered then listed a bunch easily. "I crochet. Usually put on a podcast and stitch for an hour or two. Sometimes I put on a show or listen to some music. I usually go for a walk in the evening, but that's because my day jobs often require me to sit on my butt for a long time. Since coming to High Water is still recent, I haven't figured out my new routine."

"I don't usually need any more physical labour in the evening," Declan said, "but I don't mind listening to music or that sort of thing. I like to whittle, and it's nice to have something going on in the background."

Jinx frowned. "Why don't you guys just do what you always do? You don't have to change things because I'm here."

Aiden leaned forward and rested his elbows on his knees. "That's very kind, but it's not that we're going out of our way or inconveniencing ourselves, Jinx. You're part of this family now, and yeah, sometimes families do stupid things, but usually they do their best to do smart things like make it easy to spend some time together in a way that's comfortable and makes everybody happy."

"Consider it a family routine," Declan pitched in. "Who knows? Maybe you'll decide you want to learn how to whittle. Always good to have an expert to teach you."

"I'll put that on my list, then," Jake said. "Find an expert whittler to teach Jinx—"

Declan scratched between his eyes using his middle finger.

Jake snorted. "You're still swearing. You know Jeff would never let you get away with that."

Petra laughed. The awkwardness she'd felt was slowly being melted away by the strong bond between the brothers. "Okay, so we're looking for ideas for High Water family night. Right now, we don't have much on the outside calendar, so there's no reason why we can't hang together in here, or by the fire, or things like that, right? Just no work."

"No work." Jake agreed. "Emergencies will happen, and once Jinx is in school, she might have things that happen after supper, so we'll have to make some adjustments. But for now, how about we let the weather decide?"

Jinx lifted her fingers the slightest bit, as if asking for permission to speak.

Petra ignored the urge to tell the girl this wasn't school. She'd figure it out eventually. "What's up?" she asked.

"I like some music. And some podcasts, and some shows, but there's some stuff I don't…" Beside her, Dixie nuzzled in, whining softly as she looked for what was upsetting her new charge. Jinx stroked the dog's head then determinedly lifted her head and looked Petra in the eye. "There's things I won't watch. Nothing violent, or cruel, or sex stuff, just so you know."

The brothers all nodded instantly, faces grim. This time Petra had to fight to keep her own change of body language under control. This girl—damn the people who'd had Jinx before and let her world be so tainted that basic decency had to be asked for.

Jake lifted his notepad, sharing as he wrote. "Jinx has final authority on our viewing entertainment." He made an exaggerated checkmark and met her gaze. "Easiest way is if you let us know what you want to watch or listen to, then we'll take it from there."

Declan sat straighter in his chair. "Hang on. What do you

like to watch?" he asked Jinx with mock horror in his voice "I can't handle those house hunter shows. Bunch of nonsense, with people complaining about how small the closets are."

Jinx snickered, a hesitant smile lifting her lips. "How about I'll make a list of things I like, and you guys can check it."

"Music too," Aiden suggested. "List your favourite artists and genres, that sort of thing. Because we can take turns listening to each other's stuff, but I am not sitting through George Strait repeats ever again."

"We'll make a list, Jinx," Petra said, resting her hand on Aiden's and patting it with amusement. "Remember guys, earbuds are a thing. Sometimes we can listen to our own choices and just be in the same room together. That's a possibility as well."

Jinx looked around with more curiosity than fear. "So what's tonight? Since we don't have any lists yet?"

Jake glanced at his watch. "It's a nice night. How about everybody do what they need to do for a bit, and at nine o'clock, we'll meet by the fire pit to spend an hour listening to nothing but the crackle of the wood. I don't know if you can crochet out there, Petra, but Declan can whittle. Or maybe Aiden can bring his guitar."

His guitar?

Not that Petra was going to let on that she had no idea that her *fiancé* could play. "That sound okay with you, Jinx? We have a bag of clothes to go through that my sister-in-law dropped off, but we should be able to get that done in the next while. It's sort of work, but I think it's important."

"Okay."

Beside her, Aiden leaned close before Petra could stand. As the others got up and went different directions, he put his lips beside her ear and whispered quietly. "You need to tell me if you want me to grab my bunk role so I can sleep on the floor.

Or are you okay with me sharing that mattress with you? No expectations."

Petra's stomach was back to being a jittering jumbling mess.

At least she knew part of the answer without hesitating. "We're grown-ass adults. It's a queen-size bed. I think we can share, no expectations."

He nodded firmly as he sat back then pushed to his feet.

Petra walked after him to join Jinx who waited for her at the entrance to the bedroom wing.

Jinx's observant gaze danced over them, but not even knowing she should be on her best behaviour could keep Petra's eyes from falling to the smooth, muscular flex of Aiden's ass as he strolled confidently ahead of her toward their room.

The man was damn fine. Sharing a bed with no expectations?

Hell. She was going to spontaneously combust.

∼

Petra had a shitty poker face.

Aiden tucked away that knowledge and pondered the more interesting tidbit that their final short discussion provided.

She'd looked disappointed. He'd been trying to make the sharing-a-bed thing less awkward, and she'd totally been disappointed. Which was both interesting and super frustrating.

No. It was interesting. He'd go with that option.

He slipped into the primary bedroom and tucked the rest of his things away. It only took a moment before he was back in the hallway, the sound of voices in Jinx's room carrying clearly toward him.

"These are just a few things to get you through until we can find time to make it to the store. Which won't take too long," Petra promised.

"I don't mind hand-me-downs."

Petra made a rude noise. "Hand-me-downs are a yes, but you also get some new stuff. Because as the fifth girl in a family, let me tell you that nothing *but* hand-me-downs sucks."

He made sure to make some noise as he moved closer. "Excuse me, ladies." They glanced up from their task, Jinx's body language going on alert as he'd expected. "Petra, I'm going to go help with the chores. I'll meet you at the fire pit, okay?"

She looked confused for a moment before something in her expression softened as she realized he was acting the way a fiancée would. "That sounds good." She hesitated before an outright mischievous smile crossed her face. "You should bring your guitar."

Damn Jake to hell. Aiden smiled back. "I can do that."

He was still muttering curses under his breath when he bumped into his brother in the barn. Which meant he literally bumped into his brother, nearly sending Jake sprawling to the straw. "Jackass. 'Aiden can bring his guitar,' huh?"

"Hey, you're the talented one in the bunch. Figured it'd be a pity to let all your fancy training go to waste."

Jake danced out of Aiden's swing radius, but it was all in good humour.

They made the rounds together to deal with the few chores that were there for the animal shelter.

There weren't that many animals in the barn yet. The couple they'd bought the rescue from had done a great job finding homes for most of the creatures before they'd put the ranch up for sale. The fact that the Skye brothers hadn't minded the remaining animals being included had been unusual.

Not many people would want to take on a full-time nonprofit facility along with buying a ranch.

"We're waiting until next spring to get the animal rescue fully back into gear, right?" Aiden asked.

Jake nodded. "Declan already put out the word that if there's an emergency we'll take the animals on, but we need to get the rest of the renovations and moneymakers in place first."

Which meant it was barely half an hour later after taking care of the mostly cats and few horses that Declan had already added to their own rides.

Jake went off one way to get the fire started, and Aiden went the other to grab his guitar. As soon as he had helped arrange chairs around the fire pit, he ignored everything else and sat down and began to play.

His mother had started him on the guitar, and after she passed, Jeffrey had gone out of his way to make sure the lessons continued. Aiden had enough years under his belt that once he got going, he could stare into the flames and let the music flow over him.

The fire pit was tucked to the side of the building in a bit of a dip. The lay of the land cut off some of the expansive views but meant they could be here even when the wind picked up, nestled into a safe place where they could just be.

A place to relax and brush off the stress of the day.

Jinx. The first to come to High Water. The first to join the family, and the song under Aiden's fingers changed from something light and soft to mischievous and fanciful. As if fairies flitted about the place, bringing magic around him.

Which was when the girls arrived. Admiration danced in Petra's eyes as she lowered herself into the chair next to him, Jinx on her other side. Dixie twisted on the spot then settled on the girl's feet, while Petra lifted something small and woolen from a basket she placed on the ground.

His brothers arrived. Declan opened his pocketknife, sitting forward to continue working on a tree stump he'd found. He was about halfway through making the small face of a gnome peek through the rough bark.

Throughout it all, Aiden played. The classical music that shouldn't fit so well in the setting, and yet did, swirled around them with an easy rhythm. The pulse of his fingers carried on the air and created magic as the sun dipped behind the mountains and the sky slowly filled with a rich gold.

The expression on Jinx's face was as awe-inspiring as the sunset. As if she couldn't believe where she was or how much her life had changed.

When she leaned her head against the high back of the Adirondack chair and closed her eyes, fingers stroking slowly over Dixie's head, Aiden smiled.

There might be a whole hell of a lot of other things to figure out, including getting Jinx's story straight so that the lies that would have to be told to the community would work, but right here and right now?

This was the bit of family that he'd dreamed about creating. This was why they were here.

They sat for nearly an hour. Jinx wiggled to new positions a few times, including getting up, stretching, and walking around the backside of all their chairs with Dixie pacing at her side.

Aiden played. Petra stitched. A small light hung around her neck aimed down at her fingers and highlighted them as they moved with an easy rhythm. Declan's fingers flowed over the wood as well, and between the three of them, they created an artistic symphony, each in their own way.

Jake? He had a notebook in his lap, writing a few lines then closing it. Opening it, writing a little more. Between each time, he stared into the fire, head bobbing to the beat of whatever Aiden played.

Once he knew where all his people were, Aiden let himself drift with the music. An easy, contented act until he discovered he was staring at Petra most of the time, admiring the way the light shone off her hair. Appreciating the little frown she got as she recounted stitches or something then smiled contentedly and turned her work.

The fire crackled, and somewhere in the distance an owl hooted. The small noises of the fall mixed with his guitar and added to the concert.

Petra glanced up and smiled at him, and inside, something more than heat pulsed. It was odd. Her being here, pretending to be part of his family—it was a complete lie, and yet felt like an utter truth.

Aiden let the swirling confusion in his gut tangle with the music and slide away for now.

Petra was the first to make a move to end the evening. She gathered her project and slipped it into the basket. "I know Jinx doesn't have school yet, but we may as well establish a good routine. Time to get ready for bed," she informed the girl.

Which was brilliant, Aiden realized. A chance for them to escape the guys' company without Jinx getting triggered.

Jinx stood, Dixie instantly snuggling under her hand. She glanced at his brothers then met his gaze. "I didn't mind that music. You're good."

"Thanks, kiddo. You sleep tight, okay? Petra and I are down the hall if you need anything, but go ahead and lock your door. Dixie will take care of you."

She nodded then waved goodnight to Jake and Declan. "Thanks for giving me a place to live."

"You bet," Jake said softly.

"Night, Jinx. See you in the morning," Declan offered.

They walked off, Jinx glancing over her shoulder a few times before hurrying after Petra.

Aiden strummed open chords until they were out of earshot. "I hope to hell the universe gives us the wisdom to do this right."

"Amen to that," Jake muttered. Then he fixed his gaze on Aiden. "You're sleeping in the house. You need anything, any time, you text."

"And you treat Petra with respect," Declan said firmly. He shook his hand at Aiden, the move more threatening than he possibly intended because he still held his switchblade in his fingers. "She has done amazing things and dealt with so much in the past twenty-four hours. She's the key to making this work, so don't you go fucking it up."

"I know," Aiden insisted. "I know."

Jake sighed and leaned back in his chair. "We know that part, too. That you're not an ass, but dammit, this whole thing got complicated really fast."

"That's saying a mouthful." Declan shrugged. "Just make sure you're thinking hard, Aiden. That's all we ask. Petra leaving because you pissed her off would be a disaster."

It was as if his brothers thought he had no self-control. He glowered at them. "I'm not planning on fucking up. I'm not planning on *fucking* at all."

It wasn't a *total* lie. Dreaming and fantasizing about it were not the same as planning.

A short while later, after firm back pats and goodnights from his brothers, Aiden slipped into the house as quietly as possible. A light shone from under the bathroom door connected to Jinx's room. Dixie's nails clicked on the hardwood floor in a steady rhythm as the dog paced.

Better than any surveillance camera, Aiden had to admit. If Jinx did get scared and decide to run, Dixie was going to stay glued by her side.

He walked to the primary bedroom, catching himself

before he knocked. Instead, he slipped open the door and peeked inside. The sound of running water from the bathroom made him hesitate.

Petra. Naked in the shower—

Dammit. He was being punished for some past sins.

Aiden went to the walk-in closet, hauled off his clothes and hung them on the hook on the far wall. He left on his boxer briefs, then peeked back into the room.

The water was off but still no sign of Petra.

This was utter bullshit. He could either stand in the closet and hide like a blushing virgin or go brush his teeth like a fucking adult.

One step into the bathroom area, he froze. Petra stood at the counter, hair wrapped up in a towel balanced on the top of her head. She brushed her teeth vigorously, watching him in the mirror with amusement.

The dragons on her feet were back, and a shimmering robe covered the rest of her from neck to ankles. Rainbow colours and stripes danced in front of his eyes in psychedelic kaleidoscopes.

"I think I've gone blind," he said, blinking hard and marching to the second sink.

Petra smiled around her toothbrush before spitting and rinsing. She put away her things and outright grinned. "I like bright colours."

God help him. "Good for you."

She laughed again then leaned over to take the towel off her head and rub her hair dry. "Thank you from me as well for the great guitar playing. That was a nice finish to the end of a stressful day."

"You think Jinx will actually sleep tonight?" he asked.

The amusement between them softened as the question hung in the air.

Petra nodded slowly. "Dixie is a huge help. I think Jinx is *hopeful*. I think that's about the best we can expect, here at the start of all things."

Which was the perfect assurance and a terrible trigger at the same time. Because Aiden had just realized that's what he wanted not only for Jinx, but for himself as well. Possibly for him and Petra.

Hope.

Hope for a future where they could be together.

10

*E*ver since Aiden had moved his stuff into the bedroom, Petra had played through the sleeping situation a dozen ways. Each time she'd changed her mind as to what was right and what was wrong until she'd tied herself up in a tangled knot.

But while sitting by the fire, listening to Aiden's music, she'd realized the truth. She was making this far more complicated than it had to be. If right now was about getting through one day at a time for Jinx's sake, it should be the same for them. She and Aiden had managed just fine during the one night they'd had together way back when.

If they could enjoy some wonderfully distracting moments here and now, she wouldn't mind one bit.

By the way he was pretending not to watch her, Aiden's brain was obviously as messed up as hers had been. Everything about his body language as she brushed past him and headed to the bed said he was very aware of her, and very interested.

She knew what was going on. She imagined his brothers giving him the *don't screw this up* chat. Or even worse, laying down the law to Aiden about what he could or couldn't be doing.

Petra was well past the point where she let other people dictate what went on when it came to her sex life. Didn't mean she couldn't enjoy teasing the hell out of Aiden about the contrast between how he was acting now, considering how forward and playful he'd been the other night at the bar.

Case in point? The man was clearly attempting to hide the fact he had a hard on.

Enough. Time to talk about the elephant in the room. She stopped beside the bed and twisted to face him.

He stood beside the sink, back to her as he rinsed his toothbrush as if his life depended on it. His gaze stayed fixed on the taps, avoiding the mirror that showed her reflection.

"Are you hoping I'll vanish beneath the sheets and you won't have to face me until tomorrow?" Petra asked.

Aiden chuckled, but it sounded wrong. More stress reaction than true amusement.

He turned, and his gaze dropped instantly as she loosened the knot of her robe. "You said you wanted the right side of the bed."

He snatched the hand towel off the wall and made a show of drying his hands, the hanging end of the towel held suspiciously low to block the view of his groin.

Too funny. "We need to talk."

He dragged his gaze up to meet hers, forcibly keeping it there. "Yeah?"

She let the tie fall from her hands, and the front of her robe gaped open. His gaze flickered over her naked torso for the briefest of seconds before returning to her face.

The man had willpower. She had to give him that. "Remember when we met the first time?" she asked.

Heat flashed in his eyes. "Every detail."

Petra nodded. "Me, too. And you remember when we met this last Monday at Rough Cut?"

He nodded slowly, the towel still dangling in front of him. "Why do I think I'm being set up?"

She laughed, abandoning her exaggerated pose and sliding toward him. She rested a hand against his naked chest, the scent of him surrounding her as she breathed deep, delicious wood smoke and musk filling her senses. "No games, Aiden. We might have a big job to do here with Jinx and setting up High Water, but that doesn't mean it has to complicate *us*. We've shared a bed before, and it was a whole hell of a lot of fun. I'm on board with doing that again if *you're* interested."

He tossed the towel onto the counter and slid his hands onto her hips. "You know I'm interested. I'm just worried. What if we—"

His words cut off, uneasiness on his face.

Petra spoke softly. "What if we just do this thing and act like adults? Promise to talk to each other and not make assumptions. Promise not to lie to each other. What if we choose to dive in instead of trying to dream up and work through every nightmare situation before it's even happened?"

His fingers tightened for a minute before he took a deep breath. "So you're saying we're both grown up enough to be able to crawl into this bed, enjoy each other, and tomorrow we'll get up and do what needs to be done. As friends."

Petra nodded. "So long as you haven't lost any of your moves," she teased, stroking her palms up and over his chest until she curled them behind his neck. The move narrowed the gap between them, heat building.

He released his death grip on her hips, easing downward to cup her ass and pull her tight against his solid torso. "Friends. Lovers. That's for now."

She played with the hair at the back of his neck. "If either of us want to stop, we will, just like we said about the whole fake engagement. We're adult enough we can simply say it's time to do the next thing."

His eyes danced over her face, expression far too solemn considering they were talking about sex.

"Jinx is important. I get that. But this is important too. For you *and* me," Petra added.

Aiden eliminated every stitch of air between them. "I don't think I've ever been propositioned quite so prettily. But there's one more thing I need to know since we didn't cover it properly the first time we hit a mattress."

"What's that?" She barely got the words out, the final bit a little breathless. Aiden had scooped her up in his arms to carry her the final few feet back to bed. She grinned. "Other than admitting I do enjoy your caveman-like behaviour."

He tossed her on the mattress and all but threw himself over her, pinning her in place as he teased his nose along the edge of her neck. "After I get you good and relaxed and well sated, are you a cuddler? Or are you going to kick me off to my side of the bed, and woe to me if I touch you in the night?"

His weight over her caused streaks of pleasure to zip up her spine. She scraped her nails lightly down the sides of his rib cage.

Aiden hissed and set his teeth to her neck, nibbling lightly.

He was heavy enough that she was pinned in place as he teased her skin with his teeth and tongue and set her nerves craving for more. She pulled her knees farther apart, and his hips settled more intimately between her thighs.

She took a deep breath, and her breasts brushed the dusting of hair on his chest. "*Hmmmm*, nice."

A rumble of laughter washed over her as he leaned on his

left elbow and lifted far enough to look her in the eyes. "You're easily distracted, darlin'. You plan to answer the question?"

Question? "Was there one?"

He brushed his lips over hers. "Are you a cuddler or not?"

"Worry about that later," she complained. She tangled her fingers in his hair and tugged, dragging him up to kiss him again. "Right now, kiss me," she ordered.

Aiden grinned. "Close your eyes."

She didn't question, just did as he commanded.

Darkness wrapped her like a heavy blanket, and every brush of their skin together was that much more intense. Aiden didn't say anything else, but she listened.

Waited.

Felt.

He brushed a finger along her rib cage and up to her breast. Ripples of need swept ahead of his touch, over her skin, and when his palm curled over her, she arched into the connection. Aiden's breathing kicked up, but the caress stayed slow. Deliberate. An assault on her senses like the steady drip of a gentle rain.

His hand plumped her breast, thumb skating back and forth over the tight nub of her nipple. His lips reconnected with her neck, and the fluttering sensation in her core not only doubled, but doubled exponentially. A lick, a bite. The rasp of fingernails over her skin.

When he adjusted position and the mattress tilted with his weight, she squeezed her eyes shut to keep from looking because not watching was making her skin tingle like crazy.

When lips wrapped around her nipple, Petra sighed with pleasure. "Oh, God. Don't stop," she ordered. "The touching, and the kissing. All of it. Just keep going. It's *so* good."

That low, sexy rumble answered her, and she decided it

was one of her new favourite things. His amusement, wrapped up in desire and need. An auditory echo of what raced through her body.

"Keep your eyes closed," Aiden reminded softly, lips by her ear for the briefest moment. "Feel. Enjoy. Because I sure the hell will."

Then his lips were on hers and he was kissing her. Deep and hungry and demanding, as if he'd been starving for this. She knew exactly how he felt. The drift of his hands over her body continued, now a scratch, now a pinch. A smooth, gliding caress over her ribs and belly, headed toward her sex.

When his fingers eased through her folds, he hummed again, approval in his tone as he parted her and dipped his fingers to her core. "You make it damn hard to go slow."

"Then go fast." Petra smiled toward the ceiling, her eyes still firmly shut.

Aiden shifted position, cupping both her breasts and teasing the tips of her nipples with his tongue. He nipped lightly, burning away her resistance and building pleasure until she bucked under him, Needing more. Needing his mouth everywhere.

She thrust her fingers back into his hair and tugged, wordlessly trying to guide him where she wanted him.

He chuckled again, but this time it sounded evil. "Not in charge."

"Says you," Petra muttered. She wiggled, slipping down the bed. She kept her eyes closed because now it just amused the hell out of her, but she moved fast enough she flipped him to his back. The element of surprise left her sitting across his thighs, fingers teasing the firm line of his Adonis muscles. "You said something about me not being in charge?"

He caught her hips and tugged her forward. An easy move

full of so much power Petra gasped. "You want to play? Then you get to play. But only the way I allow you."

Petra tilted her head downward. "You notice I've still got my eyes closed."

"Good. Keep them like that until I tell you otherwise."

A shiver rolled outward then rebounded to settle deep in her core. "Why does that make me so hot?"

"Stop trying to analyze it, Petra. Just go with the flow."

He pulled her forward far enough her clit was centred right over the thick ridge of his cock. "*Oh*."

"You want to be in control, have at 'er." When she didn't move for a second, Aiden's fingers tightened and he tugged, rocking her perfectly over his length. Pleasure swirled and pulsed. "Like that," he suggested.

She didn't need any more encouragement. Petra eased her knees a little farther apart, pressed her hands to his chest, and tilted her pelvis. The slow glide felt amazing, and she all but heard her body sing with pleasure.

"Oh, yeah. That's it. Keep that up."

She rocked again, easing into a rhythm. His breathing kicked up, hers as well. While they weren't running a marathon, the gasps and ragged breaths escaping the two of them were close.

Aiden teased his fingers over her breasts. The additional layer of sensation ramped up the building need between her legs, and she increased tempo. Pushed harder, digging in her fingernails, the firm planes of his muscular chest giving her something to hold onto while she brought herself closer and closer. The edge hovered right *there*.

"Open your eyes," Aiden ordered.

She snapped her eyes open and met his gaze, and it happened. Desire exploded outward and she free-fell as the world dropped away. Stars and moons and all that universe stuff swirled as she stared into his laughing eyes.

An aftershock hit, and another, and she moaned, the note long and quavering as it left her throat.

A second later, her back hit the mattress as Aiden rolled them.

Petra didn't mind one bit. She had no muscles left to support herself in the first place.

∼

CHRIST, she was beautiful.

Not just dressed up in her well-worn jeans with her hair loose and soft around her shoulders. Not only when teasing him, eyes dancing with amusement.

Both of those made him sit up and take notice but seeing her explode into ecstasy was a goddamn miracle.

She lay sprawled on the bed, hair tousled on his pillow. Eyelids low and expression sated as he slipped two fingers to the second knuckle into her sex and stroked lazily, caressing the front wall of her sex. Drawing out her pleasure for as long as possible.

"That was fun." Her lips curled up like a cat who'd gotten into the dairy. "So, so, so fucking fun. Fun fucking? Both of them."

"This I also remember about you." He stroked again, curling his fingertips just right.

She breathed deep, hips jerking off the mattress. "What?"

The word breathless and barely there.

His lips twitched with amusement. "You get fuck drunk really quick."

She met his gaze and licked her lips. "Are you saying I'm easy?"

He tempered his laughter because he didn't need the sound to carry down the hall to Jinx. Which was a good solid reminder of why he was about to move this party in a different direction than Petra expected. "It means it's a pleasure to be with you, darlin'. You're a wonder."

Petra stroked her fingers through his hair then caressed the back of her knuckles along his cheek. "Your turn. *Our* turn."

"My turn," he agreed.

She'd find out soon enough there would be no *our turn* for a while.

Before she could tug him back between her legs, he knelt over her, damn near mirroring the position she'd taken on him. A little higher and holding himself off so his weight didn't crush her.

Aiden let his gaze drift. Goddamn perfection lay beneath him, her nipples tight treats on gloriously creamy mounds.

He hummed happily. "I wondered if I'd remembered wrong. There was no way you could have the most perfect tits in the world, but it appears you do."

She opened her mouth to say something, but a low groan was all that escaped as he palmed both her breasts and teased her nipples again.

This part he had also remembered in minute detail. Her breasts were sensitive, and she liked having him play with them. Which meant she should enjoy the next part nearly as much as him.

Nearly. He wasn't saint enough to not take his own pleasure as well. He eased forward and pushed his cock between the hollow of her breasts, stroking softly.

Her eyes widened and she licked her lips again. "You need some lube for that. Want me to suck you and get you wet?"

Fuck. She was a wildfire. "Hell, yeah."

He leaned up and placed the head of his cock on her lower

lip. A growl rumbled up his throat as she teased with her tongue and swiped the sensitive spot under his glans.

"Open. Suck me in," he ordered.

She did as he asked, flicking her tongue all over him. If Aiden hadn't already had an agenda, he would've gotten lost there. Feeding her his cock, pulling back, drowning in sensation.

He stroked a couple more times then pulled out with a *pop*.

She smacked her lips, a gloating smile curling her lips upward. "You don't need to stop," she teased breathlessly.

"Another time. Already made my plans," he countered.

He pushed back between her breasts and groaned at how good it felt. It took three more dips into her mouth before the glide was perfect, then Aiden stopped worrying about deadlines and the logistics of new people coming to High Water. He forgot about how they would have to walk carefully around Jinx and what things needed to happen to keep the rescue financially viable.

He forgot about everything except being in that bed with sweet, giving Petra.

She put her hands over his on her breasts, encouraging him to squeeze harder.

Then she fucking tilted her head so every time his cock popped from the valley between her breasts, her tongue lapped at the crown.

Goddamfuckinghell.

If it didn't feel so good, he'd be embarrassed at how quickly he lost control.

Thankfully, this moment wasn't about impressing anyone. It was about giving pleasure and receiving it. He gave in and accepted the gift she'd offered, hot and dirty and perfect.

Aiden forced his eyes open to stare down at Petra as she

grinned unashamedly at him. His cock jerked and his balls emptied.

Strands of semen lay on the upper part of her chest and chin, and a look of absolute amusement covered her face.

Aiden rolled off and collapsed to his back, grabbing hold of her hand where it lay between them. "Holy fuck."

She laughed but didn't move. "So much for having had my shower already," she teased.

"Yeah, bad planning on my part. Sorry about that."

But he was laughing too.

She slipped from the bed and the water turned on.

Aiden curled himself upright and headed to the bathroom as well. He grabbed a washcloth to do his own cleanup, then straightened the sheets and pillows and put the bed back to rights.

By the time Petra reappeared, this time wearing a pair of pale green pyjama shorts and a matching tank top, he was once again in bed with his briefs in place.

He pulled down the sheet beside him and patted the mattress. "As ordered. Right side of the bed is yours."

She slipped in, laying on her side to face him. Her eyelids were heavy, but her brain was still going a million miles an hour.

"Did you ever decide?" he asked.

She raised a brow.

"Are you a cuddler or no?"

Petra's expression went straight to Happyville. "I am, but I prefer to be the big spoon. Or to cuddle like this, face-to-face."

Huh. "Good by me. Let's try this first."

He tucked his right arm under his head and lifted the quilt, encouraging Petra to slide in against his torso.

She moved closer, tangling their legs together until she was nuzzled up right under his chin.

Aiden dropped a kiss on her forehead then curled her in even tighter. "Tomorrow we'll deal with the next thing. Okay?"

"Yup. Clothes for Jinx, routine for the house. School sign up and—"

He stopped the list by tilting her head back and pressing a brief kiss to her lips. She blinked when he pulled back. "*Tomorrow.*"

She snorted softly, eyelids wavering toward closed. "We also need to plan our engagement story, you realize. Because people will ask."

He didn't answer, but it was true. Things had steamrolled ahead at such an exaggerated rate they hadn't had time for those details. He firmly told *himself* they'd worry about it in the morning before his brain settled into uneasy loops.

Petra was warm in his arms, smelled like heaven, and he still had endorphins from a great sexual release buzzing through his body.

Falling asleep was like dropping into a slice of heaven.

When he woke, he'd rolled. Now facing the edge of the bed, Petra was tucked up against his back, arm draped over him. It felt as if he was wearing a warm, soft backpack. He took a moment to appreciate the situation before sliding away as carefully as possible to avoid waking her.

Eyes still closed, her mouth was open the slightest bit and the cutest little snore escaped her lips.

It only took a moment to get dressed and out of the bedroom, pacing quietly down the hall until Aiden was in the main living space.

Sunday morning. Another thing that they'd have to decide on as a family. At this point, none of them in the house were churchgoers, but that could change. Made sense to have an actual day of rest, though, even if church wasn't involved. A plan for down the road when they didn't have quite so much on the agenda.

He checked the cooking schedule. Declan's name was on the list.

To hell with it.

Aiden didn't mind pulling two days in a row, especially considering how good he felt. Sex did that to a man, he decided as he filled the coffee maker and got out the fixings for breakfast.

The coffee pot was full when dog nails clicked a warning on the hardwood behind him. Dixie bounded into the kitchen, rushing in to bump affectionately against Aiden's shins.

Jinx wandered in a second later wearing a new old pair of jeans and a bulky sweatshirt. Her face was washed and the mess of her hair pulled back into a clumpy knot. She looked at him warily but gave a little wave as Dixie raced back to her side.

"Sleep okay?" Aiden asked.

She nodded, looking around the kitchen and room as if planning the best escape route.

He gestured to the counter three feet to his left where he'd left a big mixing bowl, a dozen eggs, and a few other ingredients. "If you could give me a hand, I'd appreciate it. We're making French toast this morning. Put all dozen eggs into the bowl and add about a cup of milk. Give it a shake or two of cinnamon and one-half teaspoon of vanilla before you whisk it together. I'll get the griddle set up."

Her eyes widened, and this time it seemed with approval. "I can do that."

He continued arranging bacon on racks on cookie sheets to prep them for the oven. "We'll wait to set our official schedule for the day until Jake shows up, because that's something he enjoys. But have you been thinking about what kind of stuff you'll need over the next few days?"

"Some." The egg she held broke crooked, and some of the shell fell into the bowl. She eyed him then grabbed a spoon to fish it out.

Aiden kept on with his task, and after taking a deep breath she did the same.

What was it that Petra had said?

Two steps forward and one step back was still moving forward.

11

It wasn't the loudest or most rambunctious breakfast Petra had ever attended, but there was plenty of food and drink. Jinx looked proud as she placed a platter stacked high with French toast in front of Petra.

Most of the conversation that followed circled around the horses. All three of the brothers had brought their own rides to High Water, but it seemed that Declan was already rounding up extras. Rescues that were still in good enough shape to be ridden both for visitors and for the artists to use as models.

Petra could ride, but she hadn't ever gone crazy over it like some of her friends, so it was a nice background discussion she didn't have to take part in.

Instead, she dug into the food and examined her companions.

Jinx's eyes were tired, but she sat straighter today than yesterday. Dixie rested between Jinx and Petra, but the dog's gaze was one hundred percent on the younger woman—optimistic dog.

The guys looked mostly rested. Aiden wore a far too

satisfied smirk—but it was possible Petra wore that same expression. She'd slept like a rock, which considering the past days was saying something about the potency of a good solid orgasm.

"Petra." Aiden laid a hand on her arm to get her attention.

Dammit. She'd gotten lost in her thoughts again. "You guys must think I have the attention span of a gnat. What's up?"

Jake dipped his chin toward Jinx. "Shopping."

The girl slouched in her chair, breaking eye contact with everyone.

Yeah, shopping was a priority, but something else needed to happen first. "Jinx has enough loaner clothes for now that she and I can take care of that tomorrow. But first, I promised my sister-in-law we'd drop in this morning."

Four sets of eyes bore into her. The masculine ones displayed concern, and Jinx's bore outright consternation.

Which was just fine. None of them had to like it, but considering first impressions were important, they were not going out in public in Heart Falls until there would be no reason for anyone to take a second glance at Jinx other than because she was new.

Petra leaned toward Jinx, curling her fingers to motion her closer. Dropping her volume so the guys couldn't hear, she laid it on the line. "I think I know why you let your hair get to be such a mess. But since we plan on registering you for school, somewhere between tangled knots and dreadlocks is not going to fly. My sister-in-law has dealt with hair disasters, and while neither of us are hairdressers, if you trust us, we can get you looking presentable."

It hadn't been said loudly, but Jinx still glanced around the table at Jake, Declan, and Aiden to see if they were reacting before meeting Petra's gaze. "You'll stay with me?"

"Absolutely." Petra raised her volume to normal levels. "I

think you'll like Julia. Sometime this week, I'm also setting up a girls' night out with my two besties so you can meet them." Petra leaned back and eyed the boys. "There's a lot of testosterone in this house, so us girls have got to make sure we get doses of female power on a regular basis."

Declan's lips twitched, but he dipped his chin. "Jake will go over the numbers with you, but we have money in the budget for more than bread and water. Don't be afraid to spend money on necessities."

"What my brother is inelegantly saying is that you don't have to use the horse shampoo unless you want to." Aiden grinned at the scowl Declan tossed him. "Hey, I'm not saying you smell bad, but..."

A snort escaped Jake. "I've got a credit card for the ranch that we'll give you, Petra." He glanced at Jinx thoughtfully before adding on for her sake. "We've had the ranch in the works for a while, but you can see we're nowhere near ready to open. There's still building to do, and we're figuring out our routine, like we talked about last night."

Jinx stayed quiet, but she nodded.

"If you've got a question about something and we don't have an answer, that's good. Means you're helping us figure things out," Jake said.

The girl was all eyes and cautious hope. "I want to help."

"You will," Aiden promised. "This is going to be your home for as long as you need it. Since you'll be going to school, you'll have chores, not a full-time job. You get to be a teenager, Jinx. That's important for us, too. Not just you."

Moisture was beginning to gather in Jinx's eyes, which Petra didn't think the girl would be comfortable with sharing yet.

She squeezed Aiden's hand gratefully then stood. "Whoever is on cleanup crew with me, let's get rolling. Then

Jinx and I are out. We won't be home for lunch. Who's cooking tonight?"

"Neither of you," Jake said. "Be back by six and we'll have supper ready."

"Deal." Petra met Jinx's gaze. "Go get washed up and be ready to leave in about twenty minutes."

Cleanup went quickly with Declan and Jake both helping Petra. She scooted back to the primary bathroom and did her own morning cleanup, stepping into the living room the same time as Jinx and Dixie.

Aiden sat at the kitchen table, catalogs and paper colour samples spread in front of him. He rose to his feet and joined them on the porch, waiting as they switched their house shoes for outdoor ones. "Call me if you need anything," he said quietly.

"I'm anticipating a very relaxing day," Petra informed him with a grin as she stood. She shoved their inside shoes into a bag then slung it over her shoulder, ready to head out.

He caught her by the wrist and tugged, hands sliding against her lower back until she rested tight against his firm body. "I hope you and Jinx have a wonderful day."

His voice was low and sexy, and she blinked hard for a second before his lips met hers.

He kissed her. Sweet and slow, but it was still enough to set off firecrackers in Petra's brain. The pressure on her lower back held them locked together, and even though Aiden pulled back and released her only a moment later, her heart rate had gone into triple time.

His wide grin washed over her, and his eyes sparkled. "Bye, sweetheart."

It finally clicked. The engagement—Jinx would have wondered if they never shared any public displays of affection.

God, she was glad one of them had remembered.

"Bye." Damn, she wished she was quicker on the uptake and had come up with some annoying cutesy name for him.

They were a few steps up the walk when Aiden cleared his throat. "Petra."

She glanced back.

He held out her purse, amusement in his eyes. "You might need this."

Petra took it gratefully. "At least I wasn't already on the road."

Jinx sat quietly in the passenger seat of the truck, staring out the front window.

She'd seemed more reassured by Petra and Aiden's kiss than frightened, and that had to be a good thing. Mistakes were going to be made, but as long as they kept trying, they'd have to call it a win.

Petra had more than one thing to accomplish today. "Did Danielle show you around town before she dropped you off at the ranch?" she asked.

Jinx shook her head. "I think she was worried. I mean, she wasn't supposed to do what she did. Pick me up and take me somewhere." The girl glanced at Petra. "I'm very grateful. To her and to you guys."

Petra gave a nod of approval. "It's good to be grateful, and we know you are. But now you should concentrate on taking advantage of this fresh start you've been given. It's not always going to be easy." Instead of turning and driving straight out to Red Boot ranch where her sister-in-law was waiting, Petra turned left and headed into Heart Falls proper. "We won't stop anywhere, but I'm going to drive through town before heading to the ranch."

Jinx sat up straighter, nose all but pressed to the side window as Petra gave her a tour. She pointed out the different buildings, including Buns and Roses and where the high school was. Jinx asked a few questions, slowly warming up until it was as close to a full-on conversation as they'd had.

Petra pulled the truck to a stop outside of Julia and Zach's cabin and paused. Time to double check.

"I need to say I'm sorry," Petra began. When Jinx blinked in confusion, Petra shrugged. "I kind of steamrolled you back there at the house, talking about getting your hair straightened out. Your hair is your business. You need to do what you're comfortable with, and my job is to support you. That said, I think you'd get less negative attention if we fix it."

Jinx shook her head. She'd used a big enough scrunchie that the tangled mess was pulled back off her face instead of hiding her features, but it was lopsided and clearly pulling at her scalp in places. "It seemed smart to look as ugly as possible."

Petra shoved down her anger at the assholes who had traumatized this girl so badly that she'd chosen to hide herself away. "So, good to change it up?"

Determined eyes met her gaze. "Please. It's itchy," Jinx confessed. "But it's bad. I don't know if we can fix it. And I'm not a fan of the shaved head look."

"Bald looks good on some people, but yeah. It's not my style either." She tipped her head toward the house and smiled. "Let's see what Julia suggests before breaking out the razor."

Petra knocked on the door and pushed it open at Julia's welcoming call. "Hey, Jules, we're ready for some pampering. I brought Jinx to meet you."

Her sister-in-law stepped forward. Julia's reddish tinged hair hung in gorgeous curls past the edge of her shoulders. She wore faded old jeans with holes in a raggedy hemline and an oversized long-sleeved shirt in pale lavender with the arms pushed up to her elbows. "Hey P. Hello, Jinx. Welcome to my salon." She lifted her gaze to Petra's. "Your brother is out doing important things somewhere near the borderline of the ranch. Cody, that's our foreman, insisted Zach was an important part of planning something way the hell out there. Which means we have the place to ourselves for hours and hours."

Petra took an appreciative sniff. "Did you make cinnamon buns?"

Amusement danced over Julia's face. "Yes, if picking up the phone and calling Tansy and begging for a home delivery counts as making them."

Jinx snickered. She accepted the bag Petra handed her, glancing inside to discover the pair of house shoes. The relief in her eyes was huge as she sat to switch them over. "Thank you."

"No problem, kiddo. Remember, one step at a time, and sometimes that's easier when you got shoes on." Petra put on her own slippers—a regular pair this time in case things got wildly messy. She didn't want to ruin her birthday present dragons. "Julia. What can I do to help and where do you want us?"

Behind her, Jinx was exchanging one pair of shoes for the other. Julia's gaze danced over then back up to Petra. She nodded in approval. "I guess we need to take a look first to see how bad it is."

She'd put two chairs side by side at the kitchen table and arranged a freestanding mirror that was big enough to see all of one person directly or two if they squished.

Petra sat next to Jinx.

Julia leaned her hip on the table. "First off, I'm sure Petra and Aiden told you that my husband and I are also your safe people. We don't know everything, but we know enough that we'll do whatever we need to help keep you safe. Okay?"

She waited until Jinx nodded.

"Now comes the part that could be easy for you, or really tough, and neither one is wrong." Julia folded her arms over her chest and leaned back, making a face. "This isn't common knowledge, but I had a stalker once. When things were at their worst, I got trapped in a tough situation where I didn't have much control over taking care of myself. Not telling you this so you feel bad for me, but so you know one result of that was my hair got messed up."

"You've kind of been where I'm at?" Jinx asked.

"Only in so far that I know that I can't help you unless I touch your hair. Plus, working out the knots will cause a fair bunch of tugging and pulling. It will be uncomfortable, but if you're okay with it, we can get started."

Petra wiggled her shoulder where it pressed against Jinx's. "If you need a breather, just say that."

Jinx stared at her reflection. "I don't want to look like this anymore."

Thank God for brave young women. "Then let's get to work."

They soaked the mess down and got to work using straight combs and picks and the gentlest touch possible. Julia was amazing through it all, which made sense considering she'd worked in the emergency services area for years. She seemed to have a knack at helping Jinx to relax.

When they came up with a combination of conditioner and coconut oil that loosened the knots, Petra's hopes rose. They wouldn't have to cut it all off.

Hours later, after a few breaks to enjoy the cinnamon buns and some hot tea, and to get lunch, they were done.

Looking a little like a wet dog, long strands of untangled deep brown hair hung around Jinx's face. But this time it was not because she was hiding, but because she was trying to keep the dripping strands from getting in her eyes. "I hope you have a shower," she said.

"Absolutely," Julia said. "Plus, like we talked about, I have some more clothes that might fit you. But I think a trip to the store with my niece might be a good idea in the next couple of days."

Jinx froze with the towel in her hand held to her chest. "Your niece?"

"Sasha," Julia informed her. "She's nearly your age, so chances are you'll end up in the same class at school."

Part of Petra wanted to protect Jinx and protest that it was too soon. But part of moving forward meant keeping the momentum going.

"If you don't want to, we won't. But I can vouch for Sasha," Petra said. "Other than being a lot more horse-obsessed than you, she's a great girl with a little sister and brother she mothers like crazy. She's someone I'd want on my side."

Jinx nodded, but she still looked unhappy. "That makes sense. Can we meet her before we go shopping? You think?"

Everything was possible. Petra considered. "What about at Buns and Roses?" she suggested to Julia. "Tomorrow is a school day, but I don't think Sasha would be upset about getting taken to lunch."

"I'll talk to her mom." Julia paused. "Did you guys figure out the story you're going to tell people in town? About who you are and the rest of it?"

"Some of it," Jinx told her. "Declan said we'd do the rest of it this afternoon, so we can tell you soon."

"That works. I'll wait to hear from you, but chances are high you'll get to meet Sasha tomorrow. Then, if you're comfortable, we can go shopping as soon as school is done." Julia pointed toward the bathroom. "Go wash all that stuff out. Shampoo, then use the conditioner and leave it in for at least five minutes. I put everything you can use on the counter. It's all brand-new and yours. The clothes are loaners, but you keep them until you have your own stuff."

Jinx covered her head with the towel and stood awkwardly, glancing between them. "I know I keep saying it, but thanks for helping. And thanks for trying to make it easier. I mean it. Maybe I'm a little scared, but today is so much better than two days ago."

She vanished, leaving Petra and Julia staring after her.

"Give me thirty minutes with the bastards she was living with before." Julia said it calmly and coolly as if discussing the weather. "Fifteen, even. I'm feeling motivated."

"It's a familiar sentiment, and you'd have to join a line right now," Petra told her. She stepped closer and wrapped her sister-in-law in a hug, squeezing tightly. Letting go of some of the sadness and focusing on the good parts that had happened that morning. "I'm glad I've got you."

"Ditto. Plus I'm glad that girl's got you," Julia returned. She stepped back and looked Petra in the eyes. "I thought maybe you were getting in over your head with the fake engagement thing and the rest of it. But I see why you did it. I'm *glad* you did it, and you know we'll go to bat for you, and for Jinx, no matter what."

"Thanks."

One more change. One more step, with a whole hell of a lot more to go. But Petra realized her sister-in-law was right. Being at High Water was both necessary and vital. For Jinx and herself.

12

Petra had texted him a heads-up she and Jinx were finally on the way home, which meant Aiden and his brothers were already in the house when her truck pulled into the parking spot outside the main door.

Declan checked the temperature on the oven then went back to tossing salad in an enormous bowl. "Did Petra say it went well?"

"Well enough. Said to remind us to keep the comments about Jinx's improved appearance as brotherly as possible."

The sound of the ladies as they chatted on the porch and dealt with their footwear brought Aiden forward to the door.

First through was Petra. "Hey, guys. We're all relaxed from our spa day, but we're starving. It smells good in here."

"Lasagna," Declan informed her. "Lazy Lasagna, because I suck at the layering thing."

"Yum. You like pasta, Jinx?"

The girl stepped forward, eyes on the floor for a second before she straightened. "Pasta's good."

Without the tangled mess hanging across her face, Jinx's

pretty features were the first thing Aiden noticed. The dark circles under her eyes made her look even more delicate and breakable than before, but the sweep of long, straight, brown hair looked far more comfortable than the rat's nest she'd worn when she left the house that morning.

Time for a bit of careful complimenting. "Hey, Jinx. Looks as if Petra and Julia helped you out."

Declan hummed in approval. "Does it feel better?"

"So much better." Ignoring Aiden, Jinx focused on Declan. "It took a lot of work, but Julia's nice. She loaned me a bunch of clothes, and she said once you and I figure out my story for good to let her know, because she's going to call her older sister and then I'm supposed to meet her niece Sasha so we can go shopping."

Aiden blinked in surprise at the outpouring of words.

Thankfully, Declan kept his cool and just nodded slowly, still mixing the lettuce. "Then we'll talk that through after supper so you can give Julia a call. I wrote down a few ideas. I think we're nearly there."

Jinx stood a little straighter then unconsciously ran her fingers through her hair as if she couldn't believe the difference. "Okay." She smiled, a shocking surprise. "Julia said she'd heard about you."

"Hopefully good things." The buzzer on the stove went off, and Declan moved to shut it off. "Wash up everyone. Supper's ready."

Aiden waylaid Petra at the sink in their bedroom. "Jinx looks a million times better, but not just on the surface. She's still on edge but doesn't have that kicked puppy look in her eyes. I take it your trip went better than we could have hoped for."

Petra eased her hip against the counter and considered. "Julia's a rock star, so give her most of the credit. Between bonding over hair trauma—Julia's got one hell of a story that I'll have to tell you sometime—and her solid know-how as a trauma care worker, my sister-in-law worked magic. She had Jinx laughing by the end of the visit."

Hell, yeah. "Thank God for that. Let's hope it continues."

They sat in the same seats as that morning, which allowed Aiden to observe the entire family as they passed around the bowls filled high with crisp green salad and the steaming hot savoury pasta. Jinx talked more than she had the day before, mostly to Petra and Declan. Aiden didn't mind, and Jake seemed more distracted than usual and wasn't contributing much to the conversation anyway.

They met at the firepit a little earlier that night.

"Come give me a hand," Aiden called to Petra before she settled in with her crocheting.

She checked for Jinx first, but the girl was tossing a ball for Dixie, the retriever dancing with excitement every time the ball got scooped into the thrower.

"Jinx could be busy at that for hours," Aiden said with a smile as Petra joined him.

"That works. It's been a full day, and a positive one, but Jinx not having time to start worrying about tomorrow's trouble is good." Petra eyed the rope in Aiden's hands. "Do I want to know?"

"Relax, darling, nothing kinky. It's for a swing," he assured her. "There's a good spot in the doorway of the barn, and I thought Jinx would enjoy one. In the meantime, you and I need to decide our dating history, and I figured now is as good a time as any."

"Okay." She paced at his side to the doorway. "We should keep it simple."

"Drat. That means the costume ball where you raced off at midnight and left behind your glass slipper is out."

She snorted. "Yeah. Neither of us fit that story. I'm no Cinderella."

He paused in climbing the ladder to offer a shocked expression. "You saying I'm no Prince Charming?"

"You're more the Flynn Ryder type," she informed him with a drawl.

"Ha." Aiden hooked the rope over the beam and set to tying a solid knot. "I don't mind that. Flynn is a decent dude."

"Once you get past the thieving and lying, he's a catch," Petra agreed.

Aiden laughed. "What about online dating?"

"Maybe. Could you have worked in Manitoba recently? My parents' place is rural Brandon." She eyed him, confusion slipping into her eyes. "Wait a second. I just thought of something. Jake was working in law enforcement, but he's now your ranch manager, yes?"

"Yes." Where was she going with this?

"Declan is obviously head of the animal part of this operation." Petra raised a brow. "I can't believe it's taken until now to ask this, but what exactly is your job? When we met three years ago, you were a ranch hand."

"That title works for me." Aiden's feet hit the dirt-covered ground. Petra held the solid wooden seat in place as he worked to add knots there as well.

She didn't let the topic go. "You're a ranch hand. But you know Danielle well enough she trusts you and your family with a stranger's life..." Petra shook her head. "Heck, *I* trusted you enough to agree to this entire scheme without hesitating. What kind of magic are you tossing around?"

"I'm not that complicated, Petra. I like people of all ages, and they tend to like me." Aiden shrugged. Some people were impressed by titles and a fancy education, but she didn't strike him as that type. "I talk to everyone, and I try to shoot straight with them the way our stepdaddy taught us. Maybe having people's backs is a lost trait in this day and age, but I still believe in it. So yeah, people trust me."

Even though the lies he'd have to tell going forward would be rising exponentially.

The ball went bouncing past them, followed instantly by a blur of golden fur as Dixie raced after it.

"Sorry," Jinx called.

He waved at the girl. "Practice getting Dixie to stay for a bit before you tell her *fetch*."

"Okay." Jinx glanced around, checking where Jake and Declan were before continuing her task.

Petra looked thoughtful as she discreetly watched Jinx.

"We'll come back to our story, but I have to say it. I'm shocked at how well it's going," Aiden admitted. "Am I imagining things, or has Jinx decided Declan is okay? Or at least more okay than me and Jake? Which I don't mind at all, but..."

"No, you're right. Julia again," Petra shared. "Turns out the foreman at Red Boot ranch has been singing Declan's praises to everyone who will listen. For some reason, Cody went along as backup when Declan went to pick up a rescue horse about a month ago. The guy they took the horse from thought he could change his mind at the last minute, but Declan made it clear that treating the animal cruelly meant he'd lost all rights to the beast."

"Sounds like Declan."

"Julia said you can tell a lot about a man from how he treats animals and how animals treat him back. Jinx was quiet for a bit, but you could tell she was putting two and two together and coming up with *Declan is a good guy*."

"That's a good solid base for what we're building here at

High Water." Aiden patted the seat and held the ropes. "Hop on."

Petra twisted and sat. "Our story?"

He was enjoying this immensely, Aiden realized. Chatting with Petra, coming up with plans. Sharing bits of his past.

It helped that she took his simple job in stride, and even seemed to admire what he was able to do without a list of shiny letters behind his name. None of which was necessary for their deception, but all of it very important if he wanted to take their relationship past simply being an obligatory lie.

"Keep it simple," he suggested. "We met three years ago right here in Heart Falls—which is no lie. We just don't mention more than the public portion of the evening."

She snickered. "Let me guess. We've been messaging and getting together when we could ever since."

"Absolutely. And when my brothers and I decided to make a new home here in Heart Falls, I proposed to you." He brushed his cheek over hers from behind and whispered. "It was very romantic."

"Of course it was," Petra said with amusement.

"A horseback ride followed by a picnic. We sat by the creek and decided we'd start our lives at our new home engaged." Aiden pushed her gently. "You didn't want a ring."

"Convenient for you."

"Very." He pushed harder, and she flew higher. "Sound like enough story?"

"Yes. Especially if both of us remember the cardinal rule of lying. Less is more." Petra dragged her feet on the ground to stop. She stood and twisted to face him. "Ask more questions than you offer answers."

Aiden raised a brow. "You speak as if you have lots of experience at this," he teased.

Her expression changed for the briefest moment before her

smile returned. "Well, no more than the average person. Did you bring your guitar?"

Interesting. Aiden might not have magic, but he did have a highly tuned sense of intuition. Petra was absolutely keeping a secret, more than the one he'd tangled her into.

Now he had to decide what to do about that tidbit of information.

∼

If Petra had any doubts about how appropriate it was to ask Sasha to help Jinx, they vanished within the first five minutes of the girls meeting at Buns and Roses.

After the initial hellos and greetings were exchanged, Sasha guided Jinx through ordering at the counter before leading the entire group to a table at the side of the room. It was amusing to watch Sasha organize to her heart's content, putting Jinx in a corner spot where she could look around but not easily be stared at in return.

Sasha plied Jinx with a few questions but mostly shared everything about herself and her family. She told stories about her little sister Emma, and even littler brother Tyler, her three uncles and aunties, and her horse. She shared how the math teacher at the high school had no sense of humour at all and asked if Jinx liked math or English better.

"Sasha's like a well-trained border collie," Julia told Petra quietly but with great amusement. "Doesn't matter how many chicks she's got under her eye at one time, she tries to keep them all close enough to care for."

"Sounds like the kind of backup Jinx might need at school." Gaze still on the girls, she spoke sideways to her sister-in-law. "Anything else you need to share? How are you these days?"

Julia gave her a questioning glance.

Petra shrugged. "Every time I've seen you over the last week it's been because I've been in dire need. Just reminding you that I like you for yourself and not your emergency rescue abilities."

"I love you too," Julia assured her. "As for the rest, don't worry about it. There are times for reminiscing or getting to know people better, and others to offer a helping hand. Family doesn't keep an IOU list."

Petra squeezed her fingers. "You're awesome."

"I am. I'm also curious." Julia lowered her voice. "What's this I hear about you and Aiden sharing a room?"

Good grief. Petra's face flushed. "Fishing for information again?"

"I'm not fishing. I'm listening to what's happening on the other side of the table. Jinx just told Sasha how the house is arranged now. Sasha had been in the house before because the previous owner used to babysit her and Emma at times. Jinx said Mrs. Fallen's room is now Petra *and* Aiden's."

"The fact you heard that while we're talking means you have Superman-level hearing," Petra complained.

"Forget how I heard it, just tell me everything's okay."

Screw keeping the fooling around part secret. Although they still hadn't done the actual deed again, last night Aiden had thoroughly rocked her world by going down on her in the shower before jacking off with her help.

Petra let her grin grow wide. "Everything is better than okay."

Julia snickered. "As long as it stays that way and you're having fun, I won't ask for any more details."

"Auntie Julia." Sasha spoke louder to get their attention.

"Yes?"

"Jinx needs some new clothes, and Mom said I could go shopping with her. But it's going to have to be tomorrow after supper because we can't go tonight, and tomorrow I've got a training session with Kelli right after school. Can you take me? Mom won't be able to because of Tyler. That's my kid brother," Sasha reminded Jinx. "He's only four and he goes to bed really early."

"If your mom says it's okay, and you don't have lots of homework, I can take you. It is a school night," Julia pointed out.

Sasha shrugged. "I never have much homework." She turned to confide in Jinx. "Nothing that I can't do on the ten-minute bus ride home. It's a nice short trip."

Jinx's gaze snapped to Petra's. She swallowed hard, forcing out her question. "You ride a bus?"

Sasha waved a hand. "It's no big deal. We're one of the last picked up in the morning and the first dropped off headed home, and since you live on the next range road over, you'll have an even shorter ride. It's not like in the city where buses get separated by age. Here they pick up everybody according to area, including the kindergarten kids, so it's noisy sometimes, but not bad." Sasha frowned, noticing Jinx's discomfort. "It's okay. Haven't you ever taken a bus?"

Jinx shook her head. "I've always lived close enough to walk."

Petra didn't have to be a mind reader to know that the idea of the bus wasn't sitting comfortably with Jinx, but they could cover that one when they were alone.

"Hello, ladies. Welcome to the best café in town," Tansy announced in a cheerful voice as she brought their order to the table. She took in each of them one after the other with amusement. "Making friends and planning mischief?"

"It's always good to have mischief afoot," Petra reminded her.

"My thoughts exactly." Tansy placed dishes on the table in

front of everyone before adding a plate for herself and pulling another chair over to join them. "Which is why I'm here. Hi, Jinx. I'm Tansy. I'm the smart, funny friend to these two." She poked her thumbs in either direction to indicate Julia and Petra. "So, what are we gossiping about? Who's broken whose heart in school today, Sasha?" She glanced to her left. "You pregnant yet, Julia?"

"*Tansy*," Petra scolded in shock. "That's rude."

"What?" Tansy threw her hands in the air as a look of understanding crossed her face. "Oh, you missed this part. It's not rude; it's a tease. Well, it's sort of rude, but it's not my fault. Zach came in here two months ago and ordered peanut butter cookie ice cream sandwiches with pickles. And we all know what *that* means."

Julia let out a long-suffering sigh. "He was supposed to buy the ice cream sandwiches. Then he remembered that he broke the pickle jar the previous day and he didn't want to have to stop at the store for one item, thus the pickle request." She offered Tansy the evil eye. "Only ever since, *this* one uses it at every opportunity."

"What can I say? When I'm offered a golden ticket, I take it." Tansy grinned as she picked up her sandwich. "I was serious about heartbreaks at school, Sasha. Is José still trying to convince you to be his sweetie?"

Sasha sighed mightily. "Auntie *Julia*."

"What?" Julia echoed in protest this time.

Sasha gave her the evil eye. "You were the only person I talked to about José."

Julia lifted a hand. "Yes, you told me. But that same day Kelli told me you'd said something about him. Then your mother mentioned him to me. Plus, your Auntie Ginny told me that you told her that Katy said Jason told her that—"

Petra was laughing so hard at this point her words came out

in gasps. "Oh my God. You could just walk into the classroom with the teenage girls," she told Julia.

"Sweet," Julia offered, grinning from ear to ear.

While Sasha animatedly shared about José, it was Jinx who held Petra's attention. Her gaze darted back and forth between everyone at the table, her mouth falling open as the teasing continued. When Sasha tossed her hair like a mane to make a point, Jinx snickered, covering her mouth with her hand, but Petra spotted her brief smile.

Both heartwarming and hope filled.

The door to Buns and Roses opened, the welcome bell tinkled, and a broad-shouldered man wearing a cowboy hat marched in. Petra blinked then checked her watch. Why was Jake coming in at this time of day?

She wondered if something had gone wrong and he was trying to track them down. She waved to get his attention. "Jake. Over here."

His head snapped up, and he blinked, as if not only surprised to see her, but to discover himself inside the shop. "Hey."

Tansy snickered. She bounced upright and brushed her hands off. "Well, girls, I hope you have a lovely time shopping later. Excuse me, I have something I need to do."

She darted from the table and grabbed Jake by the hand, towing him through the swinging kitchen doors.

The table was quiet for a second before Sasha demanded, "Who was that?"

Jinx spoke, her answer quiet but clear. "That's Jake. He's a brother to my brother-in-law. Jake is the middle one, and he's very organized," Jinx informed her.

Sasha's look of concern shifted to one that was slightly more approving. "Being organized is good," she said. "Kelli says people who don't think things through are like a guy who can't organize a piss-off at a brewery."

"*Sasha.*" Both Petra and Julia scolded at the same moment, but Jinx's grin was nearly as wide as the one Petra felt stretching her lips.

"Sometime soon you'll have to visit Silver Stone ranch and meet the source of all these Kelli-isms," Julia promised Jinx.

"Kelli's awesome," Sasha agreed as she checked the time. "I need to get back. You want us to come pick you up tomorrow, or are you going to drive to our place, Ms. Sorensen?" she asked Petra.

"We'll come get you after supper," Petra offered. "If anything changes, you have my number."

Sasha nodded. "Once you get a phone, Jinx, I'll give you my number so you and I can text." She made a face. "We have a whole ton of rules about texting, so I'll have to go over them with you. My mom and dad are really strict."

It was the easy complaint of a kid who knows exactly how good they've got it.

As the girls continued to chat, a flash of understanding struck so hard Petra leaned back in her chair and groaned softly.

Julia frowned. "P?"

Petra offered a smile that was probably a little shaky around the edges. "I just realized I'm basically proxy mom to a teenager. Enforcement of rules and regulations and all the rest of it." The idea was mind-boggling. "You're supposed to break your teeth on the parental skill set when they're small. Then if you muck up, you can just lift them bodily and put them where they're supposed to go."

Julia laughed. "I think you've had enough mothering over the years to be able to deal with this just fine. Plus, you're not on your own. Remember that. There are a whole lot of people around you willing to offer more advice than you want."

They were back in the truck and headed to High Water when Jinx tugged lightly on Petra's sleeve to get her attention. "I like Sasha," she said. "Thanks for setting that up."

"No problem. I guess we're headed out shopping tomorrow, then?"

Jinx nodded. She stared out the window, gaze flitting from place to place.

Maybe it was just Petra's imagination, but Jinx's examination of the town seemed less as if she were memorizing the area in case she needed to make a fast getaway and more like she was just soaking in her surroundings.

One more step forward.

13

*P*etra and Jinx strolled into the artists' studio, a stream of happy chatter flowing between them that made Aiden smile. He didn't stop, though, other than to toss a wink Petra's way. "Everything work out?"

She nodded. "Operation shopping trip is on for tomorrow after supper."

"Awesome. I'd give you a thumbs-up, Jinx, but my hands are full." He waved with the mudding trowel in his right hand.

She walked toward him, Dixie bumping into her heels. "What're you doing?"

"Mudding. Let's me return to my inner child," he said in a teasing tone. "More importantly, it covers the screws and the seams between the sheets of drywall and turns it into one solid piece. If I do a good job, that is."

"You damn well better do a good job," Jake called from the other side before slamming his lips shut and looking embarrassed. "Sorry, ladies."

For a second, Petra had to stop to think about what he was

apologizing for before offering him an *are you kidding me* look. "You can't even say damn?"

Beside her, Jinx snickered softly. "What about *drats* or *goodness gracious?*"

"Maybe holy cow is off the list." Petra grinned at the girl before stepping closer to the wall and examining Aiden's work. "So far I see nothing but excellent results on this side of the room."

Aiden scooped up another load of mudding plaster and smeared it as smoothly as possible over the screw heads holding the drywall in place. "It's boring work," he told them. "But it's also kind of soothing."

"Can I help?" Jinx asked.

"You can help me," Jake offered from across the room. "My job isn't boring."

"I don't know if she's allowed to work with you. You've got such a potty mouth," Petra teased. "Who knows what unfortunate things will escape and fall into Jinx's ears."

Jinx bumped into Petra, giggling softly. "Stop that. I want to help."

Petra placed a hand on the girl's shoulders and pushed her gently toward where Jake stood, a pile of sanding blocks on the table beside him. "Have at 'er. I'll stick around, but I need to get some computer work done. I'll be over there," she offered.

Jinx was already off, headed determinedly toward her target.

Petra strolled to Aiden's side, staying just far enough back he could work without interruption.

"Jinx is in a good mood," he offered quietly.

"Sasha Stone was exactly what the doctor ordered. Jinx having a friend like her will work out fine." Petra watched him for a minute. "You're not bad. I've helped with house renovations a time or two, and you've got a few of the tricks down pat."

"I spent a summer doing this right after high school," Aiden told her. "My stepdad, Jeff, was a firm believer that staying busy was a good way to keep a young man out of trouble. We all got training in a trade, even Jake, who went straight into the police academy at the end of his first summer."

Petra looked thoughtful. "I'm surprised to see he beat us here. He showed up at Buns and Roses during lunch."

"Really?" Jake hadn't put it on the schedule, but then again, he was in charge of his time. "He showed up about ten minutes ago. Maybe he's gathering information for once we've got the artists' resident set up. Hosting for special events and that kind of thing. Tansy as a caterer would be great."

Happiness bloomed on Petra's face. "I love the idea of giving work to people we like. Tansy would do a great job."

Petra offered a final smile then retreated to the middle of the room where two folding chairs nestled under a small table. She pulled a tablet from her purse and set it up as a miniature computer, fingers flying over the portable keyboard.

Aiden carried on overlaying another smooth ribbon of plaster over each section Jake had already sanded smooth.

His playlist of country music pulsed softly in the background as Jake taught Jinx how to use the sanding block. She dragged one stroke after the other across the buildup of plaster, switching to a clockwise motion when Jake told her to. Slowly the fine grit paper knocked all the ridges down until the wall was smooth to the touch.

"That's perfect," Jake encouraged. "Use a little more pressure to start, and after those first few broad strokes, keep your motions small and circular. Makes it easier for me to knock off any final ridges that show up."

Jinx worked for a while. "You guys know how to do lots of things."

"That's because of our stepdad." Jake echoed Aiden's earlier admission. "He thought if it was worthwhile doing, everybody should learn how. It didn't matter what, we were supposed to do it to the best of our ability and give it long enough to see if a talent needed to be built to make it more enjoyable."

"It wasn't just about work," Aiden added. "The same thing applied to the arts. The man never blinked when he learned I was playing classical guitar. Just nodded and told me that he'd learned to play the flute when he was young."

Jinx considered. "Was he any good?"

It was not so much the question as her longing tone that said Aiden was adding music lessons to the list of things to get the girl involved in during the coming days.

Anything that made a person light up that bright was worth exploring.

"Was Jeff any good? You know, it was the damnedest thing," Jake offered. "He had just started to date our mom, Nancy. Here we are, all wondering who this man was and if he was going to be any improvement over our bio dad. Or at least Declan and I were wondering. Aiden was like a puppy dog in love from the moment Jeff arrived." Jake flashed him a grin. "Although that's not something to tease you about since it turned out you were the smartest person in the room. Still, Declan and I were worried, and not sure about the whole flute thing. But here's Aiden playing some goddamn-awful piece over and over—"

"Watch your language, bro. Also, I was *practicing*," Aiden declared. "It's supposed to sound terrible."

Jake raised a brow. "Jeff comes in and plops down beside

him. He pulls out a case and assembles his flute, listening all the time and somehow not cringing."

"Hey," Aiden complained.

Petra didn't look up from her screen, but her lips twisted into a bigger smile.

"Then he tells Aiden to go back to the beginning. After only a few seconds, Jeff starts playing along. A side melody, not quite what Aiden was playing—thank God—but something like a bird song that floated over the guitar notes. Declan and I, we stood there with our jaws hanging open, and all thoughts about how lame it was for a big tough guy to be playing something like a flute vanished. It was sheer magic."

"For me too," Aiden said softly. "I think every time I practiced after that, I was hoping that same magic would return when I played on my own."

Jinx met his gaze across the room. "I think you found it."

"Thanks, kiddo. That means a lot. Music is something that's very personal and yet a great way to share with others."

Jinx went back to sanding. "Did you learn to play an instrument, Jake?"

"I did, but my choice was more aggressive. I decided on the drums."

"Our mom was gone by then," Aiden told her. "Jake was doing his teenage rebellion thing, but he knew better than to swear or get mad at Jeff."

"He wouldn't have let me get away with it." Jake agreed. "He was tough but fair. I think we respected that more than if he'd let us get away with things or been overly strict. He's the reason I went into the police force."

Jinx stopped completely. "You're a cop?"

Jake chuckled at the disbelief in her tone. "*Was* a cop. Fifteen years, but eventually, I realized it wasn't for me. Not a forever-until-I-retire type job. I'm glad I did it, but it was time for something new."

She nodded. "I think it would be a tough job."

"Tough on everybody," he agreed. "My ex-wife would tell you it's harder on the ones who don't pull the shift."

This time Jinx glanced at Aiden. She mouthed the question at him. *He was married?*

"It's not a secret," Aiden told her out loud. "Remember, we're still getting to know each other, so you're allowed to ask questions. Jake was married, but his wife liked the idea more than the reality of being married to someone who had responsibilities other than taking care of her demands."

Not that he should answer for his brother, but Jake usually made the failed marriage about his mistakes and nothing about his wife's. Aiden was tired of it.

Jake shrugged. "We dove in too soon. We were young, and it lasted under a year. Which was good in a way," he added. "We hadn't started a family, so there were no kids involved."

"Did you want a family?" Jinx asked. "If that's not too personal to ask."

Testing the boundaries, Aiden thought. He'd said she could ask questions to find out what she was curious about.

How willing were they to follow through?

Thankfully, this was one topic Jake had zero troubles sharing. "I do want a wife and kids someday, but there's still time. Right now, I want to get High Water up and running and things solidly settled before I think about getting serious with anyone."

"That's smart."

Jake examined the wall, running a hand slowly over it. "You're doing a great job."

"Thanks." She got back to work, full concentration on her task.

Dixie moved easily under her feet, staying just far enough out of her way that Jinx didn't trip over her. The sandpaper in Jinx's hand ghosted over the wall with a steady *scratch, scratch, scratch*.

At the table, Petra worked steadily, fingers flying again now that the conversation had slowed. Aiden paused for a break to allow Jinx and Jake to get farther ahead, moving to join Petra.

She completely ignored him.

Good powers of concentration. "You're far away," he said, dropping into the chair at her side.

Petra jerked slightly as she glanced up. "Sorry. I didn't hear you."

He chuckled. "I'm obviously not distracting enough. I end up right beside you and you don't even notice."

Her gaze darted over him, lingering on his forearms. He'd rolled up his sleeves, and small splotches of grey mud clung here and there where they'd fallen while he worked. "Yeah, you're kind of invisible. That camouflage paint is doing its job."

"I'll need to wash up later," he said, lowering his tone and putting all sorts of innuendo into his words. "Might need some help."

If she hadn't been aware of the buzz of connection between them before, he could tell she absolutely was now from the way her eyes sparkled. "You *are* rather dirty."

A terrible idea struck. He slid his right hand over the mudding tray he held below the table, coating his fingers in a thin layer of slick plaster. "What are you working on?"

"Research." She said it quickly and with an uneasy expression.

So very not Petra-like. Aiden eyed her. "You'll be doing the accounting for Red Boot ranch, right?"

She nodded, that odd expression turning slightly guilty.

"I'll set up the software they'll use and do data entry, but I'm not certified for the actual tax and payroll stuff."

"You're not setting it up right now?"

More guilt. "Just exploring."

Which was as much of a *don't ask so I don't tell you any lies* as he'd ever heard.

Under the table, he made sure his hand was good and coated. She deserved what he had in mind.

He dropped the tray on the table then leaned closer, cupping her face in his hands. Pressing their lips together, he kissed her soundly. A quick nip to her lower lip, and she gasped. Aiden took full advantage, adjusting her head to the side and taking the kiss deep enough to drive them both wild.

Petra pulled away, little huffs escaping from between her open lips. "That was dangerous," she said, hands rising to touch her cheeks. She frowned, staring down at the grey dust off her cheek that now covered her fingers before glowering at him. "That was evil."

"Just wanted to make sure you were sufficiently motivated to join me in the shower later."

Petra rolled her eyes, but after checking Jinx to make sure the girl was okay, she scooted forward and caught hold of his T-shirt. "In for a penny, in for a pound," she whispered before latching on and kissing him back as good as she'd gotten. A kiss with enough fire and sass that every cell in his body stood up and took notice.

Hands brushed over his chest before she dragged her nails down his torso and his muscles clenched tight under her touch.

She unlatched, leaning her forehead against his as they both breathed rapidly. Her blue eyes held his for the longest moment before she pushed away.

"Time to get back to work," Petra announced before calmly

turning to her computer, ignoring the grey streaks drying on her cheeks.

Aiden laughed, avoiding the questioning glare his brother offered, and returned to his task.

Sexy shower time before supper. It was always good to have something to look forward to.

~

JINX WAS CURLED up in her chair with Dixie sprawled over her legs, reading a book Sasha Stone's Uncle Walker had dropped off for her to borrow.

Petra's stomach was full and happy, and little endorphins still bubbled in her bloodstream after the quick and efficient orgasm Aiden had gifted her in the shower. He'd also helped wash the mud off her cheeks, grinning evilly the entire time.

The man was trouble, but Petra was enjoying his mischief far more than she'd expected.

Aiden and Declan were doing the dishes. Jake silently sat at the table, one of his ever-present notebooks in front of him, but his gaze drifted back and forth between his younger brother and where Petra was puttering on her computer a couple chairs down the table.

She wasn't about to ask what was on Jake's mind. If he didn't approve of her and Aiden fooling around, she didn't care. They were adults. Their decision.

But when Jake's phone pinged with a message and he cursed softly without apologizing, that got her attention.

"Jake?"

He met her eyes. "Small setback. Aiden? Can you give me a hand over here?" Jake glanced at Jinx to make sure she was occupied then spoke softly as Aiden settled in the chair next to

Petra. "My contact within the ID database is out of the country right now."

Aiden made a frustrated noise. "That's the guy who's supposed to help get Jinx new ID and registered for school?"

"Yep." Jake checked his phone. "I wondered why he was slow getting back to me. Turns out, he's gone for at least two more weeks."

"That's going to make it damn awkward," Aiden complained.

Butterflies went jigging in Petra's gut. She wanted to keep her mouth shut but couldn't. Holding off on Jinx starting school could lead to a series of questions that would cause far more trouble in the long run.

She took a deep breath before softly offering her help, "I might be able to do it."

Two heads pivoted her way, intense stares in place. Jake frowned. Aiden looked puzzled.

He spoke quietly. "Petra?"

Damn. How did one confess to having hacker skills? "I work in IT. I'm very curious, also snoopy, and at one point I might have accidentally discovered a few back doors into some governmental files."

Jake's mouth hung open in shock, but if anything, Aiden looked impressed. "Seriously? You just happen to be able to hack your way into a database?"

"No promises, but chances are good." Shit. She was going to be in so much trouble if the expression on Jake's face meant he had too much straight and narrow still left in his system. "This is all hypothetical."

Aiden must've come to the same conclusion because he twisted to face his brother. "If you need to not be here for possible deniability, move your ass."

"No. I'm good. Just wrapping my brain around the new

unexpected twist." Jake raised a brow at Petra. "Hypothetically, what would you need right now?"

"Someone to distract Jinx so she doesn't accidentally interrupt what I'm doing would be a good start," Petra suggested. "Then I'll need the paperwork Danielle gave us so I can trace through the current system and make some modifications. Adjustments are always easier than starting fresh."

Aiden was already typing quickly on his phone. A second later, Declan hauled his phone from his pocket and frowned at the screen. He glanced up at Jinx then checked his watch. "I guess we should go do those chores in the barn. Jinx? You okay to give me a hand?"

Jinx slipped a bookmark between the pages of her book before checking with Petra. "You need me for anything?"

"You're good to go help Declan." Petra lifted her chin. "Tonight by the fire, I'll get you started on those beginning crochet stitches you wanted to learn."

"Okay."

Dixie stretched lazily, back arching and butt up, before daintily prancing forward to join Declan and Jinx as they headed out the door.

Aiden took off to grab the file. Jake flipped pages in his notebook before twisting it toward her. "This is everything I was going to send my contact. Jinx's new name, address, and all the info on Declan's in-laws. What else do you need?"

A bunch of luck and for her nerves to stop skittering. "Keep track of what I change so we can double check it at the end. I don't want this to fall apart because I miss something easy."

Petra took a deep breath and sent up a prayer to the gods of mischief. She closed down the main parts of her computer and opened the secret browser where no history of her Internet time would remain.

Aiden brought her the file, then the two brothers sat quietly as Petra worked. She made it into the birth registrations department in under two minutes, and relief flooded in. "Okay. I'm going to be able to do this. At least parts of it."

Shockingly, it took under an hour, including a few nerve-racking moments when the foster care system unexpectedly froze. In the end, they left the old Jennifer in the system, early history adjusted, and current whereabouts unknown.

A new person named Jennifer Jinx Tremont had been created. She had a modified foster care record with the Tremonts her only care family, followed by a legal adoption. Declan Skye was clearly listed as her legal guardian. Jinx was also registered for grade eleven at the Heart Falls high school with all her previous grades on an official transcript from Manitoba.

Jake patted Petra on the back gently. "I don't want to know how you did that, but I'm very glad that you could. Your secret is safe."

"That you didn't adjust any of Jinx's grades to be higher than before impressed him the most," Aiden teased.

"Truth." Jake offered a wink. "I'll see you guys by the fire pit. I've got a few things to deal with before I join you."

Aiden pushed back his chair and stretched his legs in front of him. He folded his arms over his broad chest before examining her carefully. "You okay?"

Petra met his gaze firmly. "You want to know how I did that."

He shrugged. "Of course I do. But only if you want to tell me."

It wasn't that interesting, Petra thought. "I was in an angry place after a friend shared that she was raising her two young daughters paycheck to paycheck while their ex kept buying expensive toys and not paying child support. One thing led to another, and I figured out how to feed his payroll records to the government so they could start garnering his wages."

"That's pretty shitty motivation, but I'm glad you developed the skills."

"I've been using it a lot to bust deadbeat dads," she confessed. "I needed to do something positive for people who felt as if they had no control."

Aiden's expression didn't change. "I am one hundred percent not judging you. Considering what we plan for High Water, you know we're on your side. Not all vigilantes act in a way that's positive for society, but like Jake, I'm very grateful for your skill set right now. Thanks for trusting us enough to let us see what you're capable of. Once again, you've made a huge difference in Jinx's life."

He rose to his feet and pulled her into his arms for a tight hug.

Gratefully, Petra let go. All of her tension, all the worry. The sheer stress of digging through those websites and worrying that she would somehow make things worse instead of better. She wadded all those negative thoughts up in a bundle and mentally tossed them to the floor, leaning wholeheartedly into Aiden's embrace.

It took a while, but the tension in her shoulders slowly eased. An enormous sigh escaped, and Petra pressed her cheek against Aiden's chest. "I'm glad I was able to do it."

She stood there for a moment longer, enjoying the two strong arms wrapped around her, holding her as the anxiety drained away.

Doing the right thing wasn't always easy. But in this case, she was very glad she knew how to do the wrong thing for the very best reasons.

14

By Friday, Petra felt as if they'd officially made progress. They'd bought Jinx a phone, some clothes, and all the items on the school checklist, an experience that had flashed Petra back to her own high school years.

With a few more days left before her first day of school, Jinx was already having fewer panic attacks, displaying the strength that had made her ask Danielle for help in the first place.

They still hadn't decided whether she'd be taking the bus or getting a ride on Monday morning. Aiden promised Jinx she could decide at the last minute, but he and Petra had both promised to drop her off if Jinx decided it would help.

And Sasha had already informed Jinx that no matter how she got to school, Sasha had her back.

A promise that made Jinx blink hard. "She doesn't even know me," Jinx told Petra as they slowly walked back from morning chores, Dixie bouncing at their feet. "I mean, I'm glad to have her around, but she just accepted me right off the bat."

Petra shrugged. "Some people hit it off immediately. If

you're happy getting to know Sasha better, I'm sure there will come a time in the future you'll be the one who helps her. It's okay to be the one taking for a while."

Jinx nodded slowly. "Can I message her? She was going to go over the math they've already reviewed with me so I'm not behind."

"Yes, but let's stay in the living room like we agreed and please check first how long Sasha has so you don't get her in trouble."

Lord. Rules about phone usage.

Petra shook her head as she settled on the opposite side of the living room and pulled out her own phone. It was past time for checking in with her besties.

> Petra: Supper tonight at High Water. It's my turn to cook and I'm conscripting both of you to help.

Tansy: You just love us for our culinary skills.

Sydney: OMG, I hope not.

Tansy: Don't knock yourself, sister. You've got the best carving skills of anyone I know.

> Petra: That she does. But not much slice and dice tonight. I want to appeal to the masses and make pizza. Tansy, can I bribe you to bring over your portable pizza oven? Sydney and I can be your sous chefs and do all the chopping if you deal with the crust.

Tansy: High Water Pizzeria. Sounds like the place to be.

Sydney: I want to come and help, but six p.m. is the earliest I can promise. I arranged to go out to Mr. Talita's this afternoon. Depending on how ornery he is, I might get back later than that.

> Petra: Talita's? Isn't he the one my brother said went off the grid back in the eighties? Every time he shows up in town he gives the guys from Duck Dynasty a run for their money on redneck style.

> Sydney: Even people with questionable fashion choices deserve quality health care.

> Petra: Are you taking backup?

> Tansy: That's what I was going to ask. Tell you what, I'll come with you.

> Sydney: Please. After years of night shift on EMS at Calgary General, I can deal with one ornery old man just fine, thanks. But I'd love to come for pizza and meet Jinx. Which I assume is the ulterior motive?

> Tansy: Nice topic change there, slick. Call if you need help. But yes, P. How's your new chica doing?

> Petra: Jinx is doing great. One little panic attack yesterday when she looked up in the middle of helping Aiden and realized there were two additional contractors in the room. She hadn't noticed when they walked in, and extra male humans in unexpected places are definitely a trigger. But she's a sweetie with a huge heart that needs filling, and I think knowing you guys better will only give her more of a sense of family.

> Tansy: You're making me blush.

> Sydney: We'll be there.

Petra got Jinx's attention. "The girls are cooking tonight," Petra informed her. "My friends Tansy and Sydney are coming over, and the four of us are hosting a family pizza party."

"Okay." Jinx glanced at the table where Declan was

working. He was listening intently but pretending not to. Jinx considered then informed him, "We'll make you pizza, too, Declan."

He peered over the top of the glasses perched on his nose. "I assumed that."

Jinx pulled her expression to deadpan and looked Petra in the eye. "I heard Declan loves liver on his pizza."

His lips twitched, which was as close to an outright smile as he seemed to get. "Best pizza ever if there's caramelized onion on there as well."

This time, Jinx outright snickered.

That bubble of hope in Petra's chest expanded another little bit. "Tansy will come over first to help us make the dough, and you and I will get started chopping ingredients. Sydney will show up when she can. She's got a house call planned to one of the local old-timers, Mr. Talita. If he's not cooperative, it might be only you and me helping Tansy."

Jinx nodded. "That's okay. I'm looking forward to meeting Sydney when it works."

"She's looking forward to seeing you, too."

The day passed quickly. Tansy showed up early as promised, and Petra and Jinx, fresh from their showers after helping Aiden and Jake in the studio, greeted her.

Tansy strolled into the house as if she lived there—probably from all the years when it had been her Grandma's place.

She shook the Rubbermaid tote in her arms. "You probably have all the stuff I'll need, but just in case, I came prepared." She tilted her head toward the door. "Hey, Jinx. Can you grab the second box from my truck?"

"Sure." Jinx headed to the door at a rapid clip with Dixie hard on her heels. "Don't start making the dough without me," she called over her shoulder.

Petra boldly seized the tote from Tansy's grasp. "Thank you

for arriving early. That girl has had ants in her pants all day waiting for you."

"I do inspire that level of excitement," Tansy offered seriously, ruining it by adding a brow waggle. She pulled a wrapped candle from her box. "Here, this is for you."

"Not suitable for Jinx to see?" Petra suggested, ripping away the paper and letting out a huge guffaw. "*What (and I can't stress this enough) the Fuck?* It's awesome. Thanks."

"It seemed appropriate," Tansy teased, accepting the hug of thanks Petra offered. "So, other than obsessing over the wonderfulness that is me, how's the kiddo doing?"

"Settling in," Petra said quietly, tucking the candle away in the cupboard for now. "I don't want to jinx it, but it seems as long as I'm around, things are going smoothly."

Tansy wrinkled her nose as she piled things on the counter. "That doesn't bode well for school on Monday."

"I know. The shopping trip with Sasha went wonderfully. I hate to rely on one nearly sixteen-year-old to watch over another, but from the sounds of it, Sasha is a bit of a mother hen to begin with."

Tansy nodded, a big, exaggerated motion. "Oh, girl. You have no idea."

Which still left Petra feeling a little kerfuffled. She suddenly had a whole lot more sympathy for those helicopter parents she'd read about who had seemed so horrible at the time. She was now mentally apologizing for every eye roll she'd offered at how ridiculous those parents had sounded because she was tempted to hold on too tight as well.

Jinx burst into the house with an open tote in her arms. "Is all the stuff in here for toppings on the pizzas?" She sounded moderately horrified.

Tansy planted her hands on her hips. "Man does not live

on pepperoni pizza alone, my girl. So, yes. Not all of them at the same time, but trust me. I'm magical in the kitchen."

Jinx placed the container on the counter then held up what looked like a miniature white log. She tilted her head slightly as she stared at it. "Goat cheese. Which I know is a thing because there's goat's milk, but *really*?"

Petra smiled. "Oh, sweetie. We look forward to expanding your tastebud repertoire."

Jinx made a face. "Fine. But there will be pepperoni, right?"

"There will be plain old pepperoni," Tansy promised.

She got the dough going, and once it was set aside to rise, the three of them wrangled the pizza oven into position by the fire.

"It's electric," Tansy explained, setting up an extension cord. "I fully plan to build one that's woodfired at some point, but it makes no sense to have that where I am now. They don't approve of open fires in apartments."

"Your restaurant is really nice," Jinx offered sincerely.

"Thank you. It's got a lot of charm," agreed Tansy. "I like it as well because my sister is either helping me or right next door dealing with the flower shop. Rose is now living with her fiancé instead of with me, though, so the only time I see her is at work."

"And at your mom and dad's for dinner every few days. Plus, when you go to visit your sister Fern. Maybe even when you go to visit your Grandma and Grandpa," Petra added helpfully.

Tansy pressed a hand to her chest. "Yes, those times, too." She offered a long-suffering sigh and head shake to Jinx. "I'm so hard done by. Everybody loves me. They can't survive without their daily dose of Tansy."

From the expression on her face, Jinx already had a serious case of hero worship.

Sydney hadn't shown up by the time they went inside to make the crusts, but it was still early enough Petra wasn't worried. Instead, she joined in with amusement as Tansy tried to teach her and Jinx how to make the crusts get bigger by spinning the dough in the air overhead for a moment.

"I'll drop it," Jinx worried.

Tansy shrugged. "Then you drop it. I made tons of dough," she said soothingly. "Trust me. I've taught all my family to make pizza, and you can't be as bad as my father. The man goes from ten fingers to two whenever it's convenient."

"Your dad is a kick," Petra teased.

"My father is an outstanding member of this community with a little bit too much starch in his shorts at times." Tansy said it with a straight face. "Which is why it's my duty, as his favourite daughter, to ensure he has lots of opportunities to lean toward the light and airy."

Tansy's father was an outright saint for some of the hijinks he'd tolerated, most instigated by Tansy. "I'm pretty sure somebody told me you put actual starch in his shorts once upon a time."

Tansy didn't deny it. "It was a science experiment."

Jinx looked up from where she was carefully cutting thin slices from a pepperoni stick. "What kind of science experiment?"

"Saturation point of a liquid or something like that." Tansy waved a hand airily then sent her dough swirling in the air again. "Of course, then I had this huge bucket of starchy water that needed to be used up instead of wasted. I probably didn't need to use his shorts. And using balloons to hold them in position until they dried was just being creative. Arranging them on the front lawn as if invisible people were holding some kind of wild dance was the logical final step. Science, you know."

Petra leaned around Tansy to firmly inform Jinx of the facts. "Mr. Fields is a saint."

"Saint Malachi. Hmm." Tansy noted. She picked up another ball of dough and thrust it at Jinx. "I've taught my dad, and I taught my little sister, Fern. Fern was born with a shortened arm on the left side, with differently formed fingers right about here." She tapped her arm about two inches past the elbow. "She has a prothesis but doesn't wear it all the time, and I have taught her to throw a mean crust." She considered. "Honestly, I think her pizza crusts are better than mine. She said she uses mathematical calculations to time her spin. Something about a speed to flight ratio."

Petra laughed. "Food science and math. Who knew?"

"Right?" Tansy agreed. "To me, cooking is not science. It's tossing things in the pot and hoping it works."

Whether she'd been convinced by the stories or not, Jinx took the dough Tansy offered her.

∽

THE SHRIEKS of laughter from the kitchen kept growing. Aiden gave his head a final rub with the towel then dragged his fingers through his hair.

In the mirror, his grin shone back huge and bright. It was good to hear Jinx joining in. Mixed with Petra's hearty laugh, the combination was quickly growing addictive.

Tomorrow would be one week since everything had changed, and High Water had gone from an idea to a reality. One week since Jinx had walked in the door.

One week that he and Petra had been sharing a bed.

All three facts astonished him, but perhaps the fact he'd managed to keep him and Petra on the slow boat instead of diving into full-out fucking might be the most miraculous.

Of course, Petra informing him on Monday evening that her period had started and that no way, no how, were they doing anything sexy had helped.

He'd insisted on cuddling, though. She'd huffed and rolled her eyes, but every night she'd willingly curled up facing him, legs entwined.

Falling asleep staring into Petra's face was an entirely new level of intimacy he hadn't expected to be quite so thrilling.

Jinx still had her moments of panic, and she eased closer to Declan every chance she got, especially when Petra wasn't around. But after only a week, none of them expected things to have gone as well as they had.

Aiden marched out to the kitchen, eager to join the ladies.

"You guys are having way too much fun," he complained jokingly.

Jinx whirled on him. She held forward a cookie sheet where a pizza crust rested on a layer of cornmeal. "I made this one. It's rising."

He stopped and took a closer look. Lopsided instead of circle, it was clearly a fine pizza crust. "It's amazing. Although I hope we're not on a raw food diet."

Jinx smiled then ducked her head. A second later, she lifted her chin. "Nope. But there will be goat cheese."

"Okay. Hopefully pepperoni as well."

He wasn't sure why that made Jinx snicker so hard, but he didn't care. Snickering was great. Aiden made his way to Petra's side, slipped a hand around her waist and leaned in to kiss her cheek. "I hope you're making my pizza extra-large."

She snickered. "Why? Overcompensating?"

She offered the tease quietly enough Jinx couldn't overhear, but Tansy did. Her friend snorted so hard she choked.

Tansy waved away help. "Nothing. It's nothing." She shook a finger at Aiden. "I like you."

"We've already established there's so much to love."

"Ego much?" But Petra smiled even as she pushed a tray with ingredients into his hands. "Okay, Mr. Everybody Loves Me. Carry this to the table beside the fire pit. We're setting up a cooking station."

Obediently following directions and acting as a delivery boy, Aiden spotted Jake already settled by the fire. "Aren't we missing some people?"

"Sydney will be here when she can," Petra promised. "I have no idea where Declan is, though."

"Hey, Jake," Aiden called. "Know where Declan is?"

His brother shrugged. "I didn't send him off. He must have gotten tied up chatting with someone, but I'm sure he'll be here."

"Text him a reminder. After that, more pizza for us," Aiden declared happily to Jinx.

The first pizza was just about ready to come out of the oven when Declan's truck roared past, stopping in the parking area on the far side of the building.

On the opposite side of the house, a second door slammed shut.

Less than a minute later, the small, very determined redhead who was Sydney came striding into view.

She went straight to Petra and gave her a hug. "Hello, all. Sorry I'm late." She raised a hand and saluted Jinx. "I'll save the hugs for down the road. Hi, Jinx. I'm Sydney."

Jinx waved. "Hi."

Sydney examined the area with a critical eye. "Jake and Aiden. Nice to meet you again." She accepted the beer that Tansy gave her and raised it in the air. "Here's to the truth that no good-deed goes unpunished."

A worried noise escaped Petra, which set Aiden on high alert. "You had trouble at old man Talita's place?" she asked.

Sydney shook her head then made a face. "I had no trouble with Talita." She paused, waiting until Declan fully emerged from behind the barn and joined them at the fire. She tilted her beer bottle at him. "*He*, on the other hand, was a royal pain in the butt."

What the hell? Aiden eyed his brother. He'd gone and interrupted Sydney's work? Declan was protective, and both he and Jake knew their big brother tended to go big when it came to watching out for others, but how in the world had he gotten involved this time?

Declan stared down Sydney's finger as if she were holding a daisy instead of a potential weapon. "I didn't say anything Talita didn't need to hear."

Jake made a rude noise. He folded his arms where he stood on the other side of the food table. "What were you doing dropping in at Sydney's house call?"

"Yes, Declan, I'm curious too. What *were* you doing dropping in while I was on a house call?" Sydney's tone went saccharinely sweet.

"Seemed like the right thing to do." Declan's gaze drifted over the group before landing on the pizza on the cutting board. "Is that pizza ready? I'm starving."

Sydney rolled her eyes then pushed past him and sat in the chair next to Jinx. "Go ahead and feed him. He probably can't think straight and it's making him hangry."

"I wasn't angry," Declan insisted. "I was reasonable but firm. Now he knows better than to pull a gun on anyone."

Holy shit. Instinctively, Aiden glanced toward Jinx to see how she was doing after that comment. Petra was doing the same, because, sure enough, Jinx had shot upright. "Someone pulled a gun on you?" she demanded of Sydney.

Jake's gaze slid over Sydney as if examining her carefully for wounds. "You okay?"

"I'm fine. There wasn't any danger. Not really." Sydney laid a gentle hand on Jinx's wrist. "Mr. Talita is a cranky old man who would never dream of hurting anyone. He's used to putting on a show to scare people off, though, trying to protect his territory. I can't take fault with that. We were well on the way to solving our communication problem when the Lone Ranger here came to my *rescue*."

Once again all eyes landed on Declan.

He helped himself to a piece of pizza and bit into it without another word. He considered while he chewed then washed the bite down with a swig of beer before speaking.

"Seemed like the right thing to do at the time," he repeated mildly. He met Sydney's annoyed gaze and lifted his chin slightly. "Would do it again in a heartbeat."

Sydney glared harder. "You know, there's names for men like you."

"Hungry?"

Aiden laughed, and the sound broke the tension. Sydney obviously didn't have a problem with her initial situation, but more of a problem with Declan showing up. But even that was washed away as Tansy continued passing out slices of steaming hot pizza, and the conversation moved to different topics.

An hour later, Jake eased back in his chair and patted his belly. "Ladies, you outdid yourselves. Thank you, that was delicious. Especially the goat cheese one."

"My favourite was the liver and onions," Declan said with a straight face.

For some reason that made Jinx snicker.

Sydney eyed Declan. "Are you drunk?" she asked.

"I'll explain," Jinx offered. She bounced to her feet, then shocked them all by extending an invitation. "Sydney, do you and Tansy want to see the rope swing Aiden made for me in the barn?"

"That sounds like an excellent idea, and one that gets us out of doing the dishes." Sydney nodded her approval. "Well done."

"Rope swings are my favourite," Tansy agreed. "Plus, I need some kitten cuddle time if you have any." She eyed Jake. "Leave the pizza oven. I'll grab it tomorrow when it's cooled off. Everything else needs to be hand washed."

"You said your baking sheets always go in the dishwasher," Petra reminded her with amusement. "Not that there's a dishwasher here yet in the first place, but..."

"She's making more work for us," Jake gave a long-suffering sigh. "I'm not the one who intruded on Sydney's visit."

"If you don't want to get shot, don't hang with the crows," Tansy teased before batting her lashes.

Jake rolled his eyes.

Jinx guided the ladies toward the barn. Jake and Declan loaded up the dirty dishes, and suddenly Aiden found himself alone with Petra by the fire.

"Shove over," Petra demanded before curling herself up comfortably in his lap.

"This is nice," he told her honestly. He rearranged her soft ass more comfortably in his lap as she draped her arms over his shoulders. It didn't seem as if she were getting cozy to spark up a sexual connection, though. She was quiet, more so than he'd ever seen her in their short time together.

Aiden brushed his fingers over her cheek. "How're you doing, darling?"

"I'm..." She hesitated. "Overwhelmed. I hate to admit that, but as good as things have been going, and as much as I know I'm in the right place, I'm teetering on the edge of too much."

As if the confession had taken every bit of her strength, she laid her head on his shoulder and let out a huge exhale.

Aiden stroked her back softly. Thinking for a moment and filtering through all the possible ways to make things better.

Because that was his first instinct. He didn't want her hurting, or worried, or overwhelmed, but something held him back from straight up diving into solutions.

They sat there quietly for a good five minutes before Petra wiggled up to meet his eyes straight on. "How are *you* doing?"

"Pretty much the same," he said honestly. "I'm worried I'll accidentally make a wrong move and scare the beejezus out of Jinx. I'm worried I'll go overboard and be too protective of her when she's obviously strong as hell and just needs a firm foundation under her feet. I'm worried High Water won't be ready soon enough to help someone else who needs it."

She listened intently as he spoke, nodding in understanding.

Aiden took a deep breath. She was already exhausted. This wasn't the time to drop the other bomb, that he was worried that he was the only one thinking maybe the thing between them could be more than a convenient lie and great sex.

Petra raised a brow. "What?"

Nope. Not going there. Not yet.

"Focus on simple," he suggested. "Let's get through the next couple of days. Jinx starts school on Monday, and that will give us more breathing room. That should help."

"That's true. You know what? Monday I'm taking a long lazy bubble bath," Petra warned. "Middle of the day, with sweet treats and candles and no agenda."

"Perfect." He brushed his lips over hers and kissed her softly. "I'll make sure that happens."

She leaned closer, returning the kiss with gentle enthusiasm. Aiden soaked in the pleasure of having her in his arms even as he plotted mischief.

Operation Bubble Bath was on for Monday. He could not wait.

15

The weekend passed in a whirl of activity and simmering anticipation. By the time Monday morning rolled around, Petra and Aiden had at least five conversations with Jinx about exactly what she wanted to happen for her entrance into high school society.

Each time, Jinx had slowly stiffened her resolve, until now they stood on the porch, a collection of four very antsy adults hovering over a sixteen-year-old as she determinedly focused on her boots.

"If you change your mind, you give us a call," Declan said.

Jinx stood and hoisted her new grey backpack over her shoulder. She straightened and met each of their eyes fearlessly. "I'm going to be okay. I like school, and I like Sasha, and I'm going to be okay."

Petra dipped her chin firmly. "Damn straight, you are."

Jinx's lips twitched as she glanced at the guys to see how they would react to Petra swearing.

"If Jinx's teachers complain about her language, we're pointing at you," Jake warned. Petra only grinned.

"Time to get a move on," Aiden informed Jinx. "Take this for later, and we'll see you at the end of the day."

Jinx frowned slightly as she accepted the brightly coloured envelope he held. "What is it?"

"Something to read when you're on the bus. If you want," Aiden told her as he snapped a salute. "You've got this."

Jinx dipped her chin. She proceeded to surprise the hell out of Petra, darting back to steal a brief hug. Petra didn't have time to do more than fight to keep her balance before Jinx was running down the stairs, Dixie racing by her side.

"Oh. Petra," she called over her shoulder. "You left your purse on the floor in the living room last night. I hung it back at the front door for you." Jinx waved one final time before marching down the long gravel road to the highway.

They all stood in silence for a moment before Aiden laughed. "We must look ridiculous."

"I don't give a shit how I look. I'm nervous as hell," Jake admitted.

Petra folded her arms over her chest and glared at Jake. "I'm going to start a swear jar, and I bet *you* are going to fill it in its entirety, Jacob Anthony Skye."

Jake looked taken aback, but Declan chuckled, soft and low. "You got second-named, bro. I'd hate to be in your shoes."

"How did she know my second name? That's what I want to know." Jake narrowed his gaze at Aiden.

He threw his hands in the air. "Not me. Remember, she's a woman of many talents."

"And on that note," Petra said brightly, because this was not the time to admit she'd been looking them up online. Curiosity was an evil gift at times. "Jinx is at the road and she's waving. Wave back, everybody."

It was the oddest sensation, watching the young woman

who'd only been in Petra's life for a week stepping onto the bright orange vehicle and vanishing from sight.

Dixie dejectedly paced back to the ranch house alone, the absolute picture of doggie sadness.

"This is going to be one hellishly long day," Declan complained.

Jake whirled, pointing a finger in his face. "Don't you dare show up at her school."

"I am her guardian," Declan offered innocently. He eyed Aiden. "What was in the envelope?"

"A *you can do this* message along with twenty bucks so she can buy herself and Sasha something from the cafeteria as a treat." Aiden winked at Petra. "I'm going to be her favourite big brother."

"You're a pain in the behind, as usual," Declan said, glancing around at the small gathering. "She's going to be fine, but in the meantime we should all keep ourselves busy. Easiest way to make this day pass quickly."

"I have plans," Petra assured him.

"I won't be around for lunch, but I'll be back by the time the school bus arrives," Jake said.

"Same for me." Declan sighed heavily. "Guess I should get started."

Aiden walked back inside the house with Petra as Jake and Declan headed toward the barn and studio. "We're all going to be there when the school bus arrives," Aiden said softly. "It's going to feel like forever, isn't it?"

"Yeah. It seems so odd to know she's not in the house or with one of you guys." Petra twisted and pulled herself against him. "How did that happen so quickly? The feeling as if she belongs here?"

His strong arms wrapped around her and held her tight.

"As if she's been around for a split second, and yet all of forever."

"Pretty much."

Aiden pressed a kiss to Petra's forehead. "There's a strange magic when things are right."

She nodded. No use keeping him from his tasks as well. "I'll see you later."

"Hope you have a great day." He squeezed her one final time before slipping out the door.

As Declan had suggested, distraction was a good idea. Petra booted up her computer and got to work on the accounting system for Red Boot ranch. While her brother and his business partner might have no timeline expectations, sitting on her butt and worrying for the entire day wasn't going to help anyone.

She had just finished setting up the initial data links when her phone pinged with a message.

> Jinx: Everything is going great. Thought you should know. Sasha says hi.

She'd attached a selfie showing her and Sasha sitting on the bleachers in the school gymnasium. Both girls were smiling, their innocent faces shining with happiness.

Relief rushed in, and Petra carefully considered her response to not let on exactly how worried she'd been.

> Petra: Glad to hear it. Have fun, work hard, and you can tell me all about it at supper.

> Jinx: Okay. Putting my phone away now because RULES. Give Dixie a pet from me.

Petra sent a quick message to all three Skye brothers, letting them know Jinx was doing fine. Then she dove headlong into programming, relief and happiness making her fingers work double-time.

By one o'clock, she was nowhere near done but had accomplished enough she decided it was time for her treat. She tidied the small desk Aiden had set up for her in the room they were using as an office, closed her computer, and headed to the bedroom. The soaker tub in the corner of the primary bath was about to get a workout.

She stripped off her clothes and wandered into the bathroom, pausing when she spotted three bright red boxes lined up on the edge of the tub.

"What the hell?" She lifted the first and pulled the card with Aiden's handwriting from under the ribbon.

> THANKS FOR EVERYTHING YOU'VE DONE. BUT MOSTLY THANKS FOR BEING AN AWESOME PERSON. ENJOY RELAXING.

Petra lifted the lid, and the drugging scent of lilacs wafted up. Pale purple bath salts filled the box.

The second box held three doughnuts, and the third box a candle labeled *Inhale The Good Shit, Exhale The Bad Shit*. Petra grinned and got the bath water running before picking up a doughnut and taking a bite.

She groaned with happiness. It was delicious and exactly what she needed. Scalding heat made her skin tingle as she eased into the sweetly scented water. With a rolled up towel behind her neck, she closed her eyes and let the sweet goodness of the Maple Cream doughnut slide down her throat.

She'd been soaking for over half an hour when a knock clattered on the door.

"Petra? Okay if I come in?" Aiden asked.

"It's not locked," she assured him. "The water is still warm, although I have to inform you the sweets are all gone."

Aiden strolled around the corner, his expression growing heated as his gaze roamed her body. "I see something plenty sweet."

The perfect distraction of the bubble bath morphed into something even more enticing. Especially when Aiden pulled his shirt off over his head and tossed it to the floor.

"Tell me you got really dirty this morning and you're desperate for me to scrub you clean," Petra suggested.

The trim lines of his body made her fingers itch to touch. The sweep of his waist down to lean hips, the firm lines of the muscles framing his abdomen. The flex of his broad shoulders as he knelt beside the tub. All of it combined to heat her from the inside out, anticipation growing as he dipped his fingers into the bubbles floating on the water's surface.

He snatched them back instantly, cursing lightly. "Christ, woman, how hot was the water when you got in?"

Petra snickered. "Average hot for a bubble bath. Cold compared to a thermal geyser."

Aiden examined her closer, gaze dipping over her breasts. He ran a finger over her skin parallel to the water. "You're red and pink and glowing, like a sexy jellyfish."

Amusement flared. "You say the sweetest things," she informed him. "Sort of."

He hummed, slipping his hand under the water and cupping her breast. He stared into the water as his thumb caressed over her already rigid nipple. "You feeling more relaxed?"

"Yes, although at this moment, I'm decidedly tenser than five minutes ago." Petra arched into his touch as he rolled his thumb and fingers together, pinching lightly. "My period is over."

"Good to know." Fingers brushed her belly, landing between her legs. "I considered asking if I could join you, but I'm not lava resistant."

Petra widened her knees, covering his hand. "I can get out of the tub."

"In a minute," he suggested. "Right now I'm having fun. Partially boiling to death, but fun."

She laughed, the sound turning to a moan as he slicked their joined fingers over her clit. Teasing circles set a tingle rising in her core. She rested her head back on the towel and examined his face closely as he admired her. Fire danced in his eyes as he slid fingers into her yet kept up the steady brush over her clit.

Lordy, that felt good. Petra sucked for air, fighting to speak. "I'm not about to complain if you get me off like this, but I would very much like to have sex."

"This is sex," he pointed out.

Stubborn man. Talented man, too. "It's hard to think when you do that thing with the…oh God, *that*." A twist of his fingers inside her? She wasn't sure what it was except the fast road to an orgasm. "That's deliciously evil."

His grin widened. "This?"

She hissed, curling her fingers around the back of his neck and tugging him toward her. He lowered, lips hovering over hers, hand continuing to tease.

She forced out the words. "Don't think I haven't noticed that we've fooled around but not actually done the deed."

"If you're still able to think this hard, I'm doing something wrong." Aiden's smile softened. "Stop holding back. Let go."

"Promise we can have sex."

"We are—"

"Penis, then. Cock. Dick. I want yours inside me." She clamped down on his fingers, and this time he cursed.

"Be careful what you wish for," he warned.

"Put up or shut up," she taunted back.

He reached into the tub, and Petra found herself airborne. She clutched his neck as he marched to the bedroom, dripping water everywhere.

Aiden dropped her on the bed and shoved his jeans off his hips. He sat on the mattress hard enough that she bounced, his hands guiding her over his lap. One knee on either side of his hips, her butt resting on his thighs.

Stretching to the side table, Aiden snatched up a condom and rolled it over his thick cock, Petra doing her best to help.

Every brush of her fingers made him curse softly. His breath came in ragged gasps, and as he caught up her hips and levered her over him, his face turned serious. "Yes?"

Hell yes. Petra notched his cock into position then sank down one slow inch at a time.

Finally.

His fingers on her hips tightened, and he closed his eyes briefly. "So fucking good."

"Agree." But full—so full she needed a minute to adjust.

Good thing she had something else to enjoy at the same time. She cupped his face in her hands and kissed him.

∼

He might have fucked up royally by caving, but with Petra's heat wrapped around him and her tongue in his mouth, Aiden's give a damn was busted.

He squeezed her ass, enjoying the give of her curves. When he nipped her lower lip and she pulled her lips away with a gasp, he savoured his way along her jaw line to the sweet spot on her neck that made her squirm.

"Fuck yeah. Rub yourself against me. So fucking hot."

Aiden bit her neck lightly, rocking his hips and moving inside her the slightest bit.

Petra let her head fall back, fingernails digging into the tops of his shoulders. "Sweet mother of pearl."

He shouldn't find it so funny, considering the waves of pleasure rocking through him should've been enough to keep his mind fully on the here and now. But still... "I think I need to see how many swearwords I can get you to say."

She snapped her head up and smiled evilly. "Is that a challenge?"

He was about to answer with some cocky bullshit when she lifted up, dragging that sweet pussy of hers over sensitive skin and making his mind go foggy.

When she dropped in place, thighs smacking into his, Aiden cursed.

The bed bounced slightly, and Petra's smile went downright demonic. She rose and fell, setting a pace that sent his tongue tripping over itself, the heat of their bodies meshing as he turned the air blue.

"Touch me," Petra demanded, grabbing hold of his wrists and bringing them to her breasts. Aiden held on as Petra did the work, driving him deep over and over until he was holding onto his control by a thread.

Her face was tight, right on the edge of pleasure and pain, and Aiden dropped a hand between them and caught hold of her clit. She gasped as he gave it a squeeze, dropping one more time and digging her nails into his skin as she writhed over him.

Her pussy tightened around his cock, and Aiden once again caught hold of her hips, thrusting up as high as possible while holding her against him.

Petra wrapped her arms around him, clinging tightly as waves of pressure enveloped his cock...

A sharp snap sounded. The mattress tipped, dropping in

place as Aiden scrambled to catch their balance before they were flattened like a pancake.

"What the—" Petra clutched him tighter, but Aiden caught them in time. He sat on the edge of the mattress, legs straight in front of him on the floor with her still skewered on his cock.

They were two feet lower than they'd started, wooden splinters from the support base of the bed scattered at his feet.

Petra glanced around before leaning in and kissing him. Sweet and self-assured and with a hint of mischief. A final nip sank into his lip before she grinned into his face. "I can't believe we did that."

"I'm glad we did that." He bumped his nose into hers, and an aftershock sent her squirming against him briefly. "The bed's still under warranty."

Laughter bubbled up. Petra brushed a hand over his cheek as she smiled indulgently. "If you're suggesting we should test drive every bed before the warranties are up, I'm game."

He kissed her, hands stroking naked skin. He needed to deal with the condom, and he needed to not go too fast, but what he needed most of all was right here in his lap.

Petra finally broke the kiss, carefully crawling off him and onto the mattress.

Aiden dealt with the condom then pulled up his underwear and pants. He opened his arms. "Come here. I'll take you back to the tub while I clean up."

"As long as you come join me," Petra offered.

He lowered her into the water and did a quick temperature check. "This I can handle. Give me a minute."

Thankfully, there was no sign of his brothers when he grabbed the broom and dustpan, dealing with the wood splinters but leaving the broken frame for later.

He grabbed two glasses of lemonade and peanut butter cookies from the jar and made his way back to the bathroom.

Petra accepted the food and drink, chugging down half of the lemonade even as she gestured to the water in front of her. "It's big enough for two. It's big enough for three, but that's not my kink."

He stepped into the water gingerly, arranging himself with his back against the incline of the tub and her legs in his lap. "Good to know. It's not mine either."

Petra took a nip of the cookie and made a noise that made him want to go right back to the bed, broken or not. "These are really good."

"Agreed." He ran his finger up her shin, caressing her skin slowly. "I thought you made those."

She shook her head. "Not me. I thought you did."

"Well, whichever of my brothers was the mastermind, we'll request a new batch as soon as possible. These were the last two."

She licked crumbs off her fingers then stretched her arms along the top of the tub, smiling at him contentedly. "That was a most excellent bit of distracting."

"Agreed." Her skin was so soft he wanted to pull her into his lap and keep touching her. She was pink and red now for reasons other than the heat of the water, and the shine in her eyes made him all the more determined to convince her this needed to be real.

"I like that look."

Aiden lifted his gaze. "What's that?"

She wiggled her finger at his face. "You know why I went back to your hotel with you three years ago? It was mostly because of that look."

"I'm not sure what you're talking about, but I'm very happy to have that look." Aiden picked up her foot and rubbed gently. "Anything particular about it? Just in the interest of science and making sure I offer you *the look* on a regular basis."

She laughed then her expression grew thoughtful. "It was my brother's wedding weekend. Second wedding, if you count the one they can't remember that took place in Vegas."

"*Now* you tell me this story. I can't wait for the next time we see Zach and Julia."

"Mischief maker," she teased. She shook her head as if remembering. "I love my big brother, and at that point, all my other sisters were married, most with rug rats, so it was kind of as if they were all at the stage of a game that I had no interest in yet. I didn't want to settle down, but seeing Zach with Julia—they were so freaking in love, it just poured from them every time they looked at each other."

Aiden raised a brow. "So you decided having a one-night stand with a total stranger was a good way to celebrate your brother's wedding?"

"Pretty much," she agreed, but she wrinkled her nose in the most adorable fashion. "It was less about trying to counteract the wedding cootie vibes that were floating around and more about just doing something that made *me* as happy as they were at that moment."

"Well, I remember you getting happy." He smirked. "Although we didn't break a bed that time."

Her laughter rang, loud and clear. She smiled, a sweet sincere smile that made his toes curl. "But you had that look. That one that says you've got secrets. Not evil dark secrets, but delicious and naughty, and if I'm really good you might share them with me." She paused then nodded firmly. "And kind. It makes you look kind."

Aiden sighed heavily. "You had my hopes up there for a minute with secret looks and naughty looks, and then—bam, you hit me with that damn *kind* button. At least you didn't friend zone me."

She splashed him.

It seemed as good a time as any to admit this. "I picked you up because of your look as well. You were so full of life and fire I was drawn to you. That's what I remember the most about that night."

"Not the sex? Right."

"Oh, the sex too. But you shine, Petra. You really do."

She stared at him for a couple of seconds, something odd twisting her expression.

Without a word, she crawled from the tub and vanished into the bedroom.

The hell? "Petra? What's wrong?"

By the time he got out of the tub and wrapped a towel around himself, she'd vanished from the room. Cursing, he got dressed, stalking down the hallway and into the living room, looking for her.

16

*P*etra regretted bolting an instant after she'd done it, but she still didn't manage to stop her feet until she had tugged on clothes over sticky wet skin and made it onto the porch.

She left the front door open, though, and settled on the porch swing, staring at the mountains in the distance waiting until she heard his footsteps.

"I'm out here."

Aiden stepped into the doorway. "What just happened?" he asked softly.

She sniffed, dragging a hand over her cheek and brushing away tears. God, she felt like such a fool. "Not your fault. Just a bad memory surfacing at the wrong time."

Aiden sat beside her, the porch swing rocking slightly. He tucked his fingers under her chin and stared into her eyes. "I'm sorry."

She forced a smile, feeling more than a little watery. "Oh, honey. You're not the problem. It was just a reminder of exactly how much I screwed up."

The concern didn't leave his face, but he sat, leaning against the wooden backrest of the porch swing. "Want to talk about it? Or at least give me some hints of what not to say so I don't accidentally end up hurting you again?"

Well, shit. That was one of the things he'd shared that was overwhelming him—being worried he'd unintentionally upset Jinx.

Petra took a deep breath. Her parents had always emphasized the importance of honesty when they were growing up, even when it was sometimes embarrassing. With six kids in the house, lack of knowledge meant massive opportunities for small misunderstandings to bloom to unreasonable proportions. "My ex. *He* said I was shiny." When Aiden frowned, she held up a hand to hold off comments. "We met at a tech event, and when Curtis ended up interning at a company in our small town, it was as if fate had brought us together. We did everything together, just seemed to click, you know? In under a month, we were inseparable. He was so curious about everything, just like me—"

Aiden's expression went guarded. "Sounds as if you were a good pair. What went wrong?"

"He was super keen to meet my parents." Petra nodded at the way Aiden's eyes widened. "I mean, I lived right there, close to them, and we usually did all sorts of things as a family. I was so wrapped up in Curtis, though, I kept begging off on family stuff. When he pushed for us to spend time with them, I thought maybe it was a sign of an upcoming *significant moment*. You know, meet the parents, start living together, all those things. It was fast, but it didn't feel wrong."

Aiden took a deep breath. He let it out slowly, glancing away for a moment. "I want to hear this, but I simultaneously want to break the bastard's arms because I know you're not together now, which means it's his fault. I'm not going to like whatever you tell me."

"No, you're not going to like it at all," Petra agreed. "He had a girlfriend."

"What the fuck?" Aiden's scowl folded his forehead into a mass of creases.

She smoothed her fingers across it. "He had a girlfriend in another town. What's more, she knew about me. They had this convoluted plan wherein he was going to impress my father. My dad's an inventor and on the board for several businesses who offer big ol' grants. Curtis, with the full agreement of his girlfriend, decided if he made nice with my father, he'd get offered a coveted grant that would provide five years of funding for his pet project."

"And after he got the funding, he was just going to drop you?" Aiden demanded.

"I assume something of the sort. He never got a chance because I accidentally hacked into the information and dealt with him accordingly."

"Jesus fucking Christ, the fucking gall of the bastard. I hope you've blackballed him on every single grant list that there is," Aiden snapped.

The first hint of amusement she'd felt in the past few minutes slipped back in. "See? This is why you and I are friends. Of course he's blackballed. But other than that, I'm restraining myself because he and his now fiancée have a kid, so I'm not about to go make them penniless or anything."

Aiden's expression was beyond description. "I'm just— I mean— There is just no—"

His jaw hung open, completely speechless.

"Right?" Petra sighed. "I'm so sorry. You gave me what would usually be a lovely compliment. I'm glad when you looked at me you saw life and happiness and me shining.

Unfortunately, being shiny to Curtis meant a shining opportunity to take advantage of me. But it's just a word, and I know what *you* truly meant." She cupped Aiden's face and let him see the sincerity in her eyes. "I know it was an accident, and I absolutely forgive you. I hope you'll forgive me for going off the rails like that."

"*Petra.*" He kissed her. A gentle brush of his lips over hers before pulling back. He wiped his thumb under her eye, brushing away a tear. "You are a better person than me. If I had the ability to hack into records I'd be legally changing his name to Humperdinck McBastardface."

Oh my God. Amusement hit hard, and a huge snicker escaped, followed by another, especially when Aiden joined in, his laughter contagious and warm as it brushed over her. Then he pulled her into his arms and squeezed tight, holding her as she released part of the burden she'd been carrying by herself for months.

She wiped away tears again, this time from laughing too hard. She patted his chest approvingly. "Thanks. I needed that. Also, you're the only person I've told what happened. So don't share it around, please."

"Of course." He nodded slowly, peering into her eyes. "Think you should consider expanding that *in the know* list to include Tansy and Sydney. They're rock-solid friends and having them beside you would help."

"I feel like such a fool, though," Petra complained.

"You trusted someone, and they lied to you for all the wrong reasons. That makes the failure on their side, not yours." Aiden set the porch swing swaying, tucking her tighter into his embrace. "You sure you don't want his knees broken or anything?"

So very tempting, except for one fact. "Whenever thoughts of revenge rise, I remember there's an innocent kid out there who has an ass for a father and a conniving wench for a mom. She doesn't need more trouble in her life."

Aiden pressed a kiss to the top of her head. "You're a good woman, Petra."

They sat for a while longer, sunshine sneaking around the side of the house and warming them where they sat, gently rocking. A few birds sang, but mostly it was the sounds of the prairies that wrapped around them. A rush of wind, the creak of the swing. The flag beside the parking area flapping in the wind.

Aiden hummed happily then squeezed the arm around her shoulders. "I hate to interrupt this, but I have a bed to repair."

Oh God. Petra fought back against the snickers that wanted to rise. "Let me give you a hand with that."

He stood, holding her hand as he brought her to vertical. "You think it's safe for us to work together? That's what caused the bed to break in the first place."

She poked him in the belly, finger bouncing off an amazing set of ab muscles. "Don't get me restarted laughing. My stomach already hurts," she complained.

He squeezed her fingers and strolled them slowly through the living room. "I'm going to have to order a new frame. I'll leave the mattress on the floor for now if you're okay with that."

"Sounds a lot safer," she teased.

Tidying up didn't take that long, but after a half-dozen trips to carry the broken wood to the workshop area, it was rapidly approaching the end of the school day.

Aiden dipped his head toward the front of the house. "I know it might be a little overkill, but let's walk all the way up to the road. We can totally embarrass her. I'm sure that's a rite of passage she needs to go through."

"Bring Dixie," Petra reminded him.

When Aiden linked their fingers together as they walked

slowly up the Gravel drive, Petra didn't mind. She took deep breaths of the fall air and tilted her face up to the sun. "It's been a good day. I hope it's been a good day for Jinx as well."

"Me too," Aiden agreed.

They waited until the school bus had pulled to a stop. Dixie wiggled impatiently, tail wagging a million miles an hour as the door swung open and Jinx stepped down.

She smiled big as she met Petra's eyes, chin held high. "You're here."

"Too excited to wait for you to walk all the way up to the house," Petra admitted. She waved at Sasha, who had her face pressed up against the school bus window.

Jinx twisted and waved as well, then she knelt. "Come, Dixie."

Dixie pounced, slapping her tongue all over Jinx's face as if the girl had been gone for a million years instead of eight hours.

Aiden made a face. "I was going to offer you a hug, but now that you're slathered in dog germs, I'll just wait until you've decontaminated yourself."

Jinx rolled her eyes, and another knot of tension inside Petra's chest loosened.

One week. *One* week, and already this girl was beginning to show who she was, strong and resilient.

Petra tipped her head toward the house. "So, save the big stories for when we get to the house, because I know Declan and Jake want to hear them as well, but did you and Sasha still hit it off?"

"She's pretty amazing," Jinx said quietly, surprising Petra when she slipped their fingers together, pacing at Petra's side. "Did you guys have a good day?"

"Pretty good," Aiden said. "We nearly finished the walls in the studio. Next step is painting."

They chatted about paint colours and building trim all the way up to the porch, where Declan and Jake stood waiting.

Declan glanced down at the hand between Petra and Jinx and gave Petra an approving nod before focusing on the young woman. "We got your message that things were going okay."

"It was fine. A few people asked where I was from, but after I told them I'd lived in Winnipeg for a while, that seem to be enough." Jinx squeezed Petra's hand then let go. "I think it's going to work."

By executive decision, a.k.a. Jinx, they broke in different directions to deal with pre-supper chores. Jinx went with Declan and Aiden to the barn, Petra slid back to the office and left Jake to deal with supper prep.

She had no idea how he was going to pull it off considering how late he was starting, but supper was on the table promptly at five.

"Damn, this looks great." Aiden scooped a huge ladle of mashed potatoes onto his plate. "Pass the gravy when you get a chance, Declan."

Jake served up thick slices of steaming hot meatloaf, and Petra glanced around in surprise. There was also a fruit salad and green beans, and when she glanced at the counter and spotted a chocolate cake waiting there, her curiosity got the better of her.

"It looks delicious, Jake, but when did you have time to do this?"

Jake mumbled something then motioned with his spoon toward Jinx. "Is this a big enough piece for you, or do you want more?"

"That's enough, thanks," she said, loading up with salad.

Uh-uh. Petra wasn't going to let it sit. She leaned down and took a deep sniff of the meatloaf. "I like your seasoning blend. What did you put in there, Jake?"

He hesitated before letting out a lusty sigh. "I don't know. I picked it up at Buns and Roses."

Aiden slapped the table, laughing as he pointed at his brother. "I knew it. I knew you didn't have it in you to make this kind of a meal."

"You plan to have Tansy cook all your meals for you, bro?" Declan asked. He glanced at Petra and his eyes sparkled. "Because I have zero complaints about that idea as long as it's coming out of your wallet and not the ranch budget."

Jake took the teasing good-naturedly, and Petra dug into the savoury food with gusto. Like Aiden had said, it turned out to be a very good day.

∼

THE REST of the week flew past, and slowly a routine fell into place. Jinx bloomed as her confidence rose with every trip into town. Homework began. Sometimes Sasha Stone would hop off the school bus with her, the two girls sitting at the living room table to go over quadratic equations or working on English essays.

Aiden was shocked to discover he had become the designated homework helper.

On the first Wednesday when the girls had asked Declan for help, Aiden had received in emergency text telling him to get his ass into the house.

He'd rushed in all panicked only to find Declan with a stormy expression and two girls trying very hard to keep straight faces.

His brother shook his head. "Tag team. Your turn." He glanced over his shoulder at the girls and shook his head. "It was bad enough when I had to do it the first time, and back then they didn't have things like invisible numbers. You go on and torment Aiden with your questions."

"Thanks for trying, Mr. Skye," Sasha offered brightly.

"No problem. If you want help with your horses, then you come to me." Declan met Sasha's gaze. "Although I hear Kelli's pretty smart with them as well."

"Kelli says it's always good to learn new things from the best, and Jinx says horses like you."

Declan dipped his chin. "Extra dessert for you tonight, Jinx," he promised, sending both girls into a flurry of laughter as he tipped an imaginary hat then headed to the barn.

Ever since then, Aiden had made sure he was free after school in case he could help. It wasn't Declan's area of expertise, and as organized as Jake was, he still didn't feel comfortable being around Jinx without one of the rest of them there.

Aiden was doing his best to make sure that it didn't always fall on Petra, which would be too easy to do in some ways.

After homework was dealt with, he joined the girls walking the trail that connected the two properties. While both of the ranches were large, like most ranches, the actual houses themselves were walking distance apart.

They crossed over the boundary line, climbing over the stile between the well-maintained fences. Jinx and Sasha chatted easily as Aiden walked behind, enjoying the break in his day and the chance to wander. Dixie danced between him and the girls, pleased as a pig in mud to have both of them around.

When Sasha was within eyesight of her house, she turned and gave Jinx a hug. "I have a lot to do this weekend, so we can't get together. But maybe next weekend it'll work that you can come over and we can go riding." Sasha glanced at Aiden. "My mom said that you and Petra could ride with us if you'd like. I know most of the trails pretty well, but I'm still not supposed to ride by myself without an adult if we're going to go farther."

"I'll check with Petra, but I think it'll work. We'd enjoy that."

On the return journey, Jinx walked quietly at Aiden's side, Dixie prancing between them. It was the type of quiet that was less about being peaceful and more about having a million things running through your brain so quickly that they tripped over each other.

Aiden recognized it because he was pretty much facing that same sensation inside his own head these days. With so much he wanted to accomplish, and so much he hoped for, at times it felt as if the only thing he could do was sit and let his mind race faster than it was possible to plan or hope or dream.

Still, as Jeff would have done, Aiden cleared his throat. "You got anything you need to talk about? If not with me, then Petra?"

Jinx wrinkled her nose. "It just feels—" She glanced up. "How come everything's working out so well?"

Ah. Aiden considered for a moment, thinking back to when Jeff had taken control and kept their world from falling apart. "Maybe you need to consider a little harder that this is what life is supposed to be like."

She stopped walking and stared, her big grey eyes full of questions.

He shrugged. "There are a lot of things that happen in this world that shouldn't. You got into a tough place through no fault of your own. But that's not what your world was supposed to be like. If you want to use big fancy words, that was never really your destiny. You didn't deserve the bad, but you definitely deserve the good. And it's not going to go away, we promise."

They stood at the edge of the clearing with the animal

rescue and future studio in front of them. A blue autumn sky hung overhead as tears filled Jinx's eyes. She swallowed hard then nodded. "Okay. Okay, I can think about that when I start to feel scared. *This* is where I'm supposed to be, and that's why good things are happening."

Aiden wanted to shout to the sky. He wanted to sweep this girl up and swing her in a circle and ensure her that *yes*, this was where she belonged and that the good things were going to continue.

What he did was tilt his head toward the barn. "Just enough time for you to deal with the chickens before supper."

Jinx nodded and took a couple steps toward the barn before coming back and looking up at him bravely. "Thank you."

"Of course, kiddo."

He watched her all the way into the barn, Dixie sticking to her heels. Then he took a stroll to give himself time to get his emotions under control.

He was still thinking about the conversation the following week when a shiny red truck pulled up in front of the house just as he and his brothers were headed toward the barn to keep working on the renovations.

"Finally." Jake paced forward to meet the dark-skinned man climbing down from the cab. "Kevin. Welcome."

Aiden glanced at Declan. "I thought he wasn't going to make it until next week."

"Not going to complain that he's here ahead of time," Declan said, following along after Jake.

The man was lean to the point he was nothing but sinew and muscle stretched over bone. He moved smoothly, grabbing a rucksack from the truck bed and throwing it over his shoulder before turning to face the brothers.

His dark brown hair was cut short to his head, with expressive dark brown eyes and a wicked looking cut that ran down the left side of his face, narrowly missing his eye. The wound was closed but still healing.

Kevin held out a hand to Jake and shook it firmly. "Thank you for inviting me."

"Thanks for saying you'd join us." Jake shook his head and pointed at his own face. "That's new."

Kevin raised his uninjured brow. "Parting gift from my last job."

Declan stepped forward and offered his hand. "Hopefully we won't have any close calls for you here."

"People are unpredictable," Kevin said without malice. He greeted Aiden as well then stepped back to take an admiring look around the place. "I know you said you're not ready, but I don't mind swinging a hammer. Might be a nice change of pace for a while."

"We'll take any kind of help you want to give," Jake assured him, slapping a hand on his shoulder and guiding him toward the living quarters. "We do have one resident already, but we'll introduce you when the time is right."

"That's right. You warned me about that," Kevin nodded. Then he opened his hands wide. "Put me to work, boys."

Petra and Jinx were on the schedule to make supper that night. Aiden slipped in ahead of time to give them a heads-up there would be one more at the table.

"He's the therapist we told you about," Aiden reminded Jinx quietly. "But he's also here because he needs a home like High Water as well."

Jinx leaned against the counter, slipping closer to Petra without being aware of it. "I don't want to talk to him. Not tonight."

"No. Of course not. Tonight he's not a therapist," Petra assured her. "Tonight he's another hungry guy who will want at least two burgers and three servings of pie."

"Okay." Jinx made a face at Aiden. "It's hard to make enough dessert so I can take extra pieces for me and Sasha the next day at school with the way you guys eat."

"Sorry?" But Aiden grinned. "Next time bake three pies?"

Jinx rolled her eyes but she went back to peeling apples.

Petra tugged Aiden aside. He pulled her into his arms and pressed his lips to hers for a kiss. She responded, softening against him, and he kind of forgot what he was about to do and just got lost in enjoying her.

She eased back, stroking her fingers over his cheek. "That was not what I wanted to talk about."

"Too bad. It's what I wanted to start with," he teased. "Okay, serious now. What's up?"

She stroked her fingers over his chest softly, considering. "Just another turn in the road. Wanted to make sure everybody's thinking it through and hoping things go smoothly as we add Kevin to the mix." She made a face. "It's been a month since Jinx arrived, and I've grown to like the forward motion. I don't want to go back to two steps forward one step back."

"I hear you," Aiden assured her. "Jake says he's a good guy. Has a reputation of being there for his coworkers and victims as well."

"That's good, but it's still hard at this point to change our dynamic." Her smile grew a little heated. "In other news, the new bed frame is supposed to arrive tomorrow."

"Check the schedule and make sure we can do a test drive," Aiden whispered softly.

"For the warranty's sake, of course,"

"Pitter patter let's get at 'er," Jinx called, interrupting their tête-à-tête.

Petra sputtered as she tilted her head against Aiden's chest and laughed. "I cannot believe that you got her watching Letterkenny."

"It's classic Canadian comedy," Aiden protested. "Although I do have to watch it with subtitles on. The jocks' and the stoners' accents are impossible at times."

When Jake brought Kevin in to be introduced, Jinx nodded politely but stepped aside and deferred to Petra.

"Slight seating rearrangement change at Jinx's recommendation," Petra announced to everyone. "Considering we'll have new people joining us at different times. This way everyone has a spot and the new people will add on to the side. We can adjust again down the road when needed."

Jinx and Declan were still across from each other but at the edge of the table. Petra faced Jake, and across from Aiden, Kevin nodded his approval.

"Well thought out." Kevin pointed to the open space at his side. "It gives me a chance to talk to anyone new without turning it into a big deal. And if any new ladies show up, they can sit there at the head of the table, next to Jinx and Declan, who somehow manages to look very safe in spite of his size."

"I told you," Petra said to Jinx. "Stay Puft Marshmallow Man."

Declan hung his head in his hands. "I asked you not to say that in public."

"Too late, bro. We heard it, and we're never going to forget," Jake gloated.

Kevin's room wasn't ready yet, but after supper he good-naturedly set up a bedroll in what would be his space. Six of them gathered by the fire that evening, crowding in closer because the temperature dropped rapidly as the sun vanished earlier in the evening.

Aiden played his guitar. Kevin hummed along for a minute then pulled out a harmonica and began playing an accompaniment. Jinx's eyes grew wide, and Petra smiled, fingers moving steadily on yet another project.

Aiden looked around at the growing family of High Water.

So much still to do, but they were firmly on the right path.

He turned his attention to Petra, admiring the firelight dancing on her skin, the small smile curling her lips. She swayed her head to the music.

One day at a time, he reminded himself. He just needed to keep the bonds between them growing one day at a time.

17

In the middle of a girls' lunch out at Buns and Roses, Petra was utterly stunned to discover it had been a month and a half since she'd moved into High Water.

"How on earth?" she mumbled, staring down at the calendar in front of her.

Tansy raised a brow. "What's up, P?"

Petra sat back in her chair at the table. "How is it almost the end of October already?"

The other two ladies at the table, Sydney and Julia, both frowned.

Julia leaned forward. "Well, there's this big yellow thing that rises in the sky called the sun. And every time it disappears—"

"Ha-ha, very funny," Petra complained, still staring at her Day-Timer in disbelief.

From her right, Sydney laid a hand on Petra's wrist. "Is there a particular reason you're glaring at that calendar with considerable concern?"

When three faces stared intently at her, Petra finally clued in.

Shit. She shook her head vigorously. "Oh, no. No, no, no, there's nothing calendar based that I'm worried about. Other than it's been a month and a half already."

Understanding dawned on Tansy's face. "Since you moved into High Water."

"Since Jinx arrived and I moved into High Water." And since she started sleeping with Aiden, but she didn't announce that part, although it was equally shocking.

Equally satisfying, if she was being honest, at least with herself.

Her sister-in-law raised a brow. "Is there some timeline we're not aware of that's causing you distress? Are they planning on kicking you out at some point?"

"Or did you hope to *be* out by some point?" Sydney asked quietly.

"None of the above." Petra scooped up a large chunk of her pecan pie and shoved it in her mouth so she'd have some time to think.

She didn't want to leave—the time watching Jinx bloom had become a miracle in itself. Add on how much fun she was having helping now that they'd begun adding paint and trim to the artists' rooms, and Petra's days were filled with a lot of enjoyment.

Her nights were filled with just as much fun, courtesy of that shared bed with a certain enthusiastic and creative lover.

Why was time passing so shocking?

"You do need to swallow at some point," Sydney said dryly.

"Not necessarily," Tansy offered. "Spitting is a valid option."

Julia snorted so hard tea came out her nose. "Tansy Fields, you're terrible."

"What did I say?" Tansy blinked innocently.

Petra wiped her mouth with a napkin, grinning easily at her bevy of friends. "I love you guys."

Tansy waved it off. "We know that. Now spill the dirt. What's so important about a month and a half?"

She tried, but nothing came to mind other than a cold pit sat in the middle of her stomach, and Petra wasn't sure why. She shrugged. "I don't know."

They all eyed her with concern before easing back in their chairs.

"Okay, fine," Julia offered firmly. "I get it. Sometimes things won't pop to mind when you're trying to figure it out. But as soon as it does, tell us."

"Of course," Petra promised.

"In the meantime," Julia sipped her tea then stared up at the ceiling. "Let's talk about *twelve* weeks."

Petra glanced at her calendar again, trying to decide what—

"Are you serious?" Tansy said, more squeal than anything. "Are you *serious*?"

Sydney and Petra exchanged another glance. "Do you think they have Duolingo go for Tansyland? It would be handy to become more fluent," Sydney complained.

Except a second later it hit, and Petra gaped at her sister-in-law. "You're pregnant?"

Julia grinned.

The good news triggered a round of hugs while curious gazes danced over them. There were a few whispers behind hands and more than a few smiles directed toward their table as they settled back down.

"Your secret is out," Tansy warned. "Lunchtime at Buns and Roses isn't exactly the most secure moment to share tidbits of information you want to keep quiet."

Julia just grinned. "I thought Zach was going to explode

having to keep his mouth shut until now. I told him I was going to update you guys today, and he's been on the phone ever since, bragging his head off. I'm surprised no one forwarded any of you a message and beat me to the punch."

"They're probably there, but we're polite and don't check our phones while we're visiting." Sure enough, when Petra checked her phone she had messages from all three of the Skye brothers and Jinx. "Jinx says to tell you congratulations."

Julia leaned forward slightly. "Tell her thanks. We want to have you guys out again soon. How's she doing?"

"Amazing. She's blooming."

It wasn't Petra's place to share all the details, but she was very grateful for some of the changes that had happened over the past couple of weeks.

Jinx had decided to start meeting with Kevin. There'd been signs of lots of tears after the first session, and while of course Kevin wouldn't say much because of confidentiality, he had, with Jinx's permission, shared some positive news.

"She was right to leave when she did before the worst happened. She's got a good head on her shoulders, and she's very clear that the situation wasn't her fault." For some reason Kevin had looked at Aiden right then and dipped his chin before finishing. "It's still going to take time, and there will be moments when she might have upsetting flashbacks, but she's doing all the right things. Now we need to give her time."

Petra realized she'd been staring into space, lost in remembering. She smiled at her friends and focused on the good news she could share. "Jinx hasn't had a panic attack in ages. She and Sasha are setting up a children's Halloween party at Silver Stone ranch in the afternoon next Sunday. Sasha's little brother Tyler gets scared easily, and Jinx decided she was too old to go Halloweening anyway, but a non-scary event would be fun to help with."

"Sasha already arranged for me to make Halloween cake pops for the event," Tansy shared.

Conversation changed to Halloween costumes and favourite spooky dishes. Petra ate the delicious food and drank her tea and soaked in the company of three wonderful women who had her back. But she was still wondering what it was that lingered at the back of her mind and bothered her so much.

She was still thinking about it as she drove into the parking space outside High Water ranch house. She automatically glanced over to check and see whose vehicles were there. Jake's was missing, but the other three guys must be around. Although Declan's truck didn't mean he was necessarily anywhere in one of the buildings. The man took off on horseback every chance he got. Even though the weather had begun to turn and the air held a chill that warned of coming snow, Petra was pretty certain he'd be somewhere out on the land.

Kevin and Jake were putting up trim in the artists' studio. With a nail gun in Kevin's hand, and Jake at the cut saw, they moved smoothly and efficiently around each other, the bang of the brad-nailer echoing off the walls.

Petra waved but didn't bother to interrupt them. She slipped downstairs, walking past the rooms that would end up as spaces for the men who needed somewhere to stay en route to their better lives. She paused in each doorway, calculating how much still needed to be done, but everywhere signs of progress continued. Not tomorrow, not next week, but soon enough. It had all happened so quickly.

That uneasy sensation returned, and she let her feet carry her around the corner as she desperately tried to untangle the mystery.

The mini suites for the three brothers were also coming

together. One of them looked ready to move into, except for the missing plumbing hardware in the bathroom.

The second and third were stalled at an earlier stage.

Somewhere to her left, a sharp metallic *clang* rang loudly. Following the sound, she discovered Aiden cursing at a pipe in what would be the bathhouse.

When he thumped the fitting a second time with the wrench head, she laughed. "Is this a new way to use a wrench?"

He jerked to a stop an instant before smacking the pipe again. "You never saw that."

Oh, but she had. Petra glanced around the windowless room and decided she knew a good way to forget whatever it was that was bothering her. She backed up to the door and locked it behind her. "What will you give me to keep me from telling?"

Aiden's grin widened. "What do you want me to give?"

She paced toward him, draping her fingers over his shoulder as she circled slowly. "I've noticed you're getting bossier." She plucked the wrench from his hand and laid it carefully on the folding worktable.

He twisted to face her. "You like me bossy."

"Sometimes," she agreed. She traced a finger down the placket of his shirt, pausing at the top of his jeans. "Okay, usually."

He laughed, the sound turning into a hiss of pleasure as she pressed her hand over the front of his jeans and rubbed. "I don't know where you're going with this, but I approve so far."

She unsnapped the button on his jeans and lowered his zipper, face inches away from his to admire his pupils dilating, anticipation rising. "You have this bad habit of not letting me touch you."

"You have the softest skin," he complained. "It's distracting, and then one thing leads to another."

A Cowboy's Bride

She guided her hand under the waistband of his briefs and wrapped her hand around his cock. Aiden sucked for air, and his hips rocked forward slightly. Other than that, though, he stayed put. Waiting.

Watching.

Petra kissed him, hand moving slowly over his erection. Rubbing her thumb over the top, she gathered moisture to tease the sweet spot she'd discovered he loved. She tightened her grip and pulsed before returning to small strokes that made him gasp.

All the while she kissed him. Tangled their tongues, nipped his chin and his neck. Licked a heated line back up to take his mouth again.

But she was no longer in control.

She might have had her hand wrapped around him, giving him pleasure, but the kiss was no longer hers. They were falling into each other, moving together, trying for more.

Desperate for more, and Petra's head buzzed with the pleasure of it. Both the giving and the taking. Both were as right and as necessary as air.

"*Petra*," he warned.

"Let me," she whispered. "Let me," she repeated, speeding up and pulsing harder until he shook. Staring into her eyes, pleasure making his lips fall open, wet from her kisses.

His hips jerked, and moisture washed over her fingers. Aiden clutched her shoulders and held on tight. They stood there, him quivering in her arms, satisfaction rolling over her in a heated wash.

He leaned in and brushed his lips over hers. Gentle, controlled.

"I liked that," he said softly, amusement rising in his tone. "Although I do have to complain about the mess."

"Time to stop banging on that pipe and fix it, then," she

teased. She went up on her toes and kissed his cheek, pulling her hand free. When she would've stepped away, he curled his arms around her and brought them together, holding her as if he needed the assistance to stay vertical.

Petra didn't mind. She laid her head against his chest and listened to the pounding beat under her ear.

Whatever was bothering her, this wasn't it.

～

Small flakes of snow continued to fall, and Aiden sat on the porch swing, staring in admiration.

Winter had arrived with a vengeance the last day of October, and now two weeks later, everything was covered with a pristine layer of white. Clear paths in the snow had developed from where Sasha and Jinx had linked the neighbouring ranches. Trails led to the barn and artists' studio, trails to the fire pit where they continued to meet most evenings, although Petra had suggested they might want to move inside on a regular basis.

Even the air felt different. The sounds of nature were more hushed, the quieter noises of wintertime without the buzzing and chirping of little insects. The occasional birdsong rang, and excited barking when the dogs spotted something to chase. The cows in the field to the north of them carried their own brand of music.

Aiden didn't mind this time of year. There was something to be said for changing and doing the next thing.

He rocked again. One of those next things was going to happen today, and while he waited for their visitors to arrive, he pondered how to keep things rolling in the other elusive area of his agenda.

He and Petra felt right together, and he could honestly say

they were friends. She had his back—his and his brothers'—and the amount of dedication she'd put toward High Water humbled him.

They were narrowing in on the next stage, getting closer to opening their doors to other people who needed them. Petra had kept her focus firmly on Jinx, making sure that the girl not only got her feet under her but bloomed.

And every night when he pulled Petra into his arms, it felt that much more right. Was it even possible that she still assumed this was temporary?

A question he didn't want to ask.

Floorboards creaked, and Petra finally joined him. She was bundled up in her puffy coat with a long scarf and thick toque.

"Are they here yet?" she teased, landing on the seat beside him.

"Remind me never to go on a road trip with you." Aiden linked their hands together, laughing when she tucked them both under her puffy coat. "Are you really that cold?"

"I think my blood got thinner over the summer."

He tickled her side lightly. "You're from a place very close to what they affectionately call Winter-peg. It's barely below freezing right now. What are you going to do when it's officially winter?"

She trapped his fingers and held them tightly to her belly. "Keep the fire inside the house going hot enough we'll be down to shirt sleeves and shorts."

He snorted. "Thank you for the heads-up. I'll immediately order some ridiculous board shorts to annoy my brothers."

In the distance, a large SUV slowly took the turn off the highway. "There they are," Petra told him happily. "I'm so excited we're at this milestone."

They got to their feet. Aiden wrapped his arm around her

waist, pacing slowly toward the parking area to meet their guests. "Where's Jinx?"

"Already in the studio. She and Sasha had some kind of surprise they wanted to set up."

The idea should've made him nervous, considering the elegant looking man exiting the car with Rose Fields and Tansy was someone they needed to impress.

But Jinx had an idea, and he was going to support her no matter what.

"Good if I make the introductions?" Petra asked quietly.

"Of course, but I doubt you'll get a word in edgewise considering this is *Tansy's* eventual brother-in-law."

Which meant they were laughing when they arrived.

Tansy examined them with one brow raised. "Why do I have a sneaky suspicion you were talking about me?"

Petra snickered. "Because you have an overinflated sense of self?"

The tall gentleman's lips twitched. "I see you know my future sister-in-law very well."

An enormous sigh escaped Tansy. "I am *so* misunderstood. Well, not really," she added immediately before performing a grand presentation arm sweep. "Aiden Skye, this is my imminent brother-in-law, Chance Gabrielle. You know my sister, Rose. Chance, this is Aiden. Co-owner of High Water ranch and Petra's eye candy of choice."

Aiden held out a hand. "Nice to finally meet you."

"And you. There's been a lot of speculation about what you're doing here. When you called and offered a tour, I felt as if I'd won the lottery."

Another vehicle pulled in behind the SUV, and a dark-haired girl with tight curls popped out, waving her arm in the air. Sunlight glinted off the metal hook of her prothesis. "Don't start without me."

"Our youngest sister, Fern," Tansy added. "What're you doing here, short stuff?"

"I invited her," Chance said. "I hope you don't mind, but Fern is working with me at the art studio, and she's very involved in all of the educational activities we've coordinated around Heart Falls."

"Not a problem," Aiden insisted. He offered his hand to Fern as well as she joined the group. "Fern."

She had a firm grip and a sparkle in her eyes. "Good to finally meet you. I think I spotted you and Petra on the dance floor one night at Rough Cut, but that's not a place that encourages deep conversations or lasting friendships."

Aiden's mind shot back to meeting Petra there, but he focused on the task at hand. "If we're all here, let's give you that tour."

He led the way the short distance to the entrance staircase to the upper level. The staircase wrapped around the outside of the building, where a cleverly constructed angled roof protected the stairs from the snow and rain. An ample landing on the second floor gave a chance for the first step into the upper rooms to hit with full impact.

Even though Aiden had been looking at the view every day for the past couple of months, it was a sight to behold. With the walls painted a sunny yellow and sunlight reflecting off the polished pine boards underfoot, the entire place glowed. With the recessed lighting overhead, that same wall colour turned into a beautiful candlelight glow in the evening, without shadows but no longer eye-blinkingly bright. A cozy place where people could talk and visit.

Small private rooms lined the sides. The back of the main room, with its long counter, multiple sinks, and small kitchen, was accessible to the entire studio yet somehow unobtrusive.

Near the southern bank of windows, they'd set up a series

of easels, each one catching the light perfectly. In the opposite corner they'd arranged a set of comfy couches, with places to relax and share at the end of the day or sit and read a book.

From the overhead speakers, a soft lilting flute sounded, a timeless melody played a little slower than usual, but the music mixed with the presentation of the space so perfectly Aiden wanted to applaud Petra for having come up with the idea. How she had managed to organize it, he had no idea.

"Oh, wow." Fern wandered past, staring around her in awe.

"This is astonishing." Chance turned to Aiden. "Room for how many to stay on-site?"

"Five individuals, with a possible eight if there are three couples willing to share a bed. We didn't think more than that worked for the kind of atmosphere we're trying to establish."

"Oh, no. That's exactly right." Chance stepped away, ending up next to Fern, the two of them speaking quietly at a rapid pace.

Rose slipped her arm into Petra's. "Now that I see what's been keeping you so busy, I highly approve," she said.

"Oh, I wasn't involved too much with this," Petra insisted.

Rose met Aiden's gaze directly. "I wasn't talking about the artists' studio."

A soft snicker escaped Tansy. "That's my girl. Come on, I want to peek in all the rooms."

"Of course you do," Rose said, long-suffering in her tone as she winked at Petra. "I've been meaning to extend an invitation to you and Aiden to come for dinner. Tuesday this coming week?"

"I think it works, but I'll get back to you," Petra promised.

The girls stepped away, and Petra eased back beside Aiden, her shoulder bumping his. "So far so good."

"Exactly the reaction I was hoping for," Aiden admitted. Chance and Fern paced the length of the studio, still talking earnestly, but if their expressions were anything to go by, they would have the man's help in establishing the artists' part of High Water.

"I like the touch of the music," Petra whispered softly. "Well done."

Aiden frowned. "It wasn't me. I thought you did that."

They both twisted on the spot, looking for answers. Petra pointed to the one room with the door firmly shut. They casually paced over, cracking the door open.

Inside, Sasha hurriedly pressed a finger to her lips, calling for silence.

Next to her, staring intently at her sheet music, Jinx played the flute. It wasn't a simple tune, and it was well enough done that Aiden wanted to shout encouragement. Instead, he let his grin offer his approval.

When she reached the end of the song, carefully lowering the flute from her lips, Aiden broke into full applause, and Petra joined him.

Jinx dipped her chin regally before the biggest smile he'd ever seen burst free. "Was it okay? Sasha set up this app so we could play the music without being around, and she said I sounded good, but I wasn't sure—"

"You killed it," Sasha assured her, wrapping her arms around Jinx's shoulders and squeezing tight.

"You did," Petra agreed. "And I want to hear more, but first, would you like to come and meet Chance and Fern?"

"They're nice," Sasha assured Jinx quietly. "Mr. Gabrielle has done some guest lessons at the school, and he is not boring like our regular art teacher."

A soft chuckle sounded from behind Aiden's back. "I endeavour to always earn such high praise." Chance stood in the doorway, his arm wrapped around Rose's waist. "And here we have the source of the lovely music. Thank you so much for the serenade. It was well done and well selected. If I remember correctly that piece was from the unfinished symphony. And while the studio is nearly done, it still needs a few things to be finished."

"You recognize the music?" Jinx rose and transferred the flute to her left hand so she could extend her right. "Nice to meet you, Mr. Gabrielle."

"Nice to meet you too," he said. "This is Fern Fields, younger sister to Tansy and Rose, whom you already know."

Fern wiggled her fingers. "Are you an artist as well as a musician?"

"She'll say no," Sasha answered before Jinx could, "but Kelli says you can't say that until you've given it a good try."

Jinx's lips twitched. "Obviously after she's said that, I can't possibly say no."

"Wise choice," Fern agreed. She glanced around the studio again. "I like the place."

"Me too." Chance dipped his chin at Aiden. "I have a small workspace at the top of my art gallery, but it's not sufficient for the classes I'd like to offer. I'd like to sit down and come up with some plans that will work well for all of us."

"That's good to hear." Aiden's brothers were going to be so relieved. Forward motion in this area meant they were one step closer to opening their doors fully, secret or not. "Now all we need to do is officially break in the studio."

"You should host a party," Tansy suggested. "I know this great caterer and possibly some awesome people to invite."

"It's a great idea," Petra said, still more focused on Jinx than anything else. "It's too late for Thanksgiving or Halloween, and too early for Christmas. What kind of party are you going to hold so we can hire you as a caterer?"

"That's easy." Tansy met Aiden's gaze and waggled her brows. "It's Petra's birthday next Friday—"

"*Tansy,*" Petra complained.

"Oh, I like this idea," Aiden said, hopping on the train with full enthusiasm. A test run wasn't a bad idea, and if anything did go wrong, Petra wasn't going to complain.

Plus, the idea of doing something special for her made him happy.

Petra glared daggers at her friend. "You're terrible about that cone of secrecy business."

"Birthdays don't really fall under the cone of secrecy, though, do they?" Tansy shook her head. "I think not."

Aiden twisted toward Petra. He caught her hands in his and tugged to get her attention. "We won't do it if you absolutely hate the idea," he said softly. "But a bit of a party after all the work we put in isn't a bad idea."

She sighed. An enormous, dramatic thing, flopping her hands into the air. "Okay, fine. You may all celebrate my natal day. But there will be *no* presents, and I get to pick what type of cake Tansy makes me."

"Deal." Aiden shook her hand firmly then turned to the rest of them who waited eagerly in the main room. Jinx's eyes sparkled with happiness, Sasha standing close by her side. "It's official. You're all invited back next Friday for Petra's birthday party, and the official soft opening of the High Water artists' studio."

18

Sydney eyed the collection of boxes in the corner of the living room. "Are you planning on running away from home?"

Petra waved a hand. "Supplies for the art studio started to arrive, and since I haven't been allowed to go into the building for the past week, the stash has been piled here instead of being put away where they belong."

"Good thing your party is tonight, then." Sydney leaned back in her chair, extending her fingers toward the lit fireplace. "Are you ready to celebrate?"

"I suppose." It wasn't that Petra didn't want to enjoy the festivities. She completely agreed that a test run for the artist studio was a good idea.

The problem was that strange aching sensation still lingered. "Maybe I need you to prescribe something to adjust my perkiness."

"Well, if you're having troubles in the bedroom—"

"That is not it at all," Petra assured her quickly.

Sydney nodded sagely. "Ah, so you broke another bed? Or you *haven't* broken another bed?"

"You're terrible." No, the sex was just fine. Aiden was just fine. Heck, things at High Water were better than fine.

Yet something still felt so terribly off.

Petra shook her head, focusing on other things. "Did I tell you that Jinx and I had a nice long talk? Turns out she signed up on the sly for the flute lessons. She's been practicing in the barn so that none of us would know. She figured it was going to be a Christmas present until Sasha convinced her to jump the gun and play last week." The sense of pride Petra felt was out of place but undeniable. "She's good."

"Spoken like a true mama bear," Sydney said softly. "I'm glad she's doing well. I think she's doing *better* than well. When I saw her earlier today, she looked a match for any teenager, arm in arm with Sasha Stone. Brilliant matchup right there, have to tell you."

Petra was still wrapping her brain around the *mama bear* comment.

Something of what she was feeling must've shown on her face because Sydney leaned over and grabbed her fingers. "You need to never play poker. And also, as your friend—and we are good friends—I feel as if the time has come to ask if you know what you're doing."

Petra paused for a second. "Regarding what?"

Her friend shrugged. "I'll continue to support you one hundred percent, but when you told us about coming to live at High Water, it began from a place of desperation and the immediate need to get Jinx out of trouble. It's now over two months later. We're no longer in panic mode. Maybe it's time to reconsider the lies."

"Jinx is nowhere near ready for me to not be here—" Petra began before Sydney lifted a hand to stop her.

"Of course not. I'm not suggesting that at all." Her serious expression softened. "It's not you being here, helping at High Water and supporting Jinx that needs to be fixed. It's the part about pretending to be engaged to Aiden."

Shit.

Petra stared at Sydney for the longest time before her friend patted her fingers and then stood. "And that's the end of this house call. I've got a couple things I need to do before returning. I'll be back in time to join the party."

She gave Petra a hug then vanished before Petra's brain had caught up enough to even say goodbye.

A second later, the door opened again. This time Tansy rushed in, Jake hard on her heels.

"Hey, Petra," Tansy said happily. "Have a nice visit with Sydney?"

Nice? If two-by-fours to the head and heart could be considered nice, she supposed it was.

"Sure." Petra opened her mouth to ask a question, but Jake interrupted.

"Sorry, Petra. Tansy, will you stop running away?"

"Running was required because there's nothing more to talk about, but you continued to flap your gums. I figured escape was easier than breaking my hand trying to stop the babble of noise." She kept walking, headed to the kitchen. "Because if there's anything worse than being told someone doesn't think you know what you're doing, it's having somebody tell you that over and over and over again."

"I never said you don't know what you're doing," Jake snapped. "Only that we're supposed to do this together, and your approach makes no sense whatsoever."

Tansy leaned against the island, smiling at Petra even as she raised her hands in frustration. "I make no sense. That's what the man just said."

All other thoughts pushed aside, Petra ping-ponged her gaze between two of them. "What are you up to? Not that I want to organize my own party, but Tansy, I thought you were prepping things for tonight. Why are you here in the house?"

"Because *he* was in the kitchen in the studio." Tansy batted her lashes at Jake. "And *he* seems to know what needs to be done, so I'm letting him do it."

"I wasn't trying to tell you what to do," Jake insisted. He hesitated. "Well, maybe a little." He turned toward Petra for support. "I was trying to figure out when we need to start cooking the chicken wings, but Tansy seems to think that 'when they need to start' is a sufficient answer.

"Relax, Jakey. Got it under control," Tansy sing-songed.

"Is there something wrong with you writing down the times that we need to start? It seems that's what a reasonable person would do," Jake complained.

"Great, so now I'm unreasonable."

"That's not what I meant."

Tansy turned on him, fists planted on her hips as she glared daggers. "I did that once, on my final exam for level II chef training. Never again am I inflicting that level of minutia on my brain."

Petra couldn't help it. She snickered loud enough it caught both of their attention. She swallowed hard trying to hide her amusement. But really, poor Jake. "Tansy, I love you dearly. Would you please go up to the kitchen and make sure all of the things for my birthday party are ready on time?"

"I love you too, and I'll absolutely do that." Tansy blew her a kiss then marched past Jake, close enough to knock him with her shoulder.

He swayed on the spot but was smart enough not to say anything.

Petra waited until Tansy left the room before coming over

and squeezing Jake's shoulders. "You are a very organized man. I can totally understand how Tansy's seemingly scattered approach would be hard on you. But that same approach has produced all the food for a highly successful café, and also many special events around Heart Falls over the years. And, I might add, it seems to have put meals on this table at least seventy-five percent of the time when *you* were supposed to be our cook."

He opened his mouth then firmly closed it. "You're right."

That admission was only half of the battle. "If you're supposed to be working together in the kitchen, probably the easiest way to do that without you getting an ulcer is for you to ask her what you should help with."

"It's really hard not knowing what's coming next," Jake muttered softly.

"It is, but you're a big boy. I think you can handle it."

He snorted before wrapping her up in a hug. He patted her on the back the way he would've one of his brothers. "You're a good one, Petra. Thanks for the advice."

"Any time. Now," she shoved him toward the door, "would you please get out there? Because I want this to be an awesome birthday party. I'm sure Tansy's got some carrots for you to peel or something."

Jake muttered under his breath slightly, but he obediently headed for the door. The door clicked shut before Petra breathed her own sigh of relief.

Sydney's words of wisdom were still churning in Petra's gut. Being here at High Water was supposed to only be a temporary thing, but clearly, that kind of thinking couldn't continue.

Which meant starting back at square one.

What did she truly want?

She had moved all the way here to Alberta, away from what

had been her hometown, to start a new life. What she'd found were people she cared about and a young woman who was blooming because of being in a safe environment. Petra had gotten to spend time with her brother and sister-in-law, and she'd gotten to know the Skye brothers better.

But mostly, the part her brain kept turning to again and again was Aiden. Her temporary distraction, her lover who had rapidly grown into a trusted friend.

Maybe Sydney was right. Maybe something at the very core of what they were doing needed to change.

Did she want this to still be pretend? And how on earth did she change it if that's not what she wanted?

It didn't seem like the thing you up and told a guy. *Hey, you know this pretending to be engaged thing that we're doing? I think we should actually consider getting married down the road.*

Aiden would either think she was feverish or he'd be looking for the nearest exit, stat.

Frustration washed in, again, and Petra once again fell back on distraction to avoid thinking too hard. She hopped on her computer and got to work, the numbers dancing before her mixing with snippets of conversation. Moments repeated over and over, especially the ones where she and Aiden had shared tidbits from their lives. Things that had made them happy. Things that had made them think.

What was it they'd said way back then? That first day when she'd convinced him it was okay for them to be lovers—

She racked her brain, and slowly it came back. They'd said they would do this—the friends with benefits—until it wasn't working for one of them.

Well, just being friends wasn't working anymore. If Petra wanted them to stop the casual sex because she wanted it to be *more* than casual—that was within the letter of the law.

Wasn't it?

She was staring motionless at her computer screen when strong fingers landed on her shoulders, massaging lightly. Aiden bent and kissed the side of her neck.

"You're obviously jumping at the bit to put your party hat on," he teased. "Come on, it's time for the birthday girl to get ready."

She rose, kissing his cheek as she slipped past him, the start of a plan falling into place. Not now, and not until everyone had gone home, but Sydney was right. It was past time to talk about dropping the pretending.

Petra slipped on a new blue blouse and pulled herself together, then stared into the mirror and straightened her shoulders. "I think it's going to be a good evening."

Even as she crossed her fingers and hoped she wasn't about to turn her birthday party into a non-celebration of epic proportions.

∼

THE PARTY WAS A RAGING SUCCESS.

An extended group of ladies that Aiden had been informed were a large portion of the local Heart Falls girls'-night-out posse had shown up, and every one of them had brought their significant others. Zach and Julia were there, along with Sasha Stone's parents, and Chance Gabrielle and Rose Fields, and too many others to keep track of easily.

It meant a good-sized party was happening with music and impromptu dancing.

The food, plentiful and delicious, had shown up like magic right when the last of the guests arrived. For some reason, Jake's scowl deepened with every compliment, and it only got worse when Tansy had tied an apron on him boasting an image of a frazzled cat and the words *It's fine. It's all fine.*

In one corner of the room, Sasha and Jinx were playing board games with a group of other teens. Sasha had been invited to stay for a sleepover afterward, and the mere idea that Jinx felt comfortable enough to invite a friend over made everything in Aiden's heart soften.

But Aiden's gaze most often went to Petra as she wandered the room, accepting birthday wishes and hugs. She had a glow tonight, the delicate bright blue shirt making her pale eyes shine.

Aiden couldn't keep his eyes off her.

"I don't know why you're not over there standing next to Petra," Declan complained between sips from his long neck beer. "Even when you're talking to us, your mind is obviously somewhere else."

"I need a little dose of you guys," Aiden offered cheerfully. "It is her party. She needs to do the butterfly thing and give everybody a chance to enjoy her company."

"She is pretty amazing," Jake agreed, finally undoing the knot on the apron and pulling it off over his head. "And well liked. The turnout is great. People seem to be enjoying themselves, and the space is perfect for this kind of event. We should consider renting it for parties when we don't have artists in residence."

Declan began suggesting possible other parties they could arrange in the future, and as his brothers chatted back and forth, Aiden listened without hearing and went back to staring at Petra.

The outside door opened, and a rush of cold air swept in, swirling around the room. An older couple pushed through the door with wide smiles on faces that seemed eerily familiar. The woman especially looked recognizable, and all it took was a single glance between her and Petra to make the connection.

Holy shit. Petra's parents had just walked into the room.

Zach and Julia noticed before Petra did. Both of their expressions went from happiness before, as if following a cue card, flashing to panic. Their heads snapped on a swivel to Petra then across the room to Aiden.

Oh shit. Shit, shit, *shit*.

Aiden had to get to Petra's side to warn her. "Sorry guys, gotta run."

Jake didn't move out of the way, peering over his shoulder and making a fantastic roadblock. "What's got your— Oh. Who are they?"

"Petra's parents," Aiden muttered hurriedly before pushing past them.

The softly said *fucking hell* behind him was amusing and appreciated all the same.

Zach veered off and met Aiden in the middle of the room while Julia headed straight to intercept her in-laws as a greeting committee. A second later, she was enveloped in hugs and happy exclamations.

Zach tugged Aiden to the side of the room. "The congratulations about the baby will keep them distracted for a minute, but Christ, man. What are you going to do?"

"Get to Petra then make it up as we go along," Aiden said. "Who's the bigger worry? Your mom or dad?"

Zach paced at his side as they made their way across the room to where Petra stood with her back still to the door, unaware of the drama that was about to hit. "They're both equally dangerous. If it helps, both Julia and I are here for you guys."

"Thanks. That means a lot."

Zach veered away to greet his parents, and Aiden didn't

bother with the niceties, just smiled at the ladies Petra was talking to as he slipped his arm around her waist. "Sorry for interrupting, but I need to steal Petra away."

He got a bevy of amused grins in return even as he backed Petra up and leaned his lips to her ear. "Don't panic, but your parents just showed up."

She cursed softly. "Are you kidding me?"

"They're here, currently talking to Julia and Zach, but how do you want to do this? Do you want me to take off so you don't have to deal with introducing me?"

"Of course, they have to show up right now." She closed her eyes, her face contorting in a mass of frustration and confusion. "No, you're not taking off. They're reasonable people, and if I tell them that we should speak privately, they won't make a fuss." She squared her shoulders then glanced behind her. "But maybe we should try to be closer to the door than in the middle of the room to keep potential damage to a minimum."

"After you."

He kept his hands to himself, thinking that would make it easier if she decided at the last moment not to mention the fiancé thing. Although it was a roll of the dice that no one else would mention it.

Someone else dropping the bomb would probably be worse, especially springing it on them out of the blue.

So he was shocked when Petra linked her fingers in his and gripped tightly, pulling him to a stop in front of her parents. "Mom. Dad. What are you doing here?"

"You might no longer be living under our roof, but you're still our little girl. Happy birthday, Petra." Her mom threw her arms open, and Petra slipped in, accepting a massive hug.

Aiden smiled, his expression tightening slightly as he noticed Petra's dad was eyeing him oddly. But the man returned his focus to his daughter an instant later, offering her a massive hug as well. "Plus, you know it was a good excuse to come visit. We needed to celebrate the coming baby and see your brother and Julia."

Suddenly, their attention turned. "And who is this young man?" Petra's mom asked brightly.

Aiden was far too aware that there were locals watching with some confusion.

Petra laughed, a bright sound full of reassuring humour. "You're such a kidder, Mom. Hey, Aiden and I wanted to talk to you. How about we—"

A nearly deafening high-pitched clatter echoed through the room, followed by rapid clapping.

Tansy and Sydney stepped forward. Tansy held a vibrating dinner bell in the air as she glanced around the room. "Okay, everybody out of the pool. Grab your coats and head down to the fire pit. We have a surprise in a few minutes, accompanied by the best s'mores you have eaten in your entire life."

"Adult beverages will be served," Sydney added. "Nonadult ones as well, and don't think I'm not watching you, Sasha Stone."

Sasha stuck out her tongue, but she joined the others as the crowd grabbed coats and headed outside.

At first Aiden thought they'd managed to dodge a bullet when Chance Gabrielle paused to offer the older couple a warm greeting. "It's nice to finally meet you. Petra and her fiancé have been the most delightful addition to Heart Falls."

If Aiden could've dropped through a hole in the floor at that moment he totally would've.

Recovering quickly, Petra's dad smiled tightly. "That's wonderful to know."

"Come on, Chance, Tansy is waving at us." Rose dipped her head politely at the Sorensons even as she pulled her fiancé out the door.

Petra shuffled her parents to the side, waiting until the room had cleared to continue. She took a deep breath and made introductions.

"Aiden, these are my parents. Pamela and Zachary Sorenson. Mom and Dad," Petra stepped closer and slid her arm around Aiden's waist, firmly fixing him to her side. "This is Aiden Skye. Co-owner of High Water ranch with his brothers."

"I'm going to hold off on the nice to know you part." Zachary shook his head as he focused on his daughter. "Petra, what's going on?"

"Yes, that's what I'd like to know as well." Pamela eyed them with something close to horror. "You're engaged?"

Aiden opened his mouth to answer but Petra beat him to it. "We're dating. But there's a small complication that, because of confidentiality reasons, I can't share—"

"They're your parents. You can share," Aiden offered softly.

"Why does this feel like when Zach announced that he'd accidentally gotten drunk and married in Vegas?" Pamela asked. "And that he'd been pretending he and Julia were together. But they really were together..."

"It's not like that," Petra assured them.

"The complicated parts of this aside, I'm still concerned. You're already seriously dating someone?" Zachary asked. "Sweetheart, it's only been a short time. Is this some sort of rebound? Because I know that young man back home did a number on you—"

"What?" Petra demanded. She took a step back, anxiety so clear in the tension in her body that Aiden wanted to scoop her into his arms and protect her. She turned to her parents. "You knew about Curtis?"

"We knew you were seeing someone, but when you suddenly decided you didn't want to live in town anymore, we figured out things had gone sideways." Her mother spoke softly, sympathy in her voice. "It's not a failing for a relationship not to last. Not everyone is meant to be together. That's why you date."

"But that doesn't mean you should jump into another relationship immediately." Zachary eyed Aiden. "I hope you've been treating my daughter with the respect she deserves."

What a nightmare of a tangle. "Of course, sir. But at the same time, this is becoming the kind of conversation where I need to politely tell you to butt out. Petra is a grown woman, and she knows her own mind. She's not in any danger, and I would do anything to keep her safe and secure. So other than that, I don't want to be rude, but—"

"Don't stick my nose in your business?" Zachary demanded.

"Zachary, Aiden is right. Although, this is not about us telling Petra what she can or cannot do with her life." Pamela eyed Petra with a sincere love. "It's just that it's so *fast*. That's the part that worries me."

"Holy shit." Petra turned to Aiden, her expression turning from concern to one of excitement and discovery. As if she had just solved some sort of huge puzzle. "That's *it*. That's what's been bugging me."

"Excuse me?" Now Aiden felt as if he wasn't part of this conversation.

She grabbed him by the hand and tugged him toward the door. "Excuse me, Mom, Dad. Go enjoy the surprise and visit with Zach and Julia, and we'll catch up later. I'm glad you're here, and everything's going to be fine, but right now, Aiden and I need to talk."

A minute later, he had been pulled out the door into the wintry cold, dark night. Aiden went willingly, and they ended up in his rooms on the ground floor. The ones that he hadn't been doing a whole lot of work on lately because he was enjoying living in the house with Petra.

"So, that went well," he started.

She turned on him. "I figured it out. I know what's been bothering me this entire time."

Entire time? "I think you're three steps ahead of me in this conversation," Aiden warned.

"This whole fiancée thing just came up out of the blue, right? I mean, Declan threw it at us that first day when Danielle was there. *Hey, here she is, Aiden's fiancée, Petra.* And at that point we'd had, what, three hours in each other's company this go round? But we had to roll with it. Which has been a thing, but here's what gets me. I kept looking at the calendar as the days flew past. It was *Oh, we're engaged,* and then *Oh, it's one day until Jinx arrives, don't screw this up,* and then it had been a week she was there, and a month, and now it's over two months." The longer she spoke, the louder and more intense she got. "It seems as if we keep doing the next thing and never stop to realize what's really going on."

"What *is* going on?" Aiden asked loudly but with complete sincerity because he was so lost.

"Not what we should be doing." She took a deep breath and bounced a couple of paces away, looking around the room as if waiting for a cue. She spun to face him, shaking her hands in the air for emphasis as she spoke loud and clear. "Spending time pretending that we're together is the last thing I want."

Aiden froze. His stomach fell all the way down to his toes. He had not seen that one coming. "Really."

She took a deep breath then nodded firmly.

"Then I'll get out of your way. I'll do it right now." Seconds later, the door slammed shut behind him as fury whipped through his veins.

He veered away from where the partiers were gathered by

the fire pit and stomped his way back to the main house. The snow along the western path was tracked up and dirty with mud from the gravel drive. A perfect match to his suddenly foul mood.

This was not what he'd been hoping for at all. But damn if he was going to make the woman put up with his sorry ass when—

He was only feet away from the porch when something smacked into the back of his head, knocking him forward and covering him with a fine dusting of ice and cold.

He twisted on the spot, cursing whoever had the gall to hit him with a freaking snowball right now. Then he spotted Petra bearing down on him like a freight train.

19

What. The. *Hell?*

When Aiden abruptly left the room, Petra had stared after him for ten seconds before giving chase.

If nothing else she needed to knock some sense into that fat head of his. The snowball was what came naturally.

"Where are you going? We were in the middle of a conversation," she barked, her fingers tingling from the cold and wet.

"But you don't want to spend your time with me," he snapped back, "I'm getting out of your hair so you don't have to."

Her confusion deepened. "What are you talking about?"

"You just told me you don't want to be engaged anymore."

"What?" She hadn't said that. Had she? She thought back... "You're going to need to help me out here, because we seem to be in two different conversations."

His eyes flashed with anger. "Maybe it's a good thing your parents showed up unannounced. It's clarified a lot. Number one, you didn't want to tell them that we were engaged. You were horrified when Chance mentioned it. Once we were alone, you clearly said that you wanted to stop. That you didn't want to be with me anymore."

He'd lost his mind. Petra wrapped her arms around herself to try to keep out the cold, shaking her head in denial. "That's not what I said. Or if that's what I said, that's not what I meant."

"Extremely unhelpful," Aiden snapped. He stomped in a circle for seconds before tipping his head toward the house. "Get inside. We can have this argument in front of the fire so you don't freeze to death."

They kicked off their shoes in silence, shuffling forward until they stood in front of the woodburning stove. As far apart from each other as they could be while still being enveloped by heat.

She took a deep breath then lifted her gaze to his. "I wasn't embarrassed to have my parents hear Chance call you my fiancé. What I'm embarrassed about is that for days I've felt how wrong it is, this thing we're doing."

Aiden closed his eyes, frustration washing over his face. "This conversation isn't getting any better."

There was no way to do this without full-on embarrassing herself. So be it. "Fine, I'll stop trying to say this in a way that gives you an out. When we first talked about fooling around, we said that if either of us wanted to stop, we were adults. We would just say we wanted to stop being friends with benefits."

He looked at her for a long moment. "And that's what you want?" Aiden asked quietly.

"I want to stop the fake part. I want to stop the *pretending*." She closed her eyes, because looking at him while she blurted out everything was impossible. "We got shoved into this relationship through no decision of our own, but Aiden, I

A Cowboy's Bride

would've picked you. If we'd had the time to do things normally, we would've started dating."

When she opened her eyes he was staring at her, jaw dropped, speechless.

She hurried forward, because if she didn't say it now, she might lose her courage. "Part of what's had me confused is that it *has* been fast. As if part of my brain has been making the same comments that Mom and Dad did about what happened with Curtis, but the comparison felt off kilter." She took a deep breath and stepped toward him. She caught his cold hands in hers, holding them tightly. "Every time I looked at the calendar it seemed as if it was far too short of a time to care about you as much as I do. It should feel scary, like a reminder of Curtis and what went wrong, but it never did. When I think back to what I had with Curtis, and what I have with you—there is no comparison. You and I have grown so close, so fast, because we've been open and honest and ourselves—at least in private."

Aiden's mouth hung open. "You're not trying to break up with me?"

"Of course not. I'm trying to tell you what I don't like is the *pretending*." She sucked in all of her bravery and finished her confession. "Because I haven't been pretending. I care about you, Aiden. I like being with you. I like the things you do and who you are. I think we're good together."

The corner of his lips twitched. Then he tugged her toward him and wrapped his arms around her.

The hug felt amazing even if he was probably just getting ready to find some way to let her down easily. But when he tucked his strong fingers under her chin and tilted her face to his, no more anger or confusion or frustration covered his face. Just a one hundred percent Aiden smile full of amusement and mischief.

He leaned their foreheads together. "Thank God. That means I'm not the only one."

Shock, sudden and deep. "Really?"

"Really, *really*," he confirmed. "Although I'll admit that whole conversation we just had sucked. I had no idea what was going on for a big part of it. I don't like being angry and sad and worried and devastated, especially when I had hoped this evening would finish with me telling the woman I care about deeply that we should consider being more to each other than pretend."

Petra shook her head. "All that shouting and frustration was for nothing?"

"Well, I don't know about that." Aiden curled his arm around her waist, connecting their torsos. "We haven't had a fight before. That means we can have makeup sex."

"Wasn't really a fight," Petra pointed out. "It was just me making things way too convoluted. I'm sorry."

"I am too," Aiden said. "That means we can have *no more convoluted conversations* sex, yes?"

She stroked her fingers up the side of his neck and into his hair, teasing as heat wrapped around them. "I have a feeling that no matter what we decide to call the conversation, there's going to be sex involved at the end."

He pressed a series of kisses along her jaw line to under her ear and spoke quietly. "I have no problem with that plan. As there's no pretending involved."

He nipped her neck, and in spite of the fire beside them, a shiver raced up her spine.

She cupped his face in her hands and stared into his blue eyes. "I'm sorry for making things confusing. Here is me being crystal clear. I'd like to go and have sex with you, because you're an amazing guy, Aiden. You're funny, smart, and the way you move with me turns me on."

A gasp escaped as Aiden lifted her off her feet, carrying her down the hallway to their room.

He settled her on the bed, going to his knees on the carpet in front of her, pausing to stare into her eyes. "I know we probably don't need this, but I did get you a birthday present or two. Hang on."

"I don't need anything—" Petra protested, but he'd already grabbed her decorative paper bag from beside the bed, dropping it into her lap.

"I want to use them," he said, "So you have to unwrap them right this instant."

She laughed as she dug into the bag and pulled out a tissue wrapped cylinder. She ripped away the paper and discovered a candle, this one labeled *Netflix & Chill*. "Oh my God."

"They get better," he said taking the unwrapped one from her and putting it to the side.

Petra dipped back into the bag. Wrapping paper flew, and her laughter grew louder as she read the labels on three more candles.

Thanks For All The Orgasms.

Light Me When You're Horny.

Big Dick Energy Candle (when this candle is lit, give me that dick). She dragged in air, her hand pressed to her stomach. She lifted the last one in the air, tears pouring down her cheeks. "Oh. My. *God.*"

Aiden smirked. "Truth in advertising," he said as he nabbed each candle, lit it, and placed them around the room. Then he turned off the overhead lights and it was only candlelight as he came back to the bed and rolled her to the middle.

He wiped away her tears, staring at her face far too solemnly. "I know it's been a roller coaster, but I do want to wish you happy birthday. I hope this coming year is full of things that make you smile and things that make you happy, but mostly I hope it's full of *real*. No more pretending."

He pressed their lips together, brief and gentle, not as if he were teasing but as if he were savouring every moment. Every touch.

He stripped away her blouse, kissing each bit of skin as he revealed it. Coming back between over and over to her lips. He caressed her breast followed by a kiss. Licked a line down her ribcage, and another kiss.

"Aiden." She breathed his name, threading her fingers through his hair and tugging him back up when he lingered too long at her belly.

The kiss went deeper this time, more heated. Petra opened her legs and cradled him between them, naked from the waist up as his hands roamed over her, touching and caressing and teasing.

He nipped her lower lip, and when she gasped, he smiled down at her. "Stay right there," he ordered.

This time when he worked his way down her body, unsnapping her pants and easing them and her underwear off her hips, he stayed down. Fleeting licks of his tongue against her skin, small bites to the inside of her thigh. He grasped her knees and separated them.

Another touch of his tongue, easing over her clit as his fingers stroked closer and closer to her sex. A gentle taunt in a way. And as he so often did, he'd pause right before he joined them. The tips of his fingers at her entrance, watching her face as he pressed in.

Then gentleness was gone, and he took control, driving her up hard and fast with his fingers and his mouth. Petra dug her heels into his back and held onto her thighs to keep from accidentally shifting him away from where she needed him most.

"*Aiden.*" A request, a plea, a benediction as her orgasm rushed in, arching her back and driving her hips up to his mouth.

Outside the window, a bright flash of light exploded followed by a sharp rumble as the first firework went off.

Petra laughed, and the sound danced around the room, full of delight, and happiness, and everything she could've ever wished for her birthday.

∼

AIDEN HURRIEDLY STRIPPED away his clothes. He put on a condom faster than was probably wise, but sliding over a laughing Petra, naked skin to naked skin, had to happen as soon as possible.

Another firework went off, lighting the room with blues and greens. "Declan is going to give Tansy so much shit," Petra whispered. "I don't think horses like fireworks."

"Not our problem right now," Aiden pointed out. "There's no one here but us, and there's nothing I need except us. Except *you.*"

She nodded, pulling him closer to kiss him eagerly, breaking apart when her lungs demanded air. "I need you, too."

He slid into her. The heat wrapped around his cock was so fucking good, but it was the way she looked at him that drove him higher. The way she lifted her right leg and angled her hips to take him in easier. Welcoming him into her body, pleasure streaking over her face as he cupped her breast and teased her nipple. Rocking his hips slowly as he brought her up again.

It had only been a short time, but long enough they knew what each other liked. She scratched her fingernails down his back, groaning as he nipped her earlobe and neck. She pushed up against him, increasing tempo, adjusting angle to bring him in deeper, harder.

Aiden clung to his control, sliding a hand over her belly to between her legs. "I want to take you with me."

She nodded, eyes widening as she slowed the rocking motion. Made it easier for him to tease over her clit, drawing moisture from where their connection slid over and over again.

She took a deep breath, body tensing under him, and Aiden fluttered his fingers faster, pressing his cock deep in a smooth rhythm he hoped to maintain for long enough—

"*Yes.*" Petra arched, her sex fisting around him, and Aiden was gone. Lightning filled the room and streaked up his spine as he came, body shaking as he held himself high enough he didn't crush her. They both spiraled into pleasure in the reflected golden lights of a thousand sparks that danced around the room in time with the flickering candles.

Five minutes later... Ten? Time had no meaning, Aiden decided.

They were still curled around each other, Aiden staring into her eyes. In spite of everything, he hesitated.

Actually asking her to get engaged right now seemed like a *soon* thing, not a *now* thing.

"We're good?" he asked softly.

She snickered, wiggling her hips against him as her smile brightened with mischief. "If you couldn't tell, that's your loss, but yes, we're very good on so many levels." Petra took a deep breath and exhaled slowly. "I like you Aiden Skye. I like how you make me feel, and that's not just a sexual comment. Although it's totally a sexual comment," she teased.

He stared down, the ache in his heart softening. "We've done things that made us happy over the past two months, but I think you're right. The parts that were the best were the things that were truly us. And that's not just a sexual comment for me either."

She nodded, fingers slipping over his chest and shoulders in a smooth figure eight. As if she couldn't bear to stop touching him. "I don't think we truly lied to each other, except maybe lies of omission."

"Then that's the part we have to watch for going forward," he suggested. "Petra, no one is a completely wide-open book to anyone else. We'll always have some secrets or at least things we need to think about a whole lot before we talk them through. But for me, it always comes back to this—I like you as a person and I like who I am when I'm with you. That's worth having some awkward conversations and getting past misunderstandings."

Her lips quivered. "Dammit, Aiden. I do not want to become a watering can."

"I wouldn't mind avoiding that as well," he teased, brushing his nose past hers and taking a deep breath. Just breathing the same air as her because he enjoyed it so very much.

They lay together, holding close as outside the fireworks continued to go off, and the musical sound of laughter carried all the way to the main house. Slowly it quieted.

Aiden was about to suggest they should get dressed when Petra rolled him to his back and crawled over him, mischief on her face as she pressed her hands to his chest and lowered her lashes. "We were terrible hosts, but I figure everybody's heading home now. We may as well keep celebrating my birthday all on our lonesome."

She rolled her shoulders, and his gaze dropped from her eyes to her amazing breasts. Amusement hummed from her as he slid his fingers over her hips. "That is the most brilliant idea—"

A rapid knock sounded on the door. "Aiden. Sorry, bro. We

need to talk right now." Declan cleared his throat. "Petra. It's important."

Aiden sighed loud enough they probably heard it in Heart Falls. His brothers. "Really? It can't wait until the morning?"

"Dammit, Aiden." Declan's voice held restrained panic. "Jinx is missing."

20

Fear made her fingers clumsy as Petra raced to get dressed. Beside her, Aiden was hauling on jeans and socks, worry pouring off him.

"I'm sure she's okay," Petra said to reassure herself as much as him.

He caught her fingers in his and squeezed tight. "We'll figure out what happened together. No matter what." Aiden dipped his chin firmly. "We promised she'd be safe, and we will make that happen…" His voice trailed off.

They rushed into the living room to discover a full room. Everyone from High Water ranch was there, plus Zach and Julia and Petra's parents. Sasha stood slightly to one side with Tansy and Sydney surrounding her, a united front.

"Tell us," Aiden demanded, turning to Declan.

"The girls planned to sleep in the barn. Sasha went to say good night to her parents, and when she got back, Jinx was gone. Her sleeping bag and backpack are missing."

"We went through the entire barn from top to bottom," Declan said. "She's not there, and she's not in any of the stalls."

A quivering sniffle escaped Sasha, fear written all over her young face.

Petra stepped in front of her. "It's okay, honey. You didn't do anything wrong, but is there anything else you can tell us? Did Jinx say anything to you? Did she seem upset?"

Sasha shook her head. "She was quiet, but she's often quiet." She glanced at Tansy. "We had s'mores with you by the fire pit, then we sat on the swing to watch the fireworks. She said she'd meet me in the barn. I went to say good night to my mom and dad, but when I got up to the barn, Jinx wasn't there."

Aiden checked the time. "Fireworks finished less than an hour ago."

No one had yet mentioned the one horrifying possibility. "You don't think somebody from her past foster home grabbed her?" Petra asked Declan quietly, making sure Sasha didn't overhear.

He shook his head. "Jinx left her phone on a pile of neatly folded clothes. A whole bunch of new stuff you bought her. It doesn't look at all like somebody who was snatched up."

"Dixie is missing too," Jake said. "There's a good chance the dog is still with Jinx."

Or things had gone even more wrong than they knew. If someone had grabbed Jinx, they would've had to go through Dixie to do it. Fear bubbled in Petra's gut, but she fought it down. This wasn't the time to panic.

This was when she had to do everything possible for Jinx's sake.

"She left her phone." Petra paced beside Aiden then turned to the group. "Which means I can't track her through location services. What else? What else can you tell us?"

"We didn't take much out to the barn," Sasha said. "We didn't even pack any snacks because we knew there would be so much food at the birthday party."

The girl looked so miserable Petra tugged her into a hug.

Aiden joined them, wrapping his arms around Petra's and Sasha's shoulders, his voice calm and reassuring. "Any more details? You guys were going to have a sleepover. What was the plan for tomorrow? I heard something about going riding after breakfast. What else?"

"Nothing fancy. I left my riding clothes in her room because everything we needed for the sleepover fit into our backpacks. Jinx said we'd come into the house to have breakfast so we could get dressed and go as soon as Declan was ready to take us."

Petra jerked her head up and glanced toward the front door where their coats hung in an orderly fashion, courtesy of Jake's meticulous hook arrangement.

The new grey backpack Jinx had bought for school was clearly visible on its hook.

Sweet relief poured over Petra the same moment Aiden laid his hand on her shoulder. "Are you thinking what I'm thinking?" he asked.

"Definitely." Petra squeezed Sasha extra hard before stepping back, smiling her approval. "And that's the last bit of the puzzle we needed. Well done."

Sasha frowned along with the rest of them in the room. Everyone except Aiden, who instead nodded firmly as Petra grabbed her phone.

"Hacking?" Jake asked quietly.

"AirTags," Aiden answered, tilting his head toward the wall as Petra hurriedly opened the app she needed. "Jinx bought a backpack for school, but she needed a second for going on trail rides because she didn't want the school one to get all horsey. Petra lent her one of her old ones."

Tansy clapped her hands together in delight. "You didn't."

Petra nodded. "And because I'm notorious for forgetting

things somewhere and not knowing where I left them, I have AirTags sewn into *all* my bags."

Aiden leaned over her shoulder, watching as she scrolled through the app settings. "I have never been so happy for someone to be forgetful as right now." He pressed a quick kiss to her cheek then turned to Sasha. "How about we get Tansy and Sydney to take you home?"

Sasha shook her head. "I want to help find Jinx."

"If it were up to me, I'd say yes. But I think your parents need to approve as well," Sydney said bluntly. "You don't want to get them angry enough they stop you and Jinx from being friends."

The girl straightened, steel in her spine. "My parents would never do that because they know that friends help each other. I don't know why Jinx is missing, but it's not because things are bad here. She loves you, and she's so grateful to be able to live with you. So please, let me help," she begged.

Petra opened the map that indicated the location of the missing backpack. "Well, you get part of your wish." She motioned Sasha forward, increasing the size of the map. "Is this your ranch?"

Sasha examined the screen closely then nodded, pointing without touching. "That's the house. That's the main arena, and that's the old barn." She frowned. "Why is Jinx in our old barn?"

"That is the question." Aiden glanced around the room, nodding at his brothers. "Looks as if we're going on a short trip. Be prepared for anything."

∽

BEFORE THEY LEFT the house Aiden paused to give Sasha one more hug. "We're going to call your folks to explain why we're coming over. I know you want to help, but we need you to stay with Tansy and Sydney."

"As long as we're going back home, too," Sasha said firmly. "Jinx is my friend."

"Absolutely." He met Tansy's eyes. "You guys can drive her, yes?"

Tansy nodded. "We'll keep her safe," she promised. "I mean that, Sasha. We get that Jinx is your friend, but you will stay with us until I say otherwise."

The girl nodded, but fear remained in her eyes.

A mad rush began as everyone pulled themselves together and sped out the door. His brothers and Zach hopped into Declan's truck, while Julia stayed with Tansy, Sydney, and Sasha.

Aiden and Petra climbed into his truck, but before he could slam it into gear and peel off up the drive to Silver Stone ranch, the back doors opened and Petra's parents climbed in.

Aiden froze for a moment until Pamela tapped him rapidly on the shoulder. "Get going, young man. Multitasking is sometimes a necessary evil."

"Mom, Dad, this is not the time—" Petra began before Zachary interrupted her.

"Not going to do anything except apologize, sweetheart. Aiden's brother Declan pulled us aside during the fireworks and explained what you're doing here."

"We approve, and whatever reservations we have about the two of you as a couple is nothing other than the typical parental nosiness wanting what's best for our little girl. Don't worry about us, we're here to help in any way we can," Pamela assured them.

Relief over one trouble solved was wiped clean by their current situation. "Call Sasha's parents." Aiden told Petra. "A half-dozen trucks are pulling into their parking lot, and we don't want to freak them out."

Petra was on the phone within seconds. "Tamara, hi. First off, don't panic. Nothing's wrong with Sasha, but it looks as if Jinx might've decided she wanted a little alone time. She's left our place and I've tracked her down to one of your old barns. Of course nobody here will sit back and wait until we know she's fine."

Tamara responded and Petra nodded. "Yes, definitely. There were a lot of people around, and it might've been too much. We're pulling onto the Silver Stone drive now. Sasha's worried, but she's safe with Julia and the girls."

After one more final sharp nod, Petra hung up. She twisted her head toward her parents in the back. "When we get there, you two stay with Tamara and Sasha, got it?"

"It's so cute that you think you can order us around," Pamela said, once again squeezing Aiden shoulder. "You're an adorable young man, but you're a little too cautious behind the wheel. Step on it."

It was like something out of a police procedural. Aiden slid to a stop outside the main barn as Caleb Stone raced up, jerking a coat over his shoulders.

Aiden joined Caleb, ignoring the group assembling behind them. "She's somewhere in your old barn, according to what Sasha told us. If she had a panic attack, I don't want all of us going in there."

Caleb's face went as stone cold as his name. "If you need backup, you call."

"If you can keep Sasha back for right now, that's probably the best," Petra said, grabbing Aiden by the hand and tugging him toward the main doors, eyes glued to the screen of her phone.

Declan and Jake stayed hard on their heels as they wove

down neatly organized walkways, the scent of horses and clean fresh hay filling Aiden's senses, the peacefulness around them a sharp contrast to the pulse of fear racing through his veins.

Petra headed straight for the staircase, ready to race up.

Aiden caught her by the hand, holding her back. "Go slow. If by some chance there is someone with her, we need them not to panic."

She nodded, fear in her eyes.

"And I go first." He cut off all debate by stepping in front of her and gliding quietly up the wooden staircase.

In the hayloft, the light was more muted. A single beam of light shone in the casement window and across the bales. Movement in the corner of his eye made him freeze with Petra tight against his back.

A mama cat strolled into view, tail raised high. The very tip flicked with annoyance.

Aiden relaxed slightly when the cat lowered her tail and sauntered over, coming to tangle herself around his ankles affectionately.

Which meant the place was empty except for Jinx, he was almost certain.

Still, they stayed quiet as they paced forward, the app showing them closing in on the AirTag.

They stepped around the corner of the bales, and there was Jinx, arms wrapped around her knees as she sat on the floorboards, her backpack beside her and head drooped toward the ground.

"Oh my God. Jinx. You're safe," Petra whispered. She darted forward and dropped to her knees, wrapping her arms around the girl.

A soft sob escaped Jinx as she buried her chin against Petra's neck, weeping loudly.

"She okay?" Declan paused beside Aiden.

"She doesn't look hurt, but we need to talk. Maybe just Petra and me?"

"Sounds good. I'll go tell the others." Declan paused and patted his brother on the back. "You tell that girl to get her ass back home where she belongs."

He said it loud enough Jinx heard, and she turned her face toward him, eyes swimming with tears as another ragged sob escaped.

"I mean it. If you got scared or something, that's okay. But you remember we can't make things better if you don't tell us what's gone wrong." Declan dipped his chin then turned on his heel and headed down the stairs.

Jinx laid her head against Petra's chest and cried quietly for a while longer. Aiden searched his pockets but had no luck finding any sort of tissue to offer.

So what. She was a little wet and soggy, but she was there and safe, and now he needed to make this better. Aiden sat cautiously, resting a hand gently on her back. Just staying there, waiting.

It took a few minutes until her sobs turned into uneasy, shaky breaths. She dug into the backpack and pulled free a wad of Kleenex, drying her eyes and blowing her nose.

Petra leaned back, anchoring herself against Aiden. "You know what? Declan's right. We promised to talk things through, didn't we?"

A sharp, angry snort escaped Jinx. "You mean talk about things like the fact you two are only pretending to be engaged?"

Aiden bit back a curse. "Heard that, did you?"

Jinx wiggled her way upright and stared at the wall behind Petra's shoulder. "I had tucked our sleepover stuff into Declan's rooms. When everybody left to go outside for the fireworks, I slipped in so I could grab a thicker coat, and suddenly you guys were in the next room, shouting at each other."

Petra made a face. "Normally I would argue that it wasn't actually shouting but a very loud discussion, but I'm sorry we upset you. That wasn't a conversation meant for anybody else to overhear."

"Of course not. But it doesn't change anything because now I know you lied." Her voice sounded weary now, as if she'd lost all hope.

Dammit. Jeff would've said this was a clear example of why keeping to the truth was always easier. "We did lie, but with the best of intentions."

Jinx twisted, tears streaking her cheeks. "I get that. Danielle told me that she wasn't going to leave me anywhere that I wouldn't be safe. She assured me that she was leaving me with a nice couple who were engaged, and that he had two brothers, and that all of you were the salt of the earth, whatever that means. But you *lied* about being engaged."

"Because we wanted you to have somewhere safe to go," Petra insisted. "It wasn't a lie that hurt anyone. It was so that we could help you—"

"But it hurt *you*," Jinx sobbed. "It made you have to pretend to like each other and want to be with each other when that's the last thing you want. I can't do that to people I like. I can't hurt you like that."

"Well, for fuck's sake." Petra all but growled the words, and both Aiden and Jinx stared at her in shock. "Okay, I apologize for my language, but of all the conversations for you to eavesdrop on, that had to have been the worst. Not because you overheard us, but because you stopped eavesdropping before we finished."

A frown folded Jinx's brow. "You shouldn't have to be together for my sake."

"No, you're right. We shouldn't. But what you missed after you left was us getting our heads on straight as we *talked*. As we stopped pretending to ourselves that what we had wasn't real." Aiden linked his fingers with Petra's then lifted them and kissed her knuckles. "What Petra said to me once I was smart enough to listen was she didn't want to keep *pretending*. She wanted to know if I was as smart as her and had figured out that us being together was meant to be real."

Silence echoed for a moment, then another sniff sounded as Jinx considered. "But you were pretending just so that you could have me come to High Water."

"That might've been where we started, but it wasn't a lie for long." Petra smiled at Aiden. "What we should do right now is thank you, because I think we would've gotten here, but it would've taken us a lot longer. I'm so very happy I get to start forever with Aiden now instead of a couple of years down the road."

"You're staying together?" Jinx shook her head. "I don't understand."

Aiden lowered his voice. "We're really staying together, and while you're here, maybe you can do me a favour."

Jinx wiped at her eyes then pull a nearby curious kitten into her lap. "What?"

"You're my witness." He turned to Petra. "I'm not going to do anything outrageous like propose and force you into an answer before you're ready. But I want what we talked about before. About us being real. I'd be very happy if that meant the engagement as well. When it's time."

Petra's lips twitched. She turned to Jinx. "You get to be my witness as well."

Jinx wiggled upright. "What's going on?"

Petra ignored the question and took Aiden's hands in hers. "Aiden Demetri Skye, would you like to marry me?"

A gasp escaped Jinx, but all Aiden saw was Petra's shining eyes and her wicked smile. "This is me in front of a witness saying I'm not being forced into this at all, and Petra Lynn Sorenson, I would love to be yours forever."

He would've leaned in and kissed her, but at that moment Jinx threw herself at both of them, weeping and laughing and tucking herself between them. Petra joined in the crying and laughing as she gazed into Aiden's eyes.

"Happy birthday," he said. "I love you."

"I love you, too," she said back. "Happy birthday to me."

21

Christmas Eve, High Water ranch

"Move it a little further to the right. There, perfect." Pamela Sorenson smiled at Jake as he stepped back from the hanger on the wall that displayed six oversized Christmas stockings. "Now I need your help wrapping presents. Petra said all the packages I sent ahead are in the artists' studio, so if you and I go out there now, we'll have it done in no time."

Jake looked toward Petra as if hoping for her help.

Nope. Petra had other things to do, and having other people around to occupy her mother and father would make her task that much easier.

In the kitchen area, Zachary Sorenson was decorating an enormous cake with Jinx. They had numerous bags of buttercream on the counter, each with a different tip. Zachary was very carefully going through and showing Jinx how to create different kinds of flowers and rosettes, the oldest in the room and the youngest firmly focused on their task.

It wasn't Petra's typical holiday getaway—the Sorenson family usually met in Hawaii for a break in the sun and sand—but she had bowed out of the trip well before her birthday. She hadn't been about to leave Jinx during her first Christmas at High Water.

Then, with things better than right between her and Aiden, staying in Heart Falls seemed even more important. Finding out that Julia and Zach had also changed plans to stick around had made Petra teary. When her parents had outright invited themselves to High Water, their support and love had been the sweetest icing on the cake.

Next year would be soon enough to head back to the island. Maybe she and Aiden could take Jinx with them.

Declan marched in, a box of brightly wrapped presents in his hands. He paused en route to the tree and leaned in to mutter quietly. "Your parents are— How do I say this?"

"A force of nature?" Petra suggested.

He grinned. "Not the direction I was going for, but it fits. It also seems the apple doesn't fall far from the tree. I'm glad they could join us for the holidays."

"Me too," Petra said quietly, staring at her father then out the window where her mother chattered nonstop to Jake as they headed across to the studio. "I mean, they partly came to see Zach and Julia since she's building that baby over the coming year, but it's kind of nice to know my folks feel comfortable at High Water."

Declan leaned closer. "Don't kid yourself. They're here for you just as much as they are for your brother and that coming baby. They're good folks. They are a touch nosy, though. That's all I'm saying."

Petra pinched the bridge of her nose. "Did my mother give you a lecture about safe sex and the best ways you could find a future partner who will remain sexually compatible with you into your golden years?"

His eyes widened. "Not yet, but I suppose that's something to not look forward to."

They might be family, but they were a lot at times.

Petra took a deep breath and enjoyed the scent of cinnamon and orange peel that lingered on the air. Jake had cooked last night, which meant he mysteriously brought food to the table that she still suspected he'd purchased from Tansy, but at this point Petra didn't care. There'd been some kind of Peking duck along with spring rolls that were crisp and delicious.

Tonight, though, she and Aiden had been in charge and they'd gone traditional. They had cooked up a ham and mashed potatoes and green beans and a few Ukrainian dishes thrown in for good measure because it wouldn't be Christmas for her without perogies and kielbasa.

Most of the food was already in the oven, so other than putting together a salad at the final moment, no more fussing was required.

Which meant she had time to finish the one project that still needed a little work. She slipped into their bedroom, heading for the corner where Aiden had placed a comfortable loveseat. It was small enough to fit in the sunny corner beside the window, and since her birthday, they'd made sure to take time every day to sit there for a little while together. Sometimes in the morning, sometimes after they'd finished the family time. But with so many adults around all the time, they brainstormed to come up with this so they'd have a chance to keep talking about *them*.

To keep learning more and keep falling deeper in love.

Of course, with the surprise she'd put together, it wouldn't be too much longer that they'd need to use this cozy corner.

Petra sat on her side of the loveseat, curling her legs under her and picking up the final project she needed to complete. She had all her Christmas presents done for the High Water family, and a toque and mitt set for Sasha Stone that she had helped Jinx with.

She just wasn't quite done with the set of slippers she was making for her father, and she got her needle to work as she stared out the window, contentment washing over her.

The door eased open, and Aiden's bright smile appeared around the edge. "I wondered if I'd find you here."

She patted the seat beside her. "It's as good of a place as any to hide so my mother can't request I dress up like an elf or something."

He laughed, detouring to the side of the bed before joining her. He put a small, brightly coloured bag down by his feet then draped her legs across his lap. "There we go. Much better."

"Are you done with all of your cowboy things for the day?" she asked.

"Until evening chores, yes. Which means I get to relax and eat lots of food and enjoy our gift opening tonight."

Petra eyed the bag beside the couch. "Last minute item to toss under the tree?"

"Definitely not last minute, and not something I think I should put under the tree." He eased his hand down her thigh and over the arch of her foot, petting her the way that he always did when they were together. He touched as always, brushing his hands over her and making her feel as if being right beside her was the most important thing in his world.

She twisted on the spot, curled her arms around his neck, and kissed him. Because she could. Because she wanted to, even needed to.

The craving for him kept growing bigger and bigger.

He kissed her back with heat, but controlled enough that when he pulled them apart only a minute later, she sighed happily.

"I like you, Aiden Skye."

"I know." He winked, cupping her chin in his hands and brushing their lips together again. "I like you too, Petra Sorenson."

"That's good."

It was his turn to snicker.

She glanced down again because she couldn't help herself. "You going to tell me what's in the bag?"

"I'd like to know how you feel about early Christmas presents."

"I highly approve of them," she assured him. "Especially when they're for me."

He eased back far enough to pick up the package, holding it just out of reach. His expression turned serious and he took a big breath before speaking again. "Remember we promised to keep talking, so if I screwed this up, you let me know. I won't be hurt."

"Now I don't know if I want to open it," Petra said quietly.

"Oh, you want to open it," he assured her. "Here."

He all but shoved the bag into her hands.

She leaned back on the high armrest, examining him for a moment before peeking inside.

At the top, once again, was a tissue wrapped candle.

"It's exactly what I wanted," she teased, pulling it from the bag and ripping away the tissue.

The label said *Smells Like The Best Husband In The World.*

"Aww, that's so cute." Happiness swelled up inside. They were going to do this thing. Be engaged. Be together, eventually as husband and wife. "Am I supposed to light this when you've done something good?"

"That's a plan. You can also light it when I screw up to remind yourself that I'm not terrible all the time." He tipped his head toward the bag. "You didn't finish."

She put the candle on the side table next to her teacup and peeked back into the bag. A small notebook with a picture of a sunset on the front cover lay at the bottom. She laid it in her palm. "It's pretty."

He nudged her elbow. He was fidgeting so much it was like he had ants in his pants. "Open it."

"Did you write me a poem? A dirty limerick—" Petra stalled. The very center of the notebook had been cut away leaving a square barely big enough to hold a ring. "Oh my God."

She carefully lifted out the ring and turned the shining top toward her. It was a small cluster of white and blue stones, and it flashed in the sunlight shining through the window.

Petra lifted her eyes to Aiden's. "It's beautiful."

His expression went back to a smile. "I didn't screw up?"

She shook her head, slipping the ring on her finger. Holding her hand up to admire it. "It's exactly what I wanted." She considered. "How did you get that so perfect?"

"Your mom," he admitted. "We've been texting ever since your birthday, and at one point she sent me some of the pictures that you'd scrapbooked back in the day."

He linked their fingers together, pressing a kiss to her hand just above where the shiny ring sat.

"I'm glad you get along with my family, and I'm glad you're brave enough to put up with them on a regular basis," she teased, happiness still bubbling inside her.

"They're good people. Other than I've had to veer the topic

away from some blunt conversations about sex at times. Your mother is determined."

"That's one way to put it," Petra said with a smile, pressing her hand his cheek.

"Your dad said something about thank God you were the last to get hitched, because each of you got more twisted and creative. I do need to hear what happened with Julia and Zach."

"We'll make sure that happens when we go over tomorrow to spend the day with them. I bet they'd love to tell you the story." She curled herself around him, her cup of happiness nearly full to the brim. "Thank you for my ring."

His face turned suddenly serious for a moment. "I figured it was something we needed. We didn't have one before because we were pretending. But we're not pretending anymore. I love you with everything in me, no matter how quick it seems."

"I love you too." Her throat was tightening, and tears were threatening to well up, which was silly considering how happy she was. "You want to see the surprise Christmas present I got you?"

His gaze dropped to the buttons on her shirt as he undid the first snap. "It's exactly what I want."

She tugged his hands away with a laugh, crawling off the couch and pulling him with her. "It's not here, although you can totally have *that* later. Come on. I can't wait to show you."

∼

AIDEN WAS sure he was grinning from ear to ear. Every time Petra or one of her gal gang grabbed hold and towed him somewhere, it was amusing as hell.

They made it across the living room before catching the attention of Kevin and Declan who sat by the fire.

"Going somewhere?" Declan asked.

"Nothing to see here," Aiden said.

"I'm showing Aiden his surprise," Petra announced over top of him. She squeezed his fingers. "Everybody's welcome."

"Sweet." Jinx headed for the door. She paused then dashed back and grabbed Zachary by the wrist, tugging him along the same way Petra was hauling Aiden. "Come on, Grandpa Zach. You don't want to miss this."

Yep, totally amusing. Aiden exchanged a smile with his soon-to-be father-in-law then obediently switched his footwear and jerked on his winter coat, stepping into the crisp December day.

Sun sparkled off a million snowflakes, the fields around them stretching pristine and white with the new snow that had been drifting from the sky since the previous evening. The paths to the artists' studio were well defined, but it was cold enough that with each step of their winter boots, the new snow squeaked underfoot. Each inhale stabbed sharp and crisp against the back of his throat.

By the time they arrived at the base of the staircase, they had a parade following them. Jake and Pamela marched down the stairs, Pamela waving excitedly.

"Is it time?"

"It is," Petra announced happily. She tugged Aiden to a stop and fully faced him. "This is a Christmas present partly from me, but mostly from your family. To both of us," she added before blowing a kiss at Declan and Jake.

Jinx was there, bouncing on the spot. "Can I show him?" she asked eagerly.

It seemed everybody was in on the surprise except him. Minor miracle considering how closely everybody had worked together over the past weeks.

"It's okay with me," Aiden offered. "As long as I get to see it soon, because the suspense is killing me."

Jinx hurried past them to the end of the building and the farthest door.

The door to his future mini suite. The one where they'd started their fight and set off a whole chain of events that changed his world completely.

Petra slipped her hands around Aiden's arm and slowed their pace, head leaning in to speak privately. "Again, if there something you don't like about it, it can be changed. But I'm pleased, and I think you will be too."

Jinx pushed the door open and stood back, grinning as she continued to bounce. Behind them, everyone seemed to slow enough that when they stepped through the doorway, it was him and Petra alone.

He'd thought maybe the painting would be done. Maybe the window trim and baseboards would be up, but what he saw in front of him was a completely furnished home.

With windows to the south and east, the living room and kitchen were small but perfectly sized for a couple in love. A small table with four chairs around it was arranged next to a couch that faced a big-screen TV. Tucked in the corner between the windows was a loveseat—identical to the one currently in their bedroom, with side tables and lights and a view over the prairies.

"How did you do this?" Aiden asked in amazement. He kicked off his shoes without thinking, pacing forward over hardwood flooring and soft area rugs.

"You've been preoccupied planning with Jake and helping with the ranch hand quarters. Every time you worked on that, we worked in here," Petra shared, love in her voice.

He ran a hand over the small island and admired the very basic kitchen. "You did a fantastic job."

She joined him, slipping their fingers together. "We don't need much of a kitchen or dining room because this is mostly for when we want to do things by ourselves. Or maybe have Jinx over, or a couple at our place for cards. But we'll be doing most of that at the ranch house. This is *our* place."

Everyone crowded in the door and stood watching.

It suddenly hit. Aiden glanced at the three inside doors. "How is there so much room in here?" He paced toward the most northernly door and peeked in to find a sparsely decorated office space. "This was supposed to be the bedroom."

Declan cleared his throat. "Always good to change plans when it's necessary. I don't need that much room and there are two of you. We punched down one wall and put it up a little farther to the north."

"With an extra sound barrier built in." Jake offered dryly. "So you can have *loud discussions* if necessary."

Aiden laughed, and he hurried to the second door, poking his head into a Jack and Jill bathroom. One door off the living room and one door that looked as if it led into a second bedroom.

"If we have guests, then we share the bath. Otherwise we can lock this one." Petra came to his side and pointed at the south wall. Instead of being solid, a windowpane partially covered with a stained-glass image let natural light into the windowless bathroom. "Jinx came up with that idea."

Aiden whistled in admiration then turned back and offered Jinx a thumbs-up. "I like it. Good job."

He let his curiosity carry him into the bedroom. It was perfect, this place for him and Petra, with a dark brown quilt on the queen-size bed and a board over the bed with the handwritten saying, *Family is forever.*

He turned, grabbed Petra, and pulled her back into the living room, shaking his head as he met every one of his family's eyes one after the other. "This is fantastic. Thank you. I never expected this in a million years." He twisted to Petra. "And you. Holy secrets."

She grinned. "You like it?"

He shook his head. "No, I love it."

She wiggled nearly as hard as Jinx. "One more thing."

She tugged him to the wall beside the front door where a collection of eight by eight pictures were arranged neatly in exact rows. Aiden suspected that was Jake's handiwork.

Then he looked a little closer, because it wasn't only the straight-as-a-ruler frames that impressed him—it was the pictures. One of each of his brothers. A smiling picture of Jinx. There was one of Kevin, and one of Dixie with her tongue hanging out—that one made him laugh—then more pictures of familiar faces from the past months and straight from memory.

Sydney. Tansy. Zach and Julia, Caleb and Tamara. Chance and Rose. People they were getting to know better. People who were making a difference in his life.

The image in the center was him and Petra, and he squeezed her happily as he admired how good they looked together.

When he hit the picture in the upper right corner that held his mom and Jeff, arms wrapped around each other and their heads thrown back with laughter, Aiden turned to Petra and pulled her in for a hug. Mostly so he could bury his face in her neck and try to get a hold of himself.

She squeezed him close, and he stood there, letting happiness leak through his eyes.

When he finally got himself together, wiping at his face with his knuckles, they were alone. Out the window, the High Water family walked together, snow gently falling around them.

A Cowboy's Bride

"I would say that was awkward, but it wasn't really, was it?" He brushed his nose against Petra's.

"It was not awkward. It was beautiful, to be honest." She slid her thumb over his cheek. "What was the part that got to you the most?"

"That we're doing it." He said it softly as he tilted his head toward the wall. "We promised that we'd make a difference. That we would pay it forward, and we're doing it. I know we've still got a long way to go, and there are going to be hard times mixed in with the good. But here's the thing I didn't realize." He smiled, taking her hand and brushing his thumb over the spot where his ring sat. "I never realized exactly how much this was going to change *my* life. I kept thinking about how good it would be to give to others, to change their worlds. I feel as if I've gotten far more than I deserve."

"I'm glad you're happy, but I think you deserve it."

"I'm hanging onto it, no matter what." He tipped his chin toward the picture of his mom and dad. "They didn't raise a fool. I'm holding on with both hands. That means to you, Petra. Thanks for being willing to build a home with me."

She wrapped her arms around his neck and squeezed so tight he had to pick her up and spin her in a circle, just because.

They headed outside, eager to rejoin the rest of the family. Aiden held her hand tightly in his as they walked, "We're not going to move into our new room yet, though, right? I don't want to leave Jinx all alone in the big house by herself."

"Soon," she said, mischief dancing in her eyes. "Declan and I have a plan."

Aiden shook his head. "Why do I get the feeling that means Jake isn't going to like this plan?"

Petra's jaw dropped. "Wow, you're good. Now stay quiet." She pressed a finger to her lips.

"I have no idea what's going on, so trust me. That'll be

easy." Aiden curled his arm around her and tucked her close as they neared where the family were now engaged in an impromptu snowball fight. "The only thing that we need to do right now is discuss dates."

Petra hummed, laughing as Jinx's well-aimed snowball knocked Jake's toque off. "What date is that?"

Aiden tapped on Petra's ring finger. With the sun shining down on them, her eyes sparkled as much as the ring did. "We need to set a date for the wedding so that you can officially become this cowboy's bride."

EPILOGUE

The longer the night went on, the louder the music got. Jake didn't mind, mostly. Loud music meant he didn't have to talk to anybody, and he wasn't in the best of moods these days.

Which wasn't anybody's fault, but until he got his shit together, it was far better to keep his mouth shut.

Thankfully, it was pretty easy to do it at home. The to-do list was almost done, with the things that still needed to be accomplished to get High Water operational under control by the end of January. There would be no holding back after that. Jake could not wait. He needed more to occupy his time because…

Just because.

Lying to myself is such a mature option.

He finished his beer, making his way across the floor to where the rest of the family had started their New Year's Eve gathered around a high top.

Jinx had asked if she could spend it with Sasha at Silver

Stone ranch. With the girl happily celebrating with her friend, all the adults had been free to go out for the night.

Petra and Aiden were bundled together like the lovebirds they were. Jake couldn't find it in him to be annoyed at how sickeningly sweet and happy they were. His brother deserved an amazing woman, and Petra was that.

Declan was on the dance floor. He never danced more than once with anyone, but he was in high demand because he apparently actually knew how to lead. Plus some nonsense about him being a *golden retriever* kept being mentioned, which sent Petra's friends into gales of laughter.

Jake figured everybody needed to get the fuck off social media for a while.

He couldn't help it. He took a quick scan around the area, looking for the other women who inevitably appeared when Petra was around. No sign of them, and he wasn't sure if he was happy or annoyed that he was considering if he was happy or annoyed they weren't there.

Petra shook him by the sleeve and leaned in close. "Who are you looking for?" she shouted.

"An ear doctor," Jake told her.

She grinned. "Good one. *My* doctor isn't here tonight. She offered to work a shift at emergency in Diamond Valley. But Tansy's around somewhere."

Jake nodded, forcing a smile as he gave her a thumbs-up.

It shouldn't happen. That flare of excitement in his belly at the mere mention of that woman's name.

Of course, the next second he saw her, twirling on the dance floor in the arms of a short cowboy who was unsuccessfully trying to grow a beard. It almost hurt to watch them, but Tansy held her smile intact in spite of the number of times she was jerked in a new direction as her partner failed to keep them from colliding with others on the full floor.

A waitress brought Jake his beer and he firmly turned his back on the dancers and gave the girl a twenty along with a wink. "Keep them coming."

She sparkled then flitted away.

He spent the next hour pretty much doing that. Smiling, and drinking, and nodding, and wondering over and over why he was so damn attracted to *that* woman.

The music broke off briefly and a deep voice boomed over the speakers. "It's time, folks. Join me as we get ready for the final stroke of midnight and welcome in the new year."

The countdown began.

Ten, nine...

Jake found himself twisting on the spot, focusing on the smiling faces around him. Good people who had begun to be more than simply neighbours and acquaintances, but real friends.

Eight.

Seven.

To Jake's left, his brother Aiden tugged a laughing Petra close, ignored the clock, and planted a huge kiss on her.

Six.

Five.

Jake kept turning and came face-to-face with Tansy. Infuriating, dangerous, confusing Tansy.

Four.

Three.

The cowboy next to Tansy opened his arms as if inviting her in to celebrate the New Year, and Jake lost all sense. He darted forward, nabbed Tansy by the wrist and twirled her straight into his arms.

Two.

One.

"Happy New Year!"

The cry went up from all around them, but all Jake could do was stare into Tansy's shocked face.

Then he couldn't see what she was thinking because his lips were on hers and he was kissing her. Thoroughly, and deeply, and it was a damn good thing that they were in the center of a crowded room because she was kissing him back. She clung to his neck and lifted her legs, and the next second she was wrapped around him like a wayward rope on a fence post, and it felt so fucking amazing.

Jake resisted the urge to stumble them somewhere private. Instead, he kept kissing her as his entire body strummed with desire. When they finally broke apart, gasping for breath, Jake was stunned.

Infuriating to the core, Tansy grinned. "See? Sometimes spontaneity is fun."

He focused on staying upright as she shimmied her feet back to the ground. He needed to say something, anything. Maybe even apologize.

Nope, couldn't do it.

"Thanks for the great start to the new year. I'll see you around." Tansy patted his cheek then vanished between one breath and the next.

Jake stood there and tried to figure out what the hell had just happened.

He was still trying to decide the next morning as he stared at the coffee maker, willing it to spit out liquid faster.

Ten o'clock, and no one else had appeared in the house yet. He figured Aiden and Petra had a good reason to be MIA—with Jinx out of the house, they'd spent the night in their new apartment. They were probably still cozied up together. Declan was up, but still in the barn.

Jake was regretting his New Year's Eve choices more than a

little, and he stood by the coffee maker and drank an entire cup before refilling and easing his way to the table.

He stared out the window and watched as an old beat up minivan turned off the highway and down the drive. Probably somebody dropping Jinx off after her night away.

Well, to hell with it. New Year's Day. It was time to set some goals. That's what people did on New Year's Day, right?

He nabbed his notebook and turned to a fresh, clean page. He wrote GOALS at the top and a set of numbers to the side, one all the way to ten. He stared at the page for a moment then in the first spot wrote down, crisp and clear…

1. Learn to be more spontaneous.

What the fuck?

He all but glared at the journal. *That* was not what he wanted to write. That wasn't what he'd been thinking about at all, and he pressed his hands to his temples, begging for the pounding to die down.

Tansy's fault. The word she'd used the night before had still been echoing in his head.

He examined the notebook page with disgust. Everyone had their quirks, and he was honest enough to admit this was one of his. Either he crossed it out or he ripped out the damn page, neither of which sat well. He decided to just leave the damn sentence there for now and let it be annoying.

Someone knocked on the door. Jake was already on his feet even as he checked the time. New Year's Day and they had a visitor?

Oh. What if it was Danielle? What if somebody else needed their help?

He hurried forward and jerked the door open, staring down

in shock at a wildly grinning Tansy. She held a plastic container toward him, jamming it into his hands.

"What's this?" he demanded.

"Welcome to High Water brownies," she announced happily, slipping past him and hauling a rolling suitcase after her.

She closed the door then turned back, tugging the container from his fingers. "Thanks. Those are for me."

"You said they were welcome brownies," he repeated.

She nodded eagerly. "They are. You don't know how to bake that well, and I wanted brownies. Since I'm now living here, they're *welcome home, Tansy* brownies."

She twirled and headed farther into the house.

Jake shook his head, trying to get her words to settle in his brain and make sense. Nope, wasn't working.

He stomped after her into the kitchen. "What do you mean, you're living here?"

She put the brownies on the counter before twisting to face him. She brushed her hands together as if knocking off crumbs then thrust one forward. "Declan and Petra hired me. Hi, I'm your new live-in cook."

New York Times Bestselling Author Vivian Arend invites you to Heart Falls. These contemporary ranchers live in a tiny town in central Alberta, tucked into the rolling foothills. Enjoy the ride as they each find their happily-ever-afters.

The Skyes of Heart Falls
A Cowboy's Bride
A Cowboy's Trust
A Cowboy's Claim

The Stones of Heart Falls
A Rancher's Heart
A Rancher's Song
A Rancher's Bride
A Rancher's Love
A Rancher's Vow

The Coleman's of Heart Falls
The Cowgirl's Forever Love
The Cowgirl's Secret Love
The Cowgirl's Chosen Love

ABOUT THE AUTHOR

New York Times and *USA Today* bestselling author Vivian Arend loves to share the products of her over-active imagination with her readers. She writes contemporary, western, and light-hearted paranormal romances. The stories are humorous yet emotional, usually with a large cast of family or friends, and a guaranteed happily-ever-after. Vivian lives in British Columbia, Canada, with her husband of many years—her inspiration for every hero and a willing companion for all sorts of adventures.

www.vivianarend.com

Milton Keynes UK
Ingram Content Group UK Ltd.
UKHW040638131024
449481UK00001B/44